# COURAGE TO HEAL

# COURAGE TO HEAL

A Novel

Paul Bernstein, MD

SUNBELT PUBLICATIONS
SAN DIEGO, CALIFORNIA

*Courage to Heal*
Sunbelt Publications, Inc
Copyright © 2008 by the author
All rights reserved
First edition 2008. Second Printing 2009.

Edited by Jennifer Redmond
Cover and book design by Kathleen Wise
Project management by Jennifer Redmond
Printed in the United States by BookMasters, Inc.

Sunbelt Publications, Inc.
P.O. Box 191126
San Diego, CA 92159-1126
(619) 258-4911, fax: (619) 258-4916
www.sunbeltbooks.com

12 11 10 09     6 5 4 3 2

"Adventures in the Natural History and Cultural Heritage of the Californias"
A Series Edited by Lowell Lindsay

Library of Congress Cataloging-in-Publication Data

Bernstein, Paul, 1951–
  Courage to heal : a novel / Paul Bernstein. — 1st ed.
    p. cm. — (Adventures in the natural history and cultural heritage of the Californias)
  ISBN-13: 978-0-932653-85-7
  ISBN-10: 0-932653-85-5
  1. Garfield, Sidney R., 1906–1984 — Fiction. 2. Kaiser Permanente — Fiction. I. Title.

PS3602.E76286C68 2007
813'.6 — dc22
                                                                    2007030810

Cover photo courtesy of the Kaiser Permanente Archives

This novel is dedicated to the doctors who have modeled their careers

after Sidney Garfield and have served as inspirations to me and their

fellow physicians: Jeffrey Weisz, Oliver Goldsmith, Robert Pearl,

Jeffrey Selevan, Arthur Flippin, and Maurice Alfaro.

Author royalties from *Courage to Heal* are being donated to the

Sidney Garfield Memorial Fund and the Permanente Federation

to continue Dr. Garfield's legacy by encouraging innovation

that will improve health care for all.

Find out more at www.couragetoheal.org

"That any sane nation, having observed that you could provide for the supply

of bread by giving bakers a pecuniary interest in baking for you, should go on

to give a surgeon a pecuniary interest in cutting off your leg, is enough to make

one despair of political humanity. But that is precisely what we have done."

GEORGE BERNARD SHAW, 1906
INTRODUCTION TO "THE DOCTOR'S DILEMMA"

# Foreword

*"Courage to Heal" is a compelling story based on the birth and development of the Kaiser Permanente medical care program. Although fictional at times, Dr. Bernstein has captured the true character of its leader, Dr. Sidney Garfield: his courage, his integrity, and his passionate conviction that the combining of prepayment with group practice was advantageous to both patient and physician alike.*

*Those of us who participated in the early development of the program were ostracized by community physicians and medical organizations who sought the extermination of our unconventional program. At the same time, we found ourselves contending with Mr. Henry Kaiser. We were determined to preserve the physician's control and responsibility for medical decisions against any lay interference. It was our firm belief that voluntary enrollment in our prepayment program and the group form of practice combined to provide good medical care, encouraged preventive measures and was entirely ethical. It was that conviction that compelled us to continue.*

*Cecil Cutting, MD (Age 96)*
*Medical Director Emeritus*
*The Permanente Medical Group*
*September 23, 2005*

"Mom, what's wrong?" In answer, my mother buries her mouth in the crook of her elbow, stifling her cough. When she moves her arm, the white cloth mask over her mouth is wet.

"Cripes, Mom, you're okay? Right?"

She squeezes my hand. "Of course, Pumpkin." She's called me that since my first red curl sprouted on my head. I'm eight now and too old to be a pumpkin.

She leans down as if to kiss my cheek, then pulls away. "Why don't you run in and buy some candy while I get the brisket?" She places three pennies in my hand. Her fingers look like bones…pure white bones.

"Gee, thanks," I say, but I'm not hungry.

Mom coughs again and a pink stain now seeps through the cloth over her mouth.

"Forget the brisket," she says, "let's go home." She grabs my hand as we walk the one block to our apartment over my father's clothing store. "Go upstairs and play."

I pretend to go upstairs, but crouch down and watch her go in the store. Does Mom have the flu? The thought hits me like a stone against my heart. My father is wearing a suit; he always wears one. He hugs her, then picks up the phone and dials. I can't hear what he's saying, but he looks worried. He comes out the back door with Mom, holding her like she's too weak to walk.

"Sidney Garfield, go to your room and play." His voice is rushed, stern. "Now."

I race up the stairs and watch as Mom follows and barely makes it into her room.

"You'll be fine, Share-Voney," my father says. Share-Voney is her nickname, Polish for her red hair. I wonder if she hates it as much as I hate being called Pumpkin.

My father looks down the hall at me. "Sidney, close your door."

I lean against my door and hold my breath so I can listen.

The doorbell rings. "Doctor Foster?" Father says. "Yes...yes, it's an emergency. She can't breathe."

They walk down the hall into Mom's room. My heart beats so loudly, I worry my father can hear it.

Minutes pass and Mom's cough is worse; she sounds like she's drowning.

The door opens. "Dr. Foster, please!" my father pleads.

I crack open my door. The doctor is younger than my father, blond, with a red spot, like a mole, under his chin in the shape of a moon.

"Doctor, I can't pay you now, but I promise—"

I open my door and run out to the doctor. I hold up the three pennies Mom gave me.

The doctor pats my head. I watch the red spot on his chin move back and forth.

"I'll get you the money," Father says.

"Sorry. There is the Charity Hospital." The doctor walks out.

Father slams the door behind him. How can the doctor refuse to help Mom? Father hugs me and I wrap my arms around him. "Please, Sidney. Go outside in the fresh air."

"No, I want to see Mom." I break free and race into her room. She's sitting up in bed, sweat running down her forehead, her eyes surrounded by circles of coal. She gently strokes my hair with icy hands. "I'm sorry, Pumpkin. I'm so sorry."

"Please don't, Mom...please don't..." I can't say the word die. A drop of blood bubbles from her nostrils and spatters her chin. She gulps for air. Her eyes close.

"No, Mom," I yell. "Mom!" An awful, horrible odor of unsweet flowers— funeral flowers—a smell I'll never forget, fills my head.

"Breathe, Share-Voney," my father screams. "Breathe!"

# BOOK ONE

## THE DESERT

# CHAPTER 1

Los Angeles County Hospital

June 3, 1940

I was up to my elbows in blood.

"Pressure's down to sixty," anesthesia resident Donny Rand called out, through the hiss of the deflating blood pressure cuff.

After twenty-six hours on call, exhaustion and futility let in that little voice of panic. "Sixty?" My tone wavered. "Where's Chandler?"

From above her mask, the scrub nurse's eyes said hurry up. "Sorry, Dr. Garfield. He's still not answering."

I'd been called stat to the OR without time to examine the patient or talk to his family. If he had a family. "What's his name?"

"Who?"

"The patient. I like to know who I'm operating on."

"Mike Everett," Rand said. "An aqueduct construction foreman…" He tapped the gauge. "Hurry, his pressure's fifty." He tapped again as if that would somehow change the reading.

Everett was dying, bleeding to death, and I had two, maybe three minutes to find the source and stop it. Time to concentrate and stop wishing Dwight Chandler, my attending surgeon, was there to hold my hand. Chandler had a habit of disappearing in an emergency. That was too kind. He had a habit of never being around at all.

After three years of surgical training, I knew the textbooks, the anatomy.

"Suction, turn up the suction," I snapped, unable to keep the edge from my voice. The first rule of surgery is to see what you are cutting before you cut.

I was operating blind in a pool of blood. I adjusted the overhead OR lamp. No use. The reflection off the blood only made things worse. There was nothing else to do but operate by feel. I ran my rubber-gloved hand in the left upper quadrant and over the capsule of the spleen. My finger reached a deep gash and slid into the spleen's normally smooth surface like it was made of Jell-O. Of course. The spleen was ruptured. I brought up my hand, blood dripping from the rubber glove. Without asking, Joan, the scrub nurse, slapped a hemostat on my palm.

"Pressure's forty." Rand fidgeted with his stethoscope. "You'd better hurry, his heart sounds are getting distant."

"IV fluids…what about the fluids?"

"Dripping in fast, but they can't touch the blood loss."

With my left hand feeling for the pedicle where the splenic artery entered the spleen like a melon on a vine, I dove in with the hemostat in my right hand. *Snap*. As the suction drained the blood from the abdomen, the fractured rib that had torn the spleen to shreds came into view. Joan nodded, her eyes meeting mine as if she were giving me a congratulatory handshake.

"Pressure's down to thirty."

"What?" My heart pounded against my chest. "But the bleeding's stopped."

"No blood volume," Rand said. "Maybe enough IV fluid, but nothing to circulate."

The construction worker was dying. The six-hour, two hundred mile ambulance ride from the Mojave Desert to LA had been too long. I'd spent years studying anatomy and physiology, just for a moment like this. I couldn't just give up…

Joan's eyebrows lifted. "Dr. Garfield?"

I said nothing. The bleeding had stopped and the peritoneal cavity was dry. Only one alternative. One final hope. I'd read about it in textbooks, but it had never been done at County or anywhere in California. England had started a blood bank when the war with Germany began a few weeks ago. There was talk of starting one here.

Rand pulled down his cloth mask. "Can't hear a pressure or heart sounds. What…what do you—?"

The OR door swung open. Dwight Chandler, mask around his neck, strode in. "Need some help?"

"Get a glass syringe. The largest you can find." I ripped off my surgical gown and Chandler stepped back, obviously worried he'd look bad taking an order from a lowly third-year resident.

"Hurry," I yelled, "I'm not letting this patient die."

"Hold your horses, Sid. Rand, pressure?"

"Faint heart sounds only."

Joan, always one step ahead, handed me an eight-ounce glass syringe the size of a soup can. I grabbed a large bore needle from the anesthesia cart and gave them both to Rand. Extending my forearm, muscular from summers of construction work, I tapped on a vein and said, "Fill the syringe with my blood."

"You're kidding," Chandler said. "You can't experiment in my OR."

My face flushed with heat. "Then get the hell out."

Chandler held up both hands. "Think, Garfield. You can't do this."

"Can't? You're right, I can't let him die. Now, help or leave, we're wasting time."

"I'll report this to the Dean—"

I turned away and rested my arm on the OR table next to the dying worker's head.

Rand removed his stethoscope from his ears. "It's your call."

"Draw it up."

Rand plunged the needle into my vein. The pain shot up my shoulder and blood streamed into the glass vial.

"You'll be responsible for his death." Chandler threw his surgical hat on the floor. "It's your funeral, Garfield." He kicked open the door and stormed out.

The patient needed blood not fluids. No one had ever done a blood transfusion at LA County before. Blood to carry oxygen to his dying organs. Blood to expand his fluid volume and restore his pressure. Life-giving blood... I looked down; the syringe was full. "I'll give it to him. I don't want any of you involved."

Rand glanced up at me, his mask pulled down below his nose, his eyes flat and defeated. We were wasting our time, his expression was saying. "You don't know his blood type."

He was right, of course. Only a few labs in the US could do blood typing and LA County wasn't one of them. It didn't matter. I knew my blood type, O negative, the universal donor. My blood couldn't cause a transfusion reaction or do him any harm.

I pierced the rubber IV tubing with the needle, clamped off the bottle of fluids to make sure the blood went in the right direction, and quickly shoved the plunger down before it had a chance to clot.

Rand looked anxious. "Speed shock? What about speed shock…if you infuse it too fast—"

"Shock? He's almost dead. Draw some more."

I extended my arm. Rand punctured my skin with the needle and pulled back the plunger. My blood spurted again into the glass tube. Was I imagining it or was the syringe filling slower? Seconds, minutes… Rand removed the needle and I pressed gauze to stop my own bleeding, taping it around my forearm to hold it in place.

"Take his pressure."

Rand pumped up the cuff. Finding a vein in the patient's opposite arm, I squeezed the plunger, forcing my blood directly into his bloodstream. *C'mon, Mike, don't die on me.*

"Nothing," Rand said.

"Keep trying. Take his pulse."

Rand shook his head.

"Give me your stethoscope." I slid it under the sterile drapes and listened over the patient's heart. "There's something." A distant beating, but I couldn't be sure if it was the patient's heart or my own pulse pounding in my ears. "Draw more." I extended my arm again.

"You're going to pass out," Rand said.

"I'm okay. Do it…do it now."

Rand plunged the needle into my arm and pulled back. Everything swirled.

Joan grasped my shoulder. "Dr. Garfield?"

"I'm fine." I took a deep breath, steadying myself, adapting to the light-headedness. I transfused the third syringe of blood as quickly as I could, then felt for his radial pulse. Thready, but definite. "Take his pressure."

"Holy Christ," Rand tapped the blood pressure gauge again, "you did it...you did it, Sid...it's up to sixty."

"Suture, doctor?" Joan's voice caught, her eyes moist above her blue cloth mask.

"Three-O silk." I tied off both ends of the splenic artery with three quick knots and removed the ruptured spleen. It was the size of my fist and a deep purple color from the injury and clotted blood.

"Irrigation—"

The door to the OR burst open. Doctor William Keating, Dean of the medical school, labored in with Chandler in tow. Keating's soft flesh bulged at every seam of his green scrubs. "Vital signs?" He demanded.

"Stabilizing," I said. "He had a ruptured spleen and I had to—"

"I see that," Keating said. "Chandler told me you infused blood?"

"It was his only chance."

"Chandler, you close," Keating ordered. "Garfield, I want you in my office, now."

"I can't do that," I said calmly. "I won't leave this patient until I'm finished."

"That's insubordination. Do you want to graduate, Dr. Garfield?"

"Dr. Keating, it was you who taught us surgery is more thinking than cutting."

"God damn it, I'm not about to debate you. Come with me now, or you can forget ever becoming a surgeon."

I turned my back and extended my gloved palm. "Suture, please."

*Vital signs stable.*

I rinsed the dried blood off my hands and splashed cold water on my face. After another all-nighter, I was disoriented. Middle of the afternoon or early morning, it all blurred into one never-ending day. *Vital signs stable.* The three words resonated through my head as I thought of how quickly Mike Everett was recovering from surgery.

The surgical floor was a four-minute fast walk from the OR changing room. I brushed past a nurse who looked at me like I'd been given a week to live. Word of my impending demise had traveled fast. My meeting with Dean Keating was in twenty minutes and since doing the blood transfusion I'd thought of little else.

Directly across from the nursing station, Mike Everett, post-op day two — no, what was I thinking, it had been three days — sat up in bed, looking a lot better than I did.

"Babs, this is the doctor who saved my life."

Mike's wife, a solid woman with crème colored hair and pale skin, sat on the edge of his bed with two boys about six and nine. *Saved my life.* Those were the only three words I could think of that meant more than *vital signs stable*. Had Dean Keating forgot the main reason for becoming a doctor? I hoped not.

This was the first time I'd made rounds during normal visiting hours since Mike's surgery and his wife hadn't been at the hospital that first night. I offered her my hand. "Sidney Garfield." She looked up, quickly averted her eyes from mine, stared at my hand, hesitated, and then grasped my palm for a second before letting go. Not quite sure what she was thinking and not wanting to embarrass her, I backpedaled to the foot of the bed and studied the clipboard. Temperature and blood pressure both normal. *Vital signs stable.*

"How're you feeling?"

"Better, Doc. I'm hungry enough to try the food."

"It's hard to mess up scrambled eggs, but they find a way."

Positioning my stethoscope over his abdomen, I listened for bowel sounds. After the trauma of an injury or surgery, the intestines develop an ileus—quitting work while they heal. The body's way of immobilizing itself in the same manner we rest our back or knee after a sprain. Gurgles came from his lower belly—a sign things were already starting to work. "Pass any gas?"

Mike smiled and nudged the older boy. "You mean fart?"

Both kids giggled.

"That's right. Did you?"

"Well, I ain't been counting them, but yeah, I'd say I've cut a few."

"Good, I'll start you on some food today. And the more you're up and around, the quicker you'll get out of here."

Mike looked ready to jump out of bed. "The sooner the better. I can't afford to lose my job. Not in times like these." His wife stroked his hand.

"You want me to call them? Broken ribs are going to hurt for weeks. You really shouldn't be lifting anything heavy for a while."

"They don't care, Doc. If one of my men faints from the heat, he's replaced the same day. Got to be at least five men in line for every job. I'll be lucky if they wait a week for me."

"So let me call."

"No thanks, Doc. Won't matter. Hey, I've been meaning to ask…well, I heard the nurses… is it…heck, did you give me some of your own blood?"

I nodded, not sure where he was going with this. His wife looked away again as if I'd broken some taboo.

"You ever do that before?"

"You're my first." I looked down at his kids. "There was no other choice."

"I know, Doc. I…uh…" He ran his fingers through his older boy's crew cut. "Well…you know, thanks…thanks for what you did."

"Sure." I could tell he was fighting back tears, not wanting to cry in front of his boys. "Tell me more about the work you do."

"We're bringing Colorado River water to LA. Working three shifts, seven days a week to get it done. Two hundred miles of aqueducts and tunnels through a hundred and ten degree hell. But we're ahead of schedule, something my boss, Henry Kaiser, is happy about. You ever hear of him?"

"Kaiser? No. Back in college, I'd thought about being an architect. Worked on some construction sites myself. Nothing in the desert though."

Mike smiled widely, exposing two chipped front teeth. "Well, I'm glad you decided to become a doctor."

*Sidney*…I could still hear one of my father's lectures. *Use your head not your back. It's what your mother would have wanted.* He'd told me so many times to study and become a doctor. But, after watching my mother choke to death on her own blood when the doctor refused to help her, I'd been afraid of blood. Afraid of even the smallest scratch. Over the years, as I thought more about that doctor, it became clear, as if by a law of nature, what my destiny should be.

"Dr. Garfield?"

Anna, the only nurse I'd broken my rule with, stood at the door. "Dr. Keating called looking for you. You were supposed to be in his office a half-hour ago. And you know him…he sounds mad."

I looked down at my watch. It still showed twenty minutes before my meeting with the Dean. Dammit. The minute hand had stopped. "I must have forgot to wind this. God, he's going to be nuts."

She looked at me like she always did: wide-eyed with a hint of a smile. Flawless skin, slightly crooked nose, long dark hair tucked under her white nurse's hat, she had grown more attractive over the years. We'd grown up in the same neighborhood and were the same age. We used to go to the same Temple on Saturdays and I knew she still cared for me, even after what I'd said to her. But I had promised myself not to get involved with a nurse I worked with. It always led to hurt feelings and bad teamwork.

"Come here," Anna said.

Just outside the door, she spoke softly. "Please, Sid, apologize to the Dean.

You're too good a surgeon. If you won't do it for yourself, do it for me." She squeezed my hand, turned and walked down the hallway.

*Too good a surgeon.* Nothing more. *Just friends.* I watched her as she went to check on another patient and wondered for the thousandth time if I'd made the right decision.

"So, Doc, is it true?" Mike interrupted my daydreaming. He was already out of bed and walking down the hallway on his own. "Are you getting fired because you saved my life?"

"That wouldn't make much sense, would it? Nice family you have there."

I waved to Mike and without allowing him another word strode twenty steps down the hall. Mike was the last patient on my morning rounds. I liked to save my best and healthiest patients—my successes—for last. It was the successes that kept me going and the failures that made me strive to improve. My other two inpatients, a man with a perforated ulcer and a young boy with a ruptured appendix were turning the corner, but both could have been home days ago if they would have come in sooner. People who couldn't afford medical care waited until the last minute to seek help. Many times they waited until it was too late. Pneumonia patients died every day who would have survived if treated early with the new sulfa medicines. There had to be a way of providing good care to more people.

Down the corridor the linoleum became carpet, and the stink of pus and urine turned to the scent of polished wood. It made no sense why Dean Keating sat in an air-conditioned office while sick patients, who needed the comfort to heal, sweated away in overcrowded wards whose only ventilation was an open window and an old electric fan. Definitely not the way I'd design a hospital.

"Dr. Garfield." Anna yelled from down the hallway. She never panicked. Without waiting to ask, I ran back to the ward, thinking something terrible had just happened to Mike.

"The Peds ward just called, they're looking for anyone, any surgeon—"

"What? Do you know what?"

"A six year old, can't breathe."

I raced to the stairs and yelled back to Anna. "Go to the OR, pick up a trach set and metal tube."

Taking two stairs at a time, I climbed the three floors to the Pediatric ward. I don't know what it was about operating on children, their size, age, parents— maybe the unfairness of being sick so young. Whatever it was, it made me nervous and there's nothing more dangerous than a panicky surgeon.

As soon as I opened the door and entered the hallway, it was easy to find the emergency. A group of nurses stood outside the room, waiting for me.

"Doctor!" One waved frantically. "Hurry."

In the room a child was sitting up in bed, leaning forward, gasping for air, his face the blue-gray of shock—just like a scene from one of my medical student nightmares. Next to him his mother held his hand, tears running down her face. "Breathe, Jimmy. Breathe."

I tried to sound calm. "You're going to be fine, Jimmy." I turned to one of the nurses at the door. "When did—"

"We admitted him yesterday." The pediatrician came into the room. "Upper respiratory symptoms, but not straightforward. Chest muscle weakness. We're working him up for both polio and croup."

The mother's breath caught at the mention of polio.

I listened to the boy's chest and watched his rib muscles strain to get in the tiniest of breaths. He was fighting, gasping for breath, tiring quickly. Where was Anna?

"Please…hurry, doctor," the mother said. "Do something."

The boy was rapidly losing consciousness. "Call for an anesthesiologist," I said, "now."

Out of breath, Anna rushed into the room and opened a tray of instruments, spreading them out at the foot of the bed. I hesitated like a first-year resident. The anesthesiologist wouldn't be able to breathe for the boy. Stridor. Upper airway obstruction, not just paralysis from polio. Any attempt to push air in through his mouth would be futile. There was only one thing to do and quickly. Jimmy's eyes rolled back in his head and he went limp. His breathing stopped.

I glanced over at the pediatrician. He looked as panicked as I felt. Anna put her hand on my shoulder. "Dr. Garfield?"

"Scalpel." I'd done an emergency tracheotomy on a dog before, but never…shit, the lighting was terrible. "Lay him down flat. Put a pillow under his shoulders, I want his neck extended." Jimmy was blue, his lips crusted and closed. I gripped the knife in my right hand and felt for the cricoid cartilage, a tiny protrusion of the trachea, the landmark I needed to make my incision. God, his neck was small; it was hard to tell for sure. If I veered off center to one side or the other, I'd slash open the carotid artery and he'd bleed to death. *Stop hesitating.*

"Doctor, do something!" Jimmy's mother grabbed my arm. "Can't you do something?"

I looked at her and wondered if she could see the panic in my eyes.

"Please, stand back." The pediatrician gently moved her away.

I took a deep breath, steadied my hand and cut through the skin, down to the cartilage in one pass. Blood filled the wound, but Anna dabbed it away with gauze. I felt the cartilage, not hard like an adult's, more spongy and soft like a newborn. I pushed down the knife. I was in.

"Give me the tube."

Anna handed me the metal trach tube and I pushed it through the opening in the trachea.

"You sure you're in?" the pediatrician asked.

He still wasn't breathing—no reassuring rush of air—nothing. Which meant he had polio and his trachea was swollen shut with pus.

"Jesus, Sid." It was Donny Rand, the anesthesia resident. He had a pediatric mask connected to an ambu bag, the kind he used in the OR to breathe for patients.

"See if you can force any air in," I said. My stomach churned and I fought back a sudden wave of nausea.

He held the mask tightly over the tube. Jimmy's chest didn't budge an inch.

"You sure you're in the trachea?" Rand said.

"Yeah…I'm in."

I tried to breathe but couldn't. I tried to blink but couldn't. My mother had died exactly like this. Suffocated to death. The moment felt surreal; it had knocked the air out of me and brought everything to a standstill.

"Suction," Rand said. "Hand me the suction."

"I'll have to go to the OR to get one," Anna said.

I started to focus. "Get a bulb syringe, we'll try and aspirate it."

"I'm not feeling a pulse," Rand said.

I pressed down on the neck and held the tube in place. "Ventilate him. As hard as you can. Maybe it will drive the pus down into the lungs and we'll—"

Jimmy's face was a lifeless blue. "Harder…breathe for him harder."

Rand shook his head. "It's like concrete."

Jimmy's mother broke out in sobs, screams I knew I'd never forget, like the cry of an animal trying to pry its cub free from a bear trap. The room felt too hot suddenly—sweat burst from my pores. Was this really happening? I'd never lost a patient before. "I'm sorry…very sorry." The words spilled out on their own.

Anna clutched my arm. I didn't know what to say. I'd always fought death before, or at least done everything anyone could. Jimmy's mother clutched his hand in hers, sobbing, crying out, "Jimmy, Jimmy, my Jimmy," over and over.

"You're late for your meeting," Anna said. "I'll stay and take care of her."

"To hell with the Dean." My feet felt glued to the floor. I didn't know what I should do to console Jimmy's mother, so I just stood there and let her sob.

"I'm sorry," I repeated, feeling like I'd said it a thousand times. She stopped crying and looked at me, with the deep sadness of immeasurable loss. Then she held Jimmy's head to her chest and just closed her eyes.

"Please, Sid. There's nothing more you can do here," Anna said. "I'll stay with her. Come back up after you talk to Keating."

"Okay." I rushed back down the stairs, sweat rolling down my forehead, my heartbeat pounding in my ears, trying to get Jimmy's blue face out of my head and think about what I'd tell the Dean. My mouth tasted like I'd sucked on an onion. In my coat pocket was an old piece of Juicy Fruit gum. I popped it in my mouth, the taste—any taste—a welcome relief from the sour taste of anguish. I opened the stairwell door to the surgical floor and almost ran over Cecil Cutting.

"Sid, what the hell happened to you?"

Cecil, my best friend and fellow surgery resident, rail thin in his clean white coat, shook his head from side to side. "You're covered in blood and pus."

The words stammered out. "A kid with polio and upper airway obstruction."

"Why didn't you call me?"

"There wasn't time. Had to do an emergency trach on a six-year-old.

Polio…goddamn polio. He didn't make it."

"Shit, holy shit, Sid. I'm sorry." Another *I'm sorry* rang in my head. He grabbed my right arm. "Sid, you did everything you could. Everything anybody could. So don't start beating yourself up, not now, not while the Dean's waiting. You trying to get kicked out of here? C'mon, Sid, I was looking forward to us graduating together. You know what you've got to do, don't you? You listening? You've got to kiss up."

I nodded.

"Play along, say yes to everything. Even you can survive three more weeks in this place."

"I'd better hurry."

"Kiss up," he repeated.

I threw him a wave, headed back down the hall to the air conditioned administration area, and knocked on the Dean's door.

"Enter."

I opened the door and cringed.

# CHAPTER 3

## Los Angeles County Hospital

## June 6, 1940

"Garfield," Dean Keating looked at me with an angry stare, "most residents come on time. Most don't come here chewing gum. But you always have to be different." He talked as if every word summed up chapters of a medical textbook.

"Yes, sir. I *am* sorry. There was an emergency." I remained in the doorway, knees weak. There was nowhere to throw out my gum and he didn't invite me to sit down. He sat at his oversized mahogany desk, behind him his wall of glory with thirty years of diplomas, awards, and photos with celebrities. I think he was waiting for me to beg for mercy.

"Do you realize your most important duty is to uphold the reputation of this hospital and our surgical program?"

"No, sir. I thought it was to my patients. To do all that I can, to do everything possible to heal them…to make them well. Isn't that—?"

"Don't you dare lecture me about caring for patients." Keating leaned forward in his chair, his face beefy red. "I've been doing it since before you were born. Medicine is about discipline. Following the rules. Following established techniques and lessons. If you do whatever you think—that's right, Garfield, *you think*—every time you're in trouble, you'll forget your training and more times than not, your patients will suffer."

"Patients don't always follow your rules, Dean. And when they don't, are we to act like sheep? That's not why I went into medicine. A good doctor has to be able to think for himself, to think what's best for his patient, to—"

"Damn it, Garfield. Don't you ever listen? If you weren't the number one resident in this program, I wouldn't bother. I've seen you in the OR and I've heard you on rounds. I'm willing to give you a final chance if you promise to obey your superiors. Listen to everything Chandler and I tell you. There's still more you need to learn—even you, Garfield."

Kiss his ass. Cecil's words. "I...I can't do that." I knew exactly what would happen next. "My patients come first and if there's anything—anything at all that can be done to help them—"

"You had better give a damn, and quick, young man." Dean Keating rose from his leather chair. "Or you'll be expelled from this residency."

"You'd expel me for doing what's best for my patients?"

"Transfusing blood was against all medical precedent. A blood reaction alone could have killed him. I want to give you a chance. But when you act like this, you leave me little choice."

"I don't think you understand, Dean. I knew my blood type. O negative. I couldn't have done any harm."

"For God's sake," Keating said. "Sit down and listen to me." He gave a long, theatrical sigh. "New procedures and treatments require a slow, gradual acceptance, and only after thorough clinical trials have been carried out. We don't experiment on patients."

"Blood transfusions have been effective for years. England started a blood bank months ago."

Keating's red face relaxed. "Sidney, how old are you?"

His sudden calmness surprised me.

"Twenty-eight."

"And what does your father do?"

"He owns a clothing store." I wasn't sure where he was going with this new line of questioning.

"Would he want you to leave with three weeks left? Have you thought about what this will mean to your career?"

"Yes." I'd thought about little else for the past few days.

"How do you propose to practice? No hospital will hire a surgeon without a certificate of training."

"I won't ask them to hire me." I swallowed hard. "I'm going on my own.

I'll provide my patients the best possible care."

The Dean opened his top drawer and took out a single page form. "I've tried to help you," he said with resignation. He signed the bottom of the page. "You're dangerous and stubborn, Garfield. You refuse to listen. You have the potential to be a great surgeon and someday you'll realize I'm right." He smiled blandly. "You have a lot of growing up to do. I'm giving you the chance…I'm giving you your residency certificate—letting you graduate—but I want you out of my hospital today. Out of my sight and out of LA." Keating picked up the phone. My signal that the interview was over.

I closed his office door and walked down the carpeted hallway to the linoleum floor of my patients' rooms. Standing outside Mike's door, I watched him smile as he held his young son on his lap, his family at his bedside. Time to forget the Dean and what he stood for, and think only of my patients—of the Mikes and Jimmys. I knew what had to be done.

# CHAPTER 4

Downtown Los Angeles

June 6, 1940

My father, Isaac Greenfield, changed his name to Garfield because he wanted to take the name of a president, any president whose last name started with a "G." He had emigrated from the pogroms of anti-Semitic Russia in the 1890s and didn't want anyone to ever doubt his patriotism. He'd learned English at night school and had become an American citizen. My father saw the world in black and white and would never understand why Keating had fired me. Ever since I could remember, ever since my mother's death, it was my father who had decided what was right and what was wrong.

Even though I was twenty-eight years old, I still feared and hated my father's disapproval. I climbed up the back stairs to the small apartment we lived in above his clothing store on Flower and Spring Streets. As usual, the alley behind the brown brick building smelled of fried won ton and spices from the Chinese restaurant next door. I glanced down at my watch. It was ticking away perfectly now that I'd wound it. Since it was still before five, my father would be in his store. He would never consider hanging the *Closed* sign until ten minutes after five, just in case a customer had been caught in traffic. Black and white. The customer always came first. Something he taught me that stuck with me as a doctor treating patients.

Inside our apartment, the smell of mothballs overpowered everything. Moths were an enemy in a clothing store and none survived here. The apartment had two bedrooms, mine a small one off the kitchen, my father's larger, with its own bathroom he'd had built just for my mother. By the front door stood my mother's mahogany cabinet, six feet tall with three sets of glass doors. Inside, at eye level, were our framed family photos, which had gone as yellow and grainy over the years as my own memory of her. When I closed my eyes her face blurred and it was harder and harder to remember what she looked like. I picked up the silver frame, the one with my mother posing in front of my father's store.

Share-Voney. My mother's nickname. Polish for her coppery-red hair. Whenever I thought of her I felt both love and emptiness, like I'd never really known her. Back in 1918, half the world was dying of the flu. Even after more than twenty years, the pain of her death and the doctor who'd let her die haunted me like a recurring nightmare.

"Are you *meshugganah*?" I hadn't heard my father come in the apartment. I put the photo back and closed the glass doors.

"What's wrong with you, Sidney?"

My father's stony blue eyes bore into mine and, just like that, I felt hot, like on that day my mother had gotten sick. "Nothing, Dad. Nothing."

"Nothing? What were you thinking? Dean Keating just called me. I'm ashamed of you. How could you quit after so many years of hard work? Quit with only a few weeks to go?"

My tongue felt dry and covered in dirt.

"Huh, Sidney? I thought I taught you better. How could you?" He took out a handkerchief from his suit pocket and wiped the sweat from his cheek. Even on the hottest summer day, my father dressed in a double-breasted coat. I couldn't decide whether to ask for forgiveness or jump out the window.

"You taught me the customer comes first. Well, for me my patients come first."

"No, Sidney. You didn't listen. Staying in business comes first. Otherwise, I'd give everything away and be on the streets tomorrow. For you, staying in school, finishing, should have come first."

I stared at my mother's cabinet, at a photo of the three of us, my mother's arm around me, my father's arms at his side.

"Let's sit down in the kitchen and talk," I said. "Maybe you'll understand."

He followed me into the kitchen and sat down across from me, his double breasted suit buttoned, his hands clenched in front of him. "Okay, tell me why."

"I had a patient who was bleeding to death. He was about to die when I decided to try something new. A blood transfusion. I gave him my own blood."

"You what?" His hands remained unmoving on the wood table.

"It's being done in England since the war started. There was no other choice."

"And?"

"He's going to be fine."

He placed his hands flat on the table now. "So why was the Dean mad?"

"Because I didn't follow the rules. I did what had to be done to save this man and I'd do it all over, even if I knew I'd be kicked out again."

He undid his jacket, got up, placed it over the chair, and lit the stove. "You want some tea?"

I nodded.

"Go apologize," he said, facing the stove. "The Dean may change his mind and let you finish."

"No, he won't and it doesn't matter. He gave me my residency certificate. I can practice as a surgeon anywhere except LA."

His tone softened. "You know, Sidney, you're a lot like your mother."

I thought of that grainy image of her in my head. "How?"

"I could never convince her to change her mind once she was set on something."

When the tea kettle whistled, I watched him fill both cups and wondered how much time would pass before we would talk like this again. He scooted his chair back, sat down and handed me my cup. "Your mother was usually right, you know."

I sipped the hot tea. "I wish I'd known her better."

"Share-Voney," he whispered. I hadn't heard him say that in years.

"I'm going to start a hospital in the desert."

"Now I know you're *meshugganah*."

"No, it's where the business is and where I'll be needed the most. The last thing they need in LA is another surgeon. In the desert, I'll start my own hospital, run it the way I want, take care of patients the way I want, and make more money than I'd ever make around here."

"Sidney, Sidney. Think what you're doing. First you try to play God. Now you're moving to the desert like Moses. Just go apologize to the Dean. Please. For me."

In the end, no matter what I said, my father thought in black and white. This was no exception. Maybe I had turned out more like my mother than him; I'd never know. The tea moistened my dry throat, making it easy to talk. "Remember Dr. Foster, the one who refused to treat Mom? I promised myself I'd never be like that—I'd go to where people needed me the most. Oh, I'm not planning on doing it for free. But I'll never refuse to help anyone. Never."

My father looked at me for a long while and I knew he was thinking about what my mother would have done, what she would have said to me. "Wait here." He stood up abruptly and walked to his bedroom. I sipped the tea and wondered what he was thinking. How disappointed he must be, that he couldn't bear to sit with me any longer.

He returned a few minutes later, his expression softer. "Come," was all he said. Not waiting for me to answer, he opened the door and I followed him down the stairs to the alley filled with the smell of Chinese food. A neon sign in the shape of a dragon buzzed like static in my ears. "How are you going to get to the desert?" He asked. "Walk?"

"Well, no."

He reached in his pants pocket and handed me a set of keys. "I know you, Sidney. What you did was right and if the Dean won't accept that, well, so be it. There," he said, pointing to his old Studebaker touring car. "It needs a new paint job but it will make it to the desert."

I took the keys and looked from him to the car. I wanted to hug him, but that was something we never did. Maybe over the years as my father's hair had grayed, I'd been too busy becoming a doctor to notice he was also capable of thinking in shades of gray.

# CHAPTER 5

Desert Center

## October 11, 1940

Funny, how things never turn out the way you hope they will.

Standing at the front door of my hospital, I squinted into the desert sunlight. Though it was after four, the sun beat down as bright and white hot as noon. A few lizards skittered around, darting from one cholla cactus to the next. Desert Center, California. An area of the Mojave Desert so hot and dry, the air felt like breathing sand. The finished framework of the hospital cast long shadows against the cement slab. Workmen plastered the walls under the finished asphalt shingled roof.

Maybe Dean Keating, sitting in his air-conditioned office, sneaking a few puffs of his cigarette was having the last laugh. Maybe I should've listened to him. Even my father thought I'd lost my mind when I withdrew my life savings of $2,500 to move to the middle of nowhere and start my own hospital.

But nothing could be farther from the truth. There were no jobs anywhere in LA, at least for me. The Depression and Dean Keating had seen to that. Here in Desert Center, there were five thousand patients without a surgeon. My surgical skills would get plenty of business and I'd make enough in a few years to move anywhere I wanted and start my own practice.

A brown dust cloud appeared on the horizon and through the stirring sand I could see a car coming my way. A convertible, definitely not the Ford my father bought after giving me his Studebaker. This car was new, a Buick with its top down.

Dwight Chandler waved from the driver's seat as he parked the car and shut off its engine. "Sid, old boy, it's good to see you." He bolted out and around to open the passenger door for a woman.

"Dwight," I managed in a tone as plastic as his grin. Some primeval reflex made me shake his extended hand. I'd agreed to meet him at my construction site for only one reason—a loan to help finish the hospital. I looked away from that grin to the young woman standing next to him; face obscured by the late afternoon shadow, her strawberry blonde hair a fiery red aura.

"This is Judy Avalon," Chandler's hand rested on her shoulder, "my nurse."

She stepped into the shade of the hospital and her blue eyes hesitated on mine before looking away. A beautiful woman in her early twenties, with skin freckled by the outdoors, full lips, and a smile punctuated by the dimpling on her cheeks.

She extended her hand. I shook it.

"I don't want to beat around the bush," Chandler said. "You've always been a good surgeon and a smart guy." Trying to be nonchalant, he nearly leaned against a cactus, but caught himself before any damage was done. I stifled a smirk. Without skipping a beat he said emphatically, "I want you to join my practice in Palm Springs."

"You're kidding, right? In case you didn't notice, you're standing next to the hospital I'm building."

"We can both use your hospital. Why compete against each other when we can be partners? Besides, sharing calls and office space will make our lives easier."

Now, the old Chandler was beginning to make sense. Call it bad luck…or call it coincidence, Chandler's practice was less than an hour away from mine and he was worried my hospital might take away some of his business.

"Mind if I look around while you two talk?" Judy asked.

"Sure. Just watch your step."

"I'll be careful," she said in the soft kind of voice that makes men want to jump tall buildings. She headed toward what would soon be my operating room.

I glanced at my watch. My father would be here any minute. "Are you planning on seeing construction workers?"

"Well, of course," Chandler said. "They have accident insurance. You know that. And for everything else it's fee-for-service. Anyone that can pay—"

"Dr. Garfield," Mike Everett yelled from just outside the hospital, "over here!" When he'd lost his job at the aqueduct, I'd hired him as my construction foreman.

"What's your answer?" Chandler persisted.

"Wait a minute. Let me see what my contractor wants."

"Sid, before you say no, I've talked to Dean Keating. He's willing to write you a letter of recommendation so you can practice in LA if you work with me for at least one year. C'mon, man, it has to be too hard to pass up."

"Doctor! In the back."

I rushed through the hospital. Chandler's nurse, Judy, was standing next to Mike. "What's wrong?"

He pointed to a large metal compressor. "The air conditioners you ordered don't have enough BTU—"

"Jesus, Mike. I thought someone had died. BTU?"

"British thermal units, Doc. They want five hundred bucks more for the right ones."

"Five hundred more? Jesus, I thought you'd figured all this out."

"Sorry, Doc. We placed the order before you changed the plans and added on the extra square feet."

"Hell, go ahead. Order them. The only reason my patients will sweat is if they have a fever."

"Okay, Doc. It's your money."

Judy gave me a look like I'd just thrown money down the drain. "Do you really think construction workers care about air conditioning? It sounds like a terrible waste of money. Build an extra two beds, enlarge your OR. I'd put the money to better use."

"Better use than comforting the sick? A nurse should understand—"

"Yes, of course I do," she said coldly.

"Sorry." I ran my hand over my forehead, wiping away the sweat. "Chandler's waiting. Feel free to look around."

Hadn't I said that to her earlier? Maybe she was right. I could use the money to enlarge the hospital...if I had the money. Hell, Chandler wasn't that bad a guy. Well, maybe he was lazy when it came to medicine, but he was sharp when it came to making money. Depending on the arrangement, I could get him to help finance the hospital as part of a partnership deal and help my initial cash flow.

I walked around a sawed off two by four and a few piles of sawdust to the front of the hospital. Chandler puffed away on a cigarette, holding it in one of those two-fingered aristocratic grips.

"Okay, Dwight. I'm interested. What do you have in mind as a salary arrangement?"

"Trust me, Sid. I'm not about to cheat you. We'll split all our billings minus overhead. I'll pay the overhead for the Palm Springs office, you pay for the hospital. I'll even pay you extra whenever I operate here, both for the OR and hospital bed. We'll work out a fee schedule."

Judy walked to the front and hesitated as if she were accidentally overhearing a secret.

"Time to go, Judy," Chandler said. "I promised the Winthrops I'd make a house call and it would be great of you to help."

"Sure, okay."

"Let me know tomorrow," Chandler said.

"You willing to put up half the money to finish the hospital?"

"Are you kidding? C'mon, Sid, I'm offering to make you a partner based on the fact you're paying for the hospital. I paid for my office. My offer applies only after you pay for it."

I felt like Chandler had cheated me and we hadn't signed an agreement yet. Helping me finish the hospital would have been too good to be true, too unlike Chandler. "I'll think about it."

"You do that. Good-bye, Garfield." With a mock salute, he was off.

To my surprise, Judy looked at me for a long moment before walking away. There was something about her eyes. Their large, green-flecked blue irises made me feel uneasy, like a high school kid around a prom queen.

I never trusted Chandler as a resident and I didn't trust him now. Which meant I knew what I was getting myself into. I'd take care of my own patients and make sure he took care of his. At the same time, going in with Chandler would ensure that I'd make a good income and pay back my hospital loans.

I had 5,000 workers and Chandler had to have that many if not more patients in Palm Springs. And knowing him, he'd already made referral arrangements with every G.P. in town. What the hell. Even the letter of recommendation from Keating was tempting. As usual, Chandler had thought of all the angles.

"It's gotta be over a hundred and fifteen." Mike cleared his throat. I hadn't seen him standing a few feet from me. "How about if we go over to Desert Center for a drink…Doc? You listening?"

"Uh…yeah." My father was driving out and wouldn't tolerate tardiness, or worse, the hint of alcohol on my breath. You'd think I was seventeen by the way he treated me. I took a few steps and almost stumbled over Judy's purse. What a dummy I'd been. That look she'd given me was probably her trying to remember where she'd left it. "Sorry, but my father's meeting me. Four o'clock sharp. How about a rain check?"

"Okay, Doc," Mike mumbled, heading over to supervise the men loading the air conditioners back onto the truck. "But around here, that could mean years."

I kept thinking of that day in the OR when Chandler had told me to stop, to not try the blood transfusion. If I'd listened, Mike wouldn't have been here today. And this was the same man I was going into business with?

My father pulled up ten minutes before four. He got out of his car and moved slower than I'd ever seen him, either stiff from the long ride or from sixty-plus years that were starting to catch up with him. We may have disagreed at times, but the thought of my father getting old bothered me. He leaned against one of the hospital's exterior walls as workmen inside pounded away, putting on the finishing touches. "What's wrong with you, Sidney?"

"Huh?" A hot wind blew off the desert floor as the late afternoon sun descended toward jagged peaks. "Nothing, Dad."

"Nothing? What are you thinking? How can you possibly make money here? Building a hospital in the middle of nowhere, spending all your money for what? Huh, Sidney? For what?"

He took out a handkerchief from his suit pocket and wiped the sweat from his cheek and the sandy grit from his eyes. Even in the desert, my father dressed in a double-breasted coat, as if he were ready to take care of one of his customers.

"Dad, remember what you taught me? It's better to make ten dollars a week on your own than one hundred dollars working for someone else? I'm taking your advice, that's exactly what I'm doing." I nudged his shoulder. "C'mon, let's get out of the sun. I'll show you how much progress we've made."

"This is your office?" he asked as we entered the small room off the entry hall.

"Office and bedroom. I plan on sleeping here until I'm busy enough to hire another surgeon." I pointed out the window to the rugged mountain peaks in the distance and a tailings pile from the tunnel being drilled for the aqueduct. "Not a bad view."

My father swallowed hard, a sign he was about to start one of his canned lectures. Before he could begin, I led him into the twelve-bed ward. I'd sketched the plans myself and hired a draftsman to draw up the blueprints. Everything was designed for patient comfort and efficiency. "Curtains will be around every bed for privacy, Venetian blinds on the windows, air-conditioning…and look here." I pointed to the four-foot tall metal box that still smelled of oil. "My very own X-ray machine."

"You bought that? How could you afford it?"

"The Depression." I ran my hand over the metal casing. "Companies are willing to negotiate. No one's buying anything anymore so I worked out a deal. Twenty dollars a month with an option to buy. Same with my surgical equipment. Republic Supply. Everything is the latest."

"You still didn't answer me."

"I borrowed the money from the bank."

"How much?"

"Ten thousand." I'd put everything I had, the $2,500 cash and the ten thousand borrowed, into building the hospital, but needed at least ten thousand more to get things up and running. "Look, Dad. I could use some help. I know you don't have the money to loan me, but…well, I was hoping you might co-sign a loan."

He gave me a stunned look. "You want me to put up my store as collateral? Everything? Tell me how you are going to pay it back out here in the desert."

He'd spent years building his business and struggled not to lose it during the Depression. But I had to make him understand. "There are five thousand workers here. Accident insurance will help pay some of their bills. I may go into partnership with another doctor in Palm Springs. That should help me pay back the loans. Dad, listen." He looked hot in his suit. Sweat dripped down his forehead, his face red from the heat. "It's the right thing to do. You taught me that. They need a doctor here. I've seen men die because they were driven to Los Angeles for emergency treatment. Others without money are turned away." I didn't have to finish the sentence by adding, *like Mom*. My father knew that all too well.

"Dr. Garfield! Quick, hurry."

What now…a plumbing problem? But this time there was genuine panic in Mike's voice.

I rushed to the front door, my father right behind me. Mike was carrying a man, screaming in pain, his right hand mostly a stump, arterial blood pumping over both of them. "Dynamite explosion." Mike's voice trembled. "His hand…he blew off his hand."

"Put him down on the floor." I removed my belt and made a makeshift tourniquet around his arm, just below the elbow. His thumb and index fingers were still intact, but only ragged sockets of tissue remained where the other fingers once existed. I had twenty minutes of tourniquet time to tie off his ulnar artery or he'd lose his whole hand. His face turned pale gray as he went into shock. His screams quieted into moans. "Lift his feet. Cover him."

I looked up at my father. Arterial blood had sprayed over his pants. He looked ashen, ready to pass out. "Dad…" I grabbed him by the shoulder and led him to the front steps where Judy Avalon stood, looking more mirage than real.

"I'm okay," he said, "go back and—"

"Can I help?" Judy asked.

"Yes, yes." I pointed to my office. "The IV set-ups. I need to get my instruments."

Two carpenters were finishing the exterior siding. "One of you, come with me." We raced to the back storeroom. All of my equipment was still packed neatly away in a wooden crate. "Your hammer, over here. I need to open this."

"Move over, Doc," the carpenter said. He used the claw end to rip open the crate, shattering the wood as he loosened the nails and pulled off the top. I sifted through the packing paper to the leather cases filled with surgical instruments. *Dammit*. They were all mixed up. Scalpels, hemostats, retractors, all wrapped separately. I started tearing off the paper…five…ten packages until

I'd found the right instruments. The tourniquet had already been on for at least ten minutes and the maximum time without causing permanent damage was twenty. That left me less than ten minutes to find the severed artery and veins and tie them off.

I nodded thanks to the workers and rushed back to the front hallway, where Mike looked as pale as the injured man. Kneeling beside the patient, Judy inserted the IV needle into a vein on the man's good arm and lifted the bottle until the saline solution flowed in freely. I'd never seen a nurse start an IV before. She was skilled and competent, the kind of assistant I'd like to have at my hospital full time.

"Okay, Mike. We'll take over now." With only minutes left to save his hand, there was no time to administer an anesthetic. I cleaned off the shreds of what was once a fully functional hand, removing bits of bone and flesh that had been blown apart by the explosion. The worker was stuperous, mumbling words incoherently as he went in and out of consciousness. "Hold him still, Judy."

Without hesitation, she lifted the man's hand from where I'd held it on my knee, rested it on her clean white nurses' skirt and retracted the skin, helping to expose the severed blood vessels. With the snap of two hemostats I had the major arteries clamped off. "I think this will do it," I said, releasing the tourniquet.

"Not bad," Judy said, smiling. "Glad I drove back for my purse." The bleeding, except for a slight ooze from the raw flesh wound, had stopped.

I wrapped a gauze bandage around the injured hand. "So am I."

"Sidney." My father stood behind us, the normal resonant boom of his voice quieted to a murmur. I got up and faced him. He curled his arm around my neck and gave my brow a single kiss. He hadn't kissed me since I was a child. "I am proud of you, Sidney. Very proud."

He gave me one of his looks like when I'd graduated high school, college, and medical school. "I'll help you build your hospital."

# CHAPTER 6

Contractor's General Hospital

## August 17, 1941

How had it come to this? My Winchester rifle rested snugly against my shoulder, my hand ready to squeeze the trigger. Behind me the hospital was quiet. Not the quiet of peace, harmony, and health. It was more like the quiet before one's last breath, a terminal silence that would soon force me to shut down. Something scurried twenty yards away. I tightened my index finger and fired. The explosion broke the calm and sent a flock of desert quail flapping into the sky against the backdrop of a fiery sun setting below jagged mountains.

I crept from the back stoop of the hospital, easing closer to my kill, ready to club it over the head if it had somehow survived the gunshot wound. Not a chance. The shot was fatal, entering the left ear and exiting just lateral to the right eye.

How had it come to this? I asked myself again. I was going bankrupt after less than six months. Creditors everywhere; I had unpaid payments to the bank and surgical supply company, couldn't afford a nurse, and hadn't paid the Hermans, the retired couple that acted as my cook and custodians, for the last three weeks. The bank was even threatening to take over my father's business, which kept me up nights worrying. I'd sell everything and move back to LA before I'd allow that.

I'd stalled signing up with Chandler, thinking I could make it on my own. But hell, principles didn't pay the bank. I hated to think going in with Chandler would compromise me, but I had to do something. The way things were going, I was becoming a better hunter than surgeon. All thanks to Industrial Indemnity

Insurance. The company that insured the workers building the aqueduct refused to pay my fees for services and most of the time denied payment altogether. Non-industrial, they'd say about every case of pneumonia, skin infection, and almost everything except a broken bone. Back pain from carrying boulders, "powder headaches" from being too close to dynamite, were all denied. What a bunch of hooey. Stephen Atwood, my one patient in the hospital would never be able to pay me back for his ten-dollar-a-day intravenous sulfa medicines. But he needed my help and pay or not, I took all comers.

The one thing on my side was the bank didn't want to repossess a hospital in the middle of nowhere. I was more worried about my father. He'd co-signed the loan and the bank wouldn't hesitate to take over his business.

My hands tightened around the rabbit's neck as I walked through the hospital, careful not to drip blood on the spotless floors. Mrs. Herman was in the kitchen, slicing carrots and broccoli, preparing to make another one of her tasty rabbit pies.

"*Ach, Doctor Gar*field." Mrs. Herman, in her sixties, looked tired; in fact, she always looked tired. "Do not sneak up when I have a knife in my hand. You would not want me to do that to you when you *op*erate." She spoke in heavily accented English, pronouncing her words with a Germanic emphasis on first syllables.

"Sorry, Mrs. Herman. Can you cook up another pie?" I placed the animal down on a wooden cutting board opposite the vegetables.

"Of course."

The door to the kitchen opened and Robert Herman walked in. He was a large man, not tall but thick in the shoulders and chest, dressed in the mechanic's overalls he'd worn since he'd retired from Ford and moved from the cold winters of Detroit to the scorching summers of the Mojave Desert. He washed his grease-covered hands in the sink and dried them on a dish rag. "One of the air conditioners busted—"

"They're brand new GE's," I interrupted. "How can they break after only…?"

He held out his hands. "It's fine now. Only a fuse. They weren't made for this heat. I'd give the *gott*damn things only a year or two." He turned to Mrs. Herman and gave her a hug.

"*Nein*, Robert, go change." She blushed as she continued chopping carrots. "Dinner will be ready soon."

"What smells so good?" Judy held out a shopping bag full of grapefruits. "Thought you all might like some." She'd been coming by almost every night to help out after working for real wages at Chandler's office during the day.

"Those look great." I looked down at the floor, embarrassed about what I had to tell her. "I'm sorry, Judy, still no check from the insurance company."

"That's okay." She put down the bag and leaned against the sink. "You're good for it. Can I help you, Mrs. Herman?"

"No, no." Mrs. Herman waved her hands to shoo Judy away.

I shrugged. "Keep track of your hours and I'll pay you back when the checks start coming in."

"Sure you will. But for now, I'll settle for Mrs. Herman's rabbit pie."

Mrs. Herman filleted the new rabbit and the fetid smell of intestines filled the kitchen. "It will take an hour to cook."

"Thanks, Mrs. Herman," Judy said in her warm, upbeat tone. "C'mon, doc, let's go check on Stephen."

We walked from the kitchen to Stephen Atwood's bed. "You know, I really am sorry I can't pay you yet."

"Stop worrying. It's not healthy, you know."

I nodded. "Nurse and psychiatrist. You're right about worrying. I borrowed money from my father and—"

"Your father, huh?" She laughed softly. "Now that's something I don't have to worry about."

Stepping into the ward, I stopped a few feet from the bed. "I'm sorry, is your father no longer—"

"No, both my parents live in Palm Springs. I meant borrowing money from him." She smiled a little. "You know, Dwight's getting busier every day."

Okay, for whatever reason, she never talked about her family. But Dwight Chandler...I'd rather she never said a word about him.

"Seems like despite the Depression," she continued, "there are still enough rich people in Los Angeles to buy second homes in the desert. And remember those workers I was telling you about?"

"The ones with the abdominal cramping?"

She nodded. "Dwight's operated on a few of them, thinking it might be appendicitis."

Dwight. For some reason her calling him by his first name bothered me. She still called me doc or Dr. Garfield even after I'd told her to call me Sid. "What did he find?"

"I'm not sure. He throws away the appendix instead of sending it to the lab."

I stood opposite her. "Throws them away, huh? They look red or full of pus?"

She shrugged. "They looked okay to me…but I'm no expert."

I didn't want her to think I was picking on Chandler. "Abdominal cramps in twenty workers going on for two weeks. Any other symptoms?"

"Thirty now," she said. "Dwight's seeing them all daily. He feels their abdomen and the ones that don't need surgery he sends home with Milk of Magnesia, telling them to come back the next day if not better. Says it's gastro-enteritis."

I handed Atwood's vital signs clipboard to Judy.

"Hi Stephen," she said. He perked up as she ran her hand over his forehead and smiled. "Feeling better?"

"Yes, Ma'am."

"Let's check that temperature of yours." She took the mercury thermometer from the cup of antiseptic next to the bed, rinsed it off with water, and placed it under his tongue. "We'll let it sit there for a few minutes."

"Look at this." I held up the X-ray I'd taken a few hours earlier and pointed to the shrinking white shadow of infection. "A few doses of sulfa and what used to take weeks happens in days."

Judy held the X-ray up to the overhead light. "It's great, really great."

I pulled out the thermometer. 98.2. "Perfect, Stephen. You should be out of here tomorrow. Just remember next time to come in sooner." Something I stressed to all the workers. But they couldn't afford paying for their non-industrial care, so they stalled coming in until their cold had become pneumonia.

Judy straightened his sheets and adjusted his pillow. "Sleep well."

"C'mon outside," I said.

We stood on the back porch in the cool ninety-degree heat, the sky a breathtaking furnace of oranges and reds. For a second I felt a fleeting intimacy, but stopped myself. I'd never broken my rule with Anna during residency and I didn't want to risk my good working relationship with Judy. But my rule had been easier to follow before I'd met Judy. And she really didn't work for me, since I'd never been able to pay her. Which made me wonder why she bothered to come at all. Somewhere in my head was the hope she was coming to see me. I swallowed hard. "Tell me more about the sick workers."

She hesitated, studying me for a moment as if she understood what I was really thinking. "They've been sick now for a few weeks. Stomach cramps, nausea, diarrhea. Almost like food poisoning, only it's going on too long."

"There'd also be more men sick," I said. All of the men ate in the large cafeteria built along with the tent dormitories by the company in charge of the project. Kaiser Construction. "Do most of the sick live near one another?"

She shook her head. "I'm not sure."

"Let's go find out."

"Now?"

"Sure, it's only a ten-minute walk. Maybe we can figure this thing out."

I gestured for her to lead the way and we strode down the dirt road toward the workers' camp. A rising full moon helped to light our way and the cooling early evening breeze carried the scent of desert mesquite and sage. What could be more romantic than a walk to check on a bunch of workers with diarrhea?

"How are you going to get by?" She looked at me like I'd just lost my last dime.

"Don't know. You work with Chandler, do you think I should go partners with him?"

She stopped and looked at me, the moonlight reflecting off her eyes. "You want me to be honest?"

Her question surprised me. "Of course."

"You two are very different."

"I know. I worked with him as a resident."

"Then you don't need my answer."

"C'mon, Judy. Don't beat around the bush."

"All right. You asked for it. Dwight is a natural at making money, but maybe not the best doctor. You're a good doctor, but don't seem to make any money." She gazed at me. "Why is that?"

"Good question. I've been asking myself the same thing every hour for the last month. Our whole medical system is crazy, you know."

"What do you mean?"

"There's an epidemic of something going on and Chandler's raking in the dough."

"Sid, that's not fair. He's trying to help them."

"It's not just him. The whole system of fee-for-service payment is upside down. Doctors shouldn't profit from sickness. They should be rewarded for keeping people well. But that's the way things are. And in between them both is the insurance company, which cares only about money."

She was quiet for a moment and I wondered if she'd gotten my point. In the dark it was hard to see anything other than her white uniform.

"I've thought about that, too." Her tone was serious, genuinely questioning. "Only can you come up with a better way?"

"That's my problem. Every one of my ideas requires the insurance company to cooperate with me. And that'll never happen since the construction company that pays them has no incentive to keep workers healthy. If one gets sick or injured, they have five more waiting to take their place. It's almost as bad as when they built the Golden Gate Bridge. Men would hang around waiting for someone to fall so they could apply for a job. Here, they wait for workers to pass out from the heat. Guess there's no choice other than working with Chandler."

She nodded. "Maybe it would be for the best. You'd make him a better doctor and he'd help you make enough money to keep your hospital going."

Made perfect sense on the surface. Only the more I thought about it, the more uneasy it made me. "I'll call him tomorrow and work out the details before the bank starts carting away my equipment."

She smiled. "Yeah, those expensive air conditioners first."

"Very funny."

We reached the first group of tents. I picked a flower off a budding ocotillo and handed it to her. "Smells nice, doesn't it?"

She held it up to her nose. "No, it doesn't smell much at all."

"Well, it looks pretty enough."

She tucked it above her ear and sauntered ahead.

The area looked like a military encampment and with the way things were going in Europe, it could soon turn into a real Army camp. Dirt roads, wide enough for two cars separated each row of five ten-by-ten foot tents. There was an electrical pole next to the main building and cafeteria in the center, but the tents only had kerosene lanterns hanging on poles inside of them. I waved down two workers walking from dinner.

"Hi, I'm Dr. Garfield," I said, "we're looking for the men who're sick… you know, the ones with the stomach problems."

"Two rows over," one of them said. "Can't miss them, the whole place smells like puke." They smiled at Judy and kept on walking.

"You remember any of their names?" I asked her.

"Sure, some of them."

"Good. Take a look as we go by the tents." The names of the four men inside each tent were written in dark ink on the white canvas front flap. When one man became too sick to work, they just brushed over his name with white paint and wrote in another one.

We walked slowly down the second row, past names like Smith, Jones, Adams, and some Irish names like O'Malley, O'Connor, Brody—

"There," she pointed. "Brody. Sean Brody. He was in today. Been sick for a week."

I let out a long breath. We headed over to the tent's open front flap. The place smelled worse than vomit. It had an overpowering fecal odor. Sean Brody, a stout man, pale with thinning red hair, sat on the edge of his cot.

"You're the nurse," Brody said. "What're you doing here?"

"Dr. Garfield and I are here to figure out what made you sick."

"This ain't no place for a lady. The men been acting crazy, you know. It's the heat. And working around the clock. Gets to you, you know."

"Uh huh," I said. How long you been—"

"Mother Mary, here it comes again." Brody turned pale and vomited into a metal basin next to the bed. Light yellow liquid filled the pot, without a trace of blood or digested food. Brody wiped his mouth and took a swig of water. "I've seen that doc in town three times. And still sick as a dog."

"We're working with him," I lied. "Trying to figure this out."

"Well, you don't have to figure hard, Doc. I know what made me sick."

"You do?"

"I already told that other doc."

Judy looked confused. "What did you tell him?"

"The water. I told doc that. They changed trucking companies and now it tastes like, pardon me Ma'am, but it tastes like crap."

"Do you have some water?" I glanced around the tent.

"Yeah, in my wash basin. Oh, it's clean, don't worry, I ain't threw up in it. Take the whole damn thing if you want."

"Thanks, but do you have anything smaller?"

"That canteen next to my cot." He poured some water from the basin into the canteen and screwed on the cap.

"I'll bring it back when I'm done."

"Sure, Doc, but like I said, don't drink it."

"Yeah, thanks."

"Anything for a fellow Irishman." He pointed to my red hair.

I smiled and lifted the canteen in a mock toast.

We walked between the rows of tents, past the loud snoring of exhausted men and back to the hospital. Overhead, stars that went on forever filled the desert sky. We strolled in silence, listening to the buzzing of millions of insects. Halfway to the hospital, I slipped my fingers around her palm. It felt like the most natural thing to do, but the sensation of her hand in mine did something to me that was far from normal. I swear my hand trembled. The desert air was so still, I worried that she heard my heart pounding.

She looked up at me and I let go. "Sorry."

"Don't be," she said.

I tried to keep my voice smooth even though I felt my face flush with embarrassment. "It just happened."

She nodded.

"I may be out of line, but answer me one thing."

She said nothing.

"Aren't you hungry?"

She smiled. "You think Mrs. Herman has finished that rabbit pie?"

"I sure hope so."

"You surprise me, Dr. Garfield."

"Why?"

"You actually have a sense of humor. I thought you were always too busy being a doctor."

"Now look who's funny. Well, if it will keep up my reputation, I want to get this water to the lab before dinner."

"Now, that's the fun doctor I'm used to."

I laughed this time. "You know, I have a real question for you."

She tilted her head. "About food?"

"No. Really. Why are you living out here in the middle of nowhere? You could work in the best hospital in LA. You're better than any nurse I've ever worked with."

She gave me a dismissive shrug. "I guess I just like the heat."

"I'm serious. Is it to be close to your parents?"

"Did you move out here to get away from yours?" she asked.

"No. I miss my father. He's a hard man to live with, but since my mother died, he's done his best…you know, no sacrifice too great for his only son and all." I realized I'd struck a nerve with my interest in her personal life. Her defenses were far too good to be pierced by my questions.

I felt her eyes on me, even though it was too dark out to see for sure. "The child is the father of the man," she said.

"And you can quote Wordsworth. Is there anything you can't do?"

She shrugged. "I can't use a microscope."

"Well, follow me then."

We went through the back door of the hospital to the closet-sized lab next to the OR. I took the dust cloth off the microscope my father had given me on the day I'd been accepted to medical school.

"Let me show you what we have here."

Judy handed me the canteen and I shook it slightly to force any contaminants to the top and placed a drop of water on a slide. A cover slip set on top of the drop flattened it and made it easier to see under magnification. I focused the ocular up and down until I could clearly make out something that shouldn't be there.

"Take a look."

"I wouldn't know what I was looking at."

"Just keep your eyes about an inch or so away from the oculars and tell me what you see."

She squinted as she stared into the microscope while holding her breath, as if she were worried she'd make the water droplet blow away like a speck of dust. "I see some tiny round…I don't know. Tiny round balls, I guess you'd call them. Next to them are some miniature creatures floating and moving around."

I pointed to a large yellow textbook on the shelf next to her. "Hand me that book, will you?"

Steinberg's *Textbook of Microbiology* had the most comprehensive collection of all known microorganisms. I thumbed through to the section on protozoa, remembering their appearance from my college biology class, and found a match.

"What do you think?" I pointed at the black and white picture.

"That's it," she said with the same excitement as if she'd just discovered gold. "I'd say we found the reason the workers are getting sick."

She read the name printed under the picture. "Giardia?"

I nodded. "Did Chandler look at samples from the men?"

"He doesn't have a lab." She stared back into the microscope. "Still believes he can diagnose everything with that black bag of his." She looked up at me. "Can you treat it with sulfa?"

"No, a different medicine, called metronidazole. But more importantly we can prevent it."

"How?"

"Simple. Just boil the water before drinking."

To my surprise, she threw her arms around me. "That's wonderful," she said.

I hugged her back and when we stepped apart, I saw her face fill with color. I tried to think of something to say, what to do next, but nothing came to mind. Rules were meant to be broken. At this moment, I didn't give a damn about my old rule on not getting involved with my nurse. I pulled her close again, feeling her chest against me, her heart beating as fast as mine.

Then just as abruptly, she moved away and looked at her wristwatch.

"It's late and I have to assist Dwight in the OR first thing. I'd better be going."

"Wait, Judy. What about dinner?"

"I'll stop by the kitchen on the way out."

"C'mon," I pressed. "Sorry about the hug."

"Listen," she said. "It's not about that...well, maybe it is." Her face looked pale, as if the blood had suddenly dropped to her feet. "I want to tell you something. Something I haven't told anyone. See if you still feel like hugging me after..."

"Okay," I said. "I'm an expert at keeping secrets."

"I want you to know something that even Dwight doesn't know." She looked away, staring at the wall behind me. "We were serious for a few months, then I realized how stupid that was." Judy broke down and dabbed at her eyes.

I wondered if she was saying that she didn't want to make the same mistake with me. I wiped a tear from her jaw line with my thumb.

She pulled away. "I'm pregnant."

# CHAPTER 7

Contractor's General Hospital

## August 31, 1941

Judy's guilt-reddened eyes met mine. "I'm pregnant," she repeated.

"How?" One of my dumber questions, but I was too stunned to think. I closed the door, hoping that Mrs. Herman wasn't holding her ear to the wall. "Chandler?"

The word came unbidden out of my mouth. I was thinking in flashes, not thoughts. A minute ago I wanted to hold her in my arms and kiss her. Now, well…*Chandler*. Jesus. "How far along?"

She gave me a look somewhere between anger and embarrassment. "Two months. Please, you have to help me."

"Sure. Only, I'm not an obstetrician. Shouldn't you see someone qualified?"

"I can't. No one will —"

"Will what?"

"You know. I'm not about to go to one of those butchers."

"You want an *abortion*?" I'd never performed one and although no doctor had been arrested recently that I knew of, they were still illegal. I put my hand on her shoulder. "Think about what you're asking. Why not have the child?"

"Because I don't love Dwight and I'm not ready to be a mother or get married." Her guilty eyes met mine. "Now that you know…please, please, you have to help me. You've done a D and C. It's no different."

She was right. A dilatation of the cervix and curettage of the uterus was a simple procedure… only there was so much at stake. I didn't know the right answer.

"Does Chandler know? Don't you think he'd—?"

"No, goddammit. He'll want to marry me and, well, I don't feel the same anymore. It was one huge mistake and I want to end it now."

"You have to tell him. It's his child, too."

Her face turned red. "No, never."

"Judy, listen. I'll do everything I can to help you. You can even stay here with Mrs. Herman and I'll deliver the baby. Only I can't do an abortion."

"Can't? You can't or won't? Dwight told me all about you. You quit your residency for principles and end up out here in this godforsaken hell. Life isn't a game. Haven't you learned that yet? Isn't it time to quit being perfect? Isn't it time to stop playing God and help out a friend? If you force me to go... well, I'll do anything to not have this baby." She stalked out of the room, fists clenched.

"Judy, wait."

The door slammed in my face. Mrs. Herman stared down the hall at me like she'd heard everything. I hesitated for a moment. Before I could stop Judy, her car's engine cranked and her wheels kicked up gravel.

What a schmuck I'd been. But, I hadn't been able to get the thought of Chandler and her together out of my head. Chandler? How could she ever have allowed herself? What a stupid question. How could I ever allow myself to think about going in business with him? I'd call her in the morning to make sure she got home okay. I fumbled in my pocket and gripped the ambulance keys in my hand. Hell, I couldn't just sit around and do nothing... if something happened to her. Well, I'd let her down. Maybe she was right. I'd catch up with her now and follow her home.

The phone rang and I picked it up on the first ring. "Sidney?"

"Dad, can I call you later?"

"No, Sidney. The bank came by my store today. They're sending an appraiser out tomorrow. You hear me?"

"An appraiser?"

"The bank is taking over my store. You hear me, Sidney? They might as well bury me." I'd never heard him so upset.

"Dad, I won't let that happen. No matter what. It won't happen." I'd been losing sleep over worrying about it and now, I'd do everything to stop the bank, even if it meant going in with Chandler.

"Then you must come home. Get a job in Los Angeles and forget that hospital of yours."

My office door opened and Steve Ragsdale stormed in. "Dr. Garfield, I'm glad you're here." Ragsdale was the founder and owner of the one-block town of Desert Center, six miles east. He liked to gab and frankly, I wasn't in the mood.

"Yes, Steve, look, I'm on the phone—"

"If my car worked I'd have brought them myself, but only the motor-cycle…Doc, you listening? You'd better get in that ambulance of yours and get to my restaurant now. I got two men, one claiming to be Henry Kaiser himself, who jumped off a train. They're bleeding pretty bad."

"Why the hell would they jump off the train?"

"Doc, we need to go. Now. Please."

I held the phone up to my ear. "I heard, Sidney. Go."

"Okay, Dad. Don't worry. I won't let the bank take—"

"Sidney, go." He hung up.

"Get the OR ready," I told Mrs. Herman. "I'll have two patients to sew up." I wished that Judy hadn't left; I sure could have used her help now.

I grabbed my coat, filled my black bag with bandages to help stem any bleed-ing during the trip back to the hospital, and hoped that the ambulance would start. I turned the key in the ignition. Nothing. Again. Not a sound. Wouldn't you know it? I finally had an emergency and the damn thing wouldn't start.

Ragsdale shook his head. "Jeez, Doc. We could have walked there by now. You want to ride on the back of my motorcycle?"

I held up my hand and turned the key. The engine revved, sputtered, and kept on running.

"I'll see you at my place," Ragsdale said. "If you're not there in five minutes, I'll come back for you."

"Funny." I took off toward Desert Center, gazing up at the star-streaked sky as I worried about Judy, driving home angry, upset, and alone.

How could I have too many principles? The guilt of not helping her ripped at me. Maybe abortion was the right thing to do. Why bring another unwanted baby into this world? But it wasn't that easy. The AMA had come out against abortion, and there was my hospital and all the workers that needed care to think about.

With the top red light flashing—the siren no longer worked—I parked next to the Desert Center Café, which had been open every day since Ragsdale started it back in '22, Christmas and New Years included.

Inside, the place smelled like chili and burgers. "Over here," Ragsdale called.

A bald man in his fifties, massive in build and heavy jawed, sat next to Ragsdale. He held a bloody towel on the right side of his scalp, his face bruised and scratched, his suit jacket torn and dirty. He rose with the quickness of a welterweight and extended his hand. "Henry Kaiser, young man. You must be the ambulance driver. Was the doctor too busy to come along?"

His hand swallowed mine. "Sidney Garfield, Mr. Kaiser. Doctor, ambulance driver, and nurse."

He grinned. "Initiative, young man. The can-do attitude I like. This is Harold Hatch, my chief engineer. The smartest man you'll ever meet." He gestured to a short man with a hunched back due to some type of spinal deformity. His jacket was off and his arms appeared to have taken the brunt of the fall, both abraded from wrist to elbow. Hard to imagine why the smartest man in the world would jump off a train.

"Either of you feel like you broke any bones?" I asked.

"I'm sore, but fully functional," Hatch said. "Before you ask, my back was like this before we took the jump."

"Can you believe these two hopped off the train?" Ragsdale said, sipping a beer. "Seen some hoboes skip off, but never in the middle of the desert, and never two guys in suits."

"Before you *jump* to any conclusions, Dr. Garfield," Kaiser grinned, "I can assure you we're not nuts."

"I'd like to hear about it on the way to my hospital," I said. "The sooner I clean up those wounds the better they'll heal."

"*Your* hospital?" Kaiser asked.

"Mine for now, at least. C'mon, I'll give you the VIP ride."

Kaiser was out the door ahead of me and into the front seat, while I helped Hatch into the back. We sped off for the ten-minute ride. Kaiser seemed oblivious to any pain, wide-eyed and grinning like a kid, enjoying the speed.

"So, tell me, Mr. Kaiser, why did you and Mr. Hatch jump off the train?"

"Have you heard of Parker Dam?"

I nodded.

"Bids were due today by five. There was no time to take the train to LA or Phoenix and then drive back here before the deadline. And I always get my bids in on time. So, I had them slow the train and we tried to land in what looked like soft sand. Only the soft part was only a few inches thick." He turned and looked at Hatch. "You doing okay now, Harold?"

"Yes, boss. I'll be fine."

"Wait a minute," I said. "You're kidding, right?"

"No, I'm not. We left Oakland late last night and barely got here before five. It took the extra time to research the costs involved. We underbid our competitors by twenty thousand and we'll do it six months quicker. We signed the contract right here an hour ago and we'll have it done before we go to war."

I'd heard about Henry Kaiser from Mike, but I'd thought most of the stories were exaggerations. Meeting the man made me think they might be true. "You really think we're going to war?"

"FDR is the only politician I've met that wasn't made from a banana. We're going to war all right. And soon."

I pulled into the back of the hospital and parked next to my Studebaker. Kaiser was out and through the back door before I helped Hatch out of the ambulance.

"Nice hospital, Doctor. Air-conditioned. Never been in one fully air-conditioned before, even in the city." Kaiser made a quick appraisal of the main ward. "Venetian blinds, flowers by your patients' beds. Shows you have a head on that shoulder of yours. Customer service is the only way to succeed. Worked for me when I owned a photo shop and is working for me now."

Mrs. Herman opened up a minor suture tray and set it on the cabinet next to the OR table. Never one to be ignored, she cleared her throat loudly.

"Thank you, Mrs. Herman. Do you mind cleaning up Mr. Hatch for me?" She nodded. "*Ja.*"

Kaiser went over to her and whispered in what sounded like German.

Mrs. Herman laughed. In fact, I'd never seen her laugh so hard before.

"Now, Mr. Kaiser, if you'd lie down on the table, I'll suture up that laceration."

"You're the boss, Doctor."

His tremendous girth barely fit on the table. I focused the OR light on his scalp and washed off the dirt and clotted blood with an iodine solution. His bald scalp made my job easier. The laceration was about three inches long and down to bone, but the skull was smooth without any step-offs or sharp edges. No need to get an X-ray.

"Hold still, please," I said. "This shot of Novocain will only burn for a moment. You're lucky you didn't fracture your skull."

"Too hard headed for that." He clenched his jaw as the local anesthetic went in. Once the wound was numb, I rinsed out the dirt with sterile saline and washed it again with iodine to lessen the chance of infection. I snapped on a pair of rubber gloves, repaired the subcutaneous tissue with three-O catgut and closed the skin with a running silk suture.

"Tell me, how did you make Mrs. Herman laugh?"

"I told her an old German joke. It loses something in the translation."

I nodded. "Hold some pressure on the bandage while I check out Mr. Hatch."

Hatch was luckier, no lacerations, all he needed was a petroleum gauze wrap around his abrasions. Afterward, we sat opposite one another at the small kitchen table while Kaiser devoured Mrs. Herman's left-over rabbit pie and Hatch picked away at the crust.

Kaiser took a gulp of water and wiped his face with a napkin. "Nice hospital, Dr. Garfield. But how can you keep it running with no patients?"

"I can't. The workers make 50 cents an hour and can't pay for their own routine care. The insurance company that's supposed to cover accidents and workman's comp discounts my bills or doesn't pay at all. Industrial Indemnity Insurance has all the money and does everything to keep it."

Hatch raised his eyebrows. "Industrial Indemnity?"

"That's right."

Kaiser smiled that infectious grin of his. "What would you have the insurance company do?"

"Well, first off, for what you're probably paying them, you're not getting your money's worth."

"And why's that?"

"Don't get me wrong, Mr. Kaiser, but I assume you're a quality builder."

He nodded.

"And just as you make sure everything you build is up to code, why not treat your workers the same way? Keeping them healthy means they'll do their best work for you. Give them health insurance that actually keeps them well instead of waiting for them to get sick and replacing them with new and inexperienced workers."

"I thought we were paying for that now. Hatch, am I wrong?"

"We're keeping costs down, boss."

Kaiser's lips tightened. "You mean we're skimping on health care for our workers?"

Hatch hesitated. "Let's just say we're not overpaying. What would you do differently, Doctor?"

"I've been thinking hard on that one," I went on, "and haven't come up with the answer. For now, I just need the insurance company to cover my fees."

"I thought we were paying for that," Kaiser said.

"No, what you're doing now is refusing to pay my bills. Why not keep your workers healthy instead of replacing them every time they get sick or injured? That has to slow you down."

"True." Kaiser stood and paced back and forth. "Why don't you think of something new? A system that's good for you, the workers and insurance company. I have to admit, Doctor, I've never liked our fee-for-service system of medicine. The rich get the best care and the rest can't afford it or lose everything they have trying to pay for it."

"I couldn't agree more. It never made much sense." I wasn't about to tell him I was ready to sign on the dotted line with Chandler to keep my hospital in business and keep the bank from taking over my father's store. I'd spent countless sleepless nights mulling over what to do. Trying to convince myself that the workers needed a good doctor and I had to do whatever it took to stay in business.

Kaiser gazed past me, his expression serious. "I haven't spoken of this in years. But, my mother died of pneumonia because we couldn't afford to go to a doctor and my father refused to take her to a charity hospital. I swore I'd do something about it one day."

The coincidence of both our mothers dying the same way...well, it seemed uncanny. Funny how, out of nowhere, things had a way of changing.

Kaiser slapped me on the back like a football coach. "Think of something new and call me," Kaiser repeated. "If I like it, I just might be able to convince Industrial Indemnity Insurance to go along."

"I'm sure you can, boss," Hatch said. "You own it."

# CHAPTER 8

## Contractor's General Hospital

## September 7, 1941

Dwight Chandler had moved his office uptown since the last time I'd driven to Palm Springs. He'd called a few hours earlier, saying it was "urgent" for us to talk and with my hospital going bankrupt, it was time we worked out a deal. Before leaving, I'd tried to get a hold of my father, but there was no answer at his house or the store. Which worried me. He must be at the bank. There was the slim chance I could work out an agreement with Kaiser's insurance company, but there was no time for that now. Not with my father about to lose his business.

I shifted the old Studebaker and made a right off Indian Avenue, the main road that circled around from the recently built highway. Chandler's office was the standard sort of white medical professional building with squared off modern lines, a rock composite roof, air conditioners hanging outside every window, and Chandler's name on top of a directory list of physicians. Chandler may make the wrong diagnoses and even operate for the wrong reasons, but he'd perfected his bedside manner enough so that everyone always forgave him. Inside, every seat in the waiting room was full. Expensive art work—original oil paintings of desert scenes—adorned the walls, and plush brown carpet covered the floors. He was doing well.

An attractive red-haired receptionist, just the sort I'd expect Chandler to hire, greeted me with a smile.

"I'm Dr. Garfield. Dr. Chandler's expecting me."

"Sorry, he's running behind, Doctor. I'm sure he'd want you to wait in his office." She opened the Dutch door that led into the exam area. "The last one at the end of the hall." She gestured with her well-manicured nails and turned to answer the phone.

The hallway smelled of alcohol mixed with a sweet fragrance, a desert flower scent of some sort. I looked around for Judy, but she must have been in one of the exam rooms; at least I hoped she was. Since she told me she was pregnant a week ago, she'd continued to come by and help out at the hospital at night, but barely said a word to me and I worried about her almost as much as I did my father. I opened the office door, not even thinking to knock, and practically mowed Chandler down. He was talking to a man who looked as if he were modeling the winter suit line for my father's clothing store. He wore wire-rimmed glasses and a three-piece suit on a one-hundred-degrees-in-the-shade day.

"Sorry, Dwight, your receptionist told me to go in."

He frowned. "Sid, this is Dr. Paul Foster, President of the LA County Medical Association. Close the door, we'd like to talk to you."

There it was again. That same feeling of doom as when Dean Keating would call me in his office. Chandler took a seat behind his desk and pointed to a chair across from him, next to Foster. I stared at the man. Something about him bothered me. The name. Foster. It had to be a coincidence.

"You'd better face the facts, Dr. Garfield," Foster said. I didn't remember Chandler mentioning my last name. "You'll never make it on your own."

"I'm doing just fine, thank you." I leaned forward, away from the cold air blasting against my already stiff neck muscles. Sure I was lying; I didn't want to seem too anxious. My father had taught me that when I'd worked in his clothing store. Too pushy meant there was something wrong and it turned off the buyer. I couldn't help staring at Foster. He was in his late fifties, which made him about the right age. "Dr. Foster, how long have you been practicing in Los Angeles?"

"Sid," Chandler interrupted. "What does that matter? Let's get to the point here. Remember my offer? Well, things have changed."

"Changed, how?"

"I'm so busy now, I'd need you here most of the time. Oh sure, you could go to your hospital a day or so a week, but the money's here, not taking care of workers."

Foster cleared his throat. "I'm willing to offer you a full membership in the LA County Medical Society if you sign up with Dwight. If the workers get sick, let them drive over here. If they can't pay, they can go to LA. Let the residents over at County practice on them."

Foster locked his eyes on mine. I blinked and then stared back. Under his chin was a moon-shaped hemangioma. A red mole. In my mind, my Father was yelling, "*I'll get you your money. Please—*"

Foster had looked down at a small boy without a trace of compassion—and patted his head. I felt like every ounce of blood in my body was squeezed into my skull. My face burned. The saddest memory of my life rose from the deep. Foster, the doctor who'd refused to help my mother, sat a couple of feet from me, after all these years.

"Ah, hell, Sid." Chandler gave me one of his best attempts at a grin. "Think about what you're doing. I know how tough things are for you going it alone. I'm offering to help."

Foster smashed his cigarette in the ashtray. "Now, young man, I suggest you listen to Dwight."

I stood, my chair screeching against the wood floor. "You're the one. You goddamn sonofabitch. You're the one that refused to help my mother!"

"Sid," Chandler said. "What's gotten into you? Are you nuts?"

Foster's body tensed as if no one had ever yelled at him before. He glared up at me. I didn't move. Then to my surprise, he smiled. "You're confusing me with someone else. I don't remember ever seeing you or your mother." He crossed his legs, removed a gold case from his inner jacket pocket and for a moment I thought he was going to offer me a cigarette. Instead he lit one and took a deep drag. "We can't make you save your career and hospital. We thought you'd want to do that on your own."

"That's right, Sid," Chandler interjected. "I'm offering you—"

Foster exhaled a puff of smoke in my direction and gave me a patronizing look. "You need to calm down. Maybe you should think it over for a few days. Even a week. Out here, the heat must make it hard to think clearly."

He was right about that. I couldn't think clearly. *Foster,* after all these years. The moment felt surreal…it knocked the breath out of me and I found it hard to speak.

"Look," Chandler went on, "I'll help you. I'm grateful to you, Sid. For all the times you helped out during your residency. I'll help you get in the medical society. I know your father's about to lose his business. Now, sit down and listen. It's time for you to do the right thing."

A loud knock on the door. "Dr. Chandler." I recognized Judy's voice. She knocked again. "Dr. Chandler."

"Not now, Judy," he said. "We're—"

"Doctor, one of your patients just passed out in the waiting room."

"Who?"

"Mr. Harris."

Chandler got up and opened the door. "I've seen him three times this week. It's a flu bug is all. I'll go check him."

I wanted to pummel Foster, choke him until he couldn't breathe. Let him know how my mother felt as she suffocated to death. I wanted to, but knew I couldn't. I had to do something to stop doctors who cared more about money than people. I'd sell my equipment and do whatever it took to keep the bank from taking over my father's store. Anything other than go into business with the likes of these bastards. Chandler followed Judy into the waiting room. She wouldn't look at me.

The other patients had moved to the opposite wall, as if Harris was about to explode.

"Mr. Harris, let me help you into one of the exam rooms," Chandler said in his reassuring doctor's voice. "You'll be more comfortable there. I'm sure it's nothing more than gastroenteritis."

"You've been seeing him every day this week," Judy said as we walked down the hall to the exam area. "It's more than an upset stomach. Even I can tell that."

Chandler glared at her. "That's it," he said to Harris, "just lie down and relax."

Harris was gripping his abdomen in obvious pain. "Where does it hurt the most?"

"Here," he groaned as he pointed to his right lower abdomen. "Right here."

"Mind if I take a feel?" Chandler said. "Promise I'll be gentle."

With two fingers Chandler pressed on his abdomen. "I'm going to lift your right leg." He brought it up and turned Harris' foot to the right, stretching his iliopsoas muscle. Harris grimaced in pain.

Chandler turned to me. "He has a ruptured appendix."

Harris had a serious complication that could have been prevented if his appendicitis had been diagnosed sooner.

"Start him on intravenous sulfa now," Chandler said. "Mr. Harris, we're going to need to take you to the hospital."

Harris stared up at us, looking scared to death.

"Don't worry," Chandler said. "We'll operate and you'll be fine."

Foster grabbed the blood pressure cuff and busied himself checking Harris' vitals.

"Dwight," Judy said.

He looked at her and smiled.

"I didn't get a chance to tell you earlier."

"What?"

For a moment I thought she was going to tell him she was pregnant with his baby.

"I'm quitting."

# CHAPTER 9

Contractor's General Hospital

September 20, 1941

Judy started working for me the next day and we barely spoke until the middle of the following week. We'd just finished making evening rounds and Mrs. Herman was cleaning up the dinner dishes.

"C'mon, Judy, let's get some fresh air." We walked outside, the sky filled with so many stars that every time I blinked another thousand appeared.

"Okay, Dr. Garfield, I know I haven't said much, but I've been thinking." She looked tired. Light gray circles had formed under her eyes. "Go on."

"I'm going to have this baby." She waved her hand over her stomach.

"Good, I—" She put her finger to my lips.

"I've talked to Mrs. Herman. She'll take care of the baby while I'm helping you with patients. What do you think, Dr. Garfield?"

I gave her a mock wince. "Sid. It's Sid."

She drew a breath and looked at me skeptically. "Then you'll let me work, even when I'm waddling around and tired?"

"You can work as long as you want to. I'll do everything I can to help."

She extended her hand and we shook. "Deal," she said. "There is one catch, though."

"I know, you want to get paid."

"Well, I'm okay now working for room and board, but with the baby, I'll need some money."

"Believe me, we both do. I've come up with a few ideas. Only I'm not sure they'll work."

53

We sat on the back porch of the hospital and listened to a lonely desert owl hooting somewhere.

"First, tell me why you became a surgeon."

"What does that have to do with anything?"

"Indulge me," she said.

"Okay. It's because of the 'Twenty-six.'"

"Huh?"

"The 'Twenty-six.' Thousands of diseases in this world and Medical Science only has a cure for twenty-six of them. The rest is guesswork. At least there's that many things I can operate on."

"Right. Name them," she challenged.

"Hernias, tonsils, gallstones, kidney stones...you want me to go into every tumor I can think of?"

"Okay, I give."

"Now it's your turn. Why did you become a nurse?"

She rolled her eyes. "Why I Became a Nurse, by Judy Avalon. I became a nurse because..."

"Yes?"

"Because when I was small and my grandmother was very sick, a nurse came every day to help her get well. She came even though my grandfather couldn't afford to pay her." She ran her hand through her hair. "Guess it left an impression on me. Seeing how appreciative my grandmother was and how much the nurse enjoyed her work; she seemed like a real-life Florence Nightingale. Although I often fantasized about being a doctor."

"So why didn't you?"

"I could never afford it. Besides, how many women were in your medical school class?"

"One."

Judy shook her head. "See? Anyway, I like nursing a lot. I'm happy with my choice. I'm not the type to sit around and be envious. Sometimes I think we do more for patients than some doctors."

"Not sometimes." I smiled. "I'd say most of the time."

Her lips tightened. "Okay, Dr. Garfield, now that I know how important it is for you to be a surgeon, tell me one more thing. How are you going to save this hospital?"

I stood and extended my hand to help her up. "Let's go to the construction site and we'll talk on the way. Can you pick up nails in the dark?"

"Well…"

"I'll grab a few flashlights. You get the gloves."

The flashlight beams cut through the dark and sent a few rabbits scurrying for cover. They might be tomorrow night's dinner. The air was warm, a hint of moisture from somewhere miles to the west.

Judy's blond hair bounced lightly against the white collar of her nurses' uniform as she walked. Less than three months pregnant, she wasn't showing. I cleared my throat. "I've been thinking about how to keep people healthy. You know, preventive medicine instead of what we do now. Just sit around and wait for patients to get sick."

"More doctors should care about prevention," she said.

"Yeah. Didn't Benjamin Franklin say something like 'an ounce of prevention is worth a pound of cure?'"

"I think he was talking about fires, not medicine."

"Oh." I aimed the flashlight onto the dirt path leading to the construction site. "It's funny how you hear those sayings over and over and never really know why they were used in the first place."

She nodded. "You promise you won't laugh?"

"Depends…no, okay, I promise."

She pointed up at the clear desert sky. "I've never flown…and it's something I can't wait to do."

"And here I thought you'd done everything."

"Not funny," she said. "Where have you flown, mister big shot?"

"I went to medical school in Iowa. I've flown back and forth a few times."

"So, what's it like?"

"Well, when the weather's nice, it's exactly like it seems. Soaring through the clouds with a view that never ends. But when the weather's bad, hold on for your life." I swept the path with the flashlight. "Time to look down."

"Does that mean you want me to shut up?"

"No, of course not. Hey look, there's some." I scooped a few nails into a leather pouch on my belt next to my waterproof first aid kit.

Judy picked up a nail that had been thrown carelessly on one of the wooden forms used to pour the concrete. "Ouch, I just cut myself."

"Didn't you bring gloves?"

"Mrs. Herman said she was going to try and plant a vegetable garden tomorrow, so I thought she'd need them more than me."

"Vegetable garden in the sand, huh? Let me see your hand."

She held it up to her mouth. "It's fine. Just a scratch."

"Okay, but I don't think saliva is a good antiseptic." I picked up another nail. "Look at all these dirty nails. All just lying around, waiting for someone to step on them and end up with a puncture wound, tetanus or worse."

"You trying to scare a pregnant woman? Here, take a look."

There was a tiny puncture wound on her right palm. I always carried a small first aid kit on my belt when I went to the construction site. I cleaned Judy's hand with an antiseptic and put on a clean bandage. "Better?"

She smiled. "Much."

I wiped my forehead with the back of my hand. God, it had to be at least ninety. A typical summer's night in the middle of the Mojave. "You know, there is a small airport near here. If you're really interested in flying, we could hire a pilot and…Judy, watch- out!"

She stumbled over one of the metal wires used to strengthen the aqueduct's concrete channels. I caught her by the shoulder.

Judy teetered for a moment in my arms. "Thanks…I'm pretty clumsy tonight." She moved away and straightened her skirt. "Sid, are you serious about taking me flying?"

She'd finally called me by my first name. I wanted to hug her, but hesitated. Better to keep things professional, considering we were living in the same building.

"Doc, what are you doing here at night?" I'd been so focused on Judy, I hadn't noticed Mike, his face covered in dirt, on the trail in front of us. Hard to stay clean when your sweat acted like a dust magnet.

"Trying to keep your men healthy." I pulled out some nails. "You know, the safer we keep this work site, the better."

"Okay, Doc. I'll have a few guys do safety patrol. Working around the clock makes them careless. Although, I've heard—excuse me for saying this, Miss Judy—but some of the men go in, saying their backs hurt just to see you. It can get a bit lonely out here, you know."

I looked at Judy. "Yeah, I know."

"You know, Doc. Henry Kaiser's staying here tonight. Sleeping in one of the workman's tents. Watching how we're doing."

Judy nudged my shoulder.

"Can you show me where?" I asked.

"Course, Doc."

We walked a few hundred yards to a tent closest to the dining room, its front flap open and a kerosene lamp hung from the central wood support.

"Good luck, Doc. I've got some things to do." Mike turned and walked away.

Henry Kaiser sat at a makeshift desk of wooden boxes with his reading glasses perched low on his nose. He looked up and waved me in.

"Ah, Dr. Garfield. My physician back in Oakland said you did a magnificent job sewing me up. Can't even see the scar."

"Well, thanks."

He stood and extended his hand to Judy. "Henry Kaiser, young lady. You must be Dr. Garfield's nurse."

She wore a white uniform so it didn't take much imagination. "Nice to meet you," she said.

"I have to hand it to you, Doctor. Air conditioned hospital, pretty nurses, these workmen are lucky."

"That's why we're here. I'm going to have to close the hospital unless—"

He straightened in his canvas sling chair. "You don't seem like a quitter. Tell me what you have in mind."

"I've been thinking hard on that one since we first talked," I went on, "and the answer that works for my hospital, patients, and the insurance company is preventive medicine."

"You've lost me, Doctor. How can we prevent people from getting sick?"

"We can't completely. But we can keep the workplace safe and encourage the workers to come in earlier. Before their cold turns into pneumonia. That's what I mean."

"Go on."

Judy straightened her skirt and sat across from Kaiser in another canvas chair. "It's the same as car insurance," she said. "You pay a small amount a month and if you get in an accident they pay to fix it. Medicine is just the opposite. If you get in an accident—you get sick—you have to come up with the money to get well."

The kerosene lantern flickered off Judy's face, casting her shadow against the far side of the tent. "Exactly. Mr. Kaiser, pay me up front and I'll keep all your workers healthy. Cover everything they need from a cold to a broken bone." I was ready for him to laugh at my idea or at the least tell me I was naive.

"So…let me understand this. You want the insurance company to pay you before the worker gets sick?" he asked with a note of incredulity. "That's like paying something for nothing."

"No, that's health insurance. Paying me to keep your workers on the job. Just like Judy said about car insurance. What we're doing now is 'sick' insurance. I bill the insurance company fee-for-service…so I'm paid to do more of everything: more visits, more tests, more hospitalizations, more surgery. The sicker the workers are, the more money I make. Not a penny goes for preventive care."

"Okay." Kaiser tapped his pen against the wooden crate table. "So even if I can budget my costs with prepayment, how do I know you'll keep up your end…and provide the care the workers need? What keeps you from skimping on quality when they do get sick?"

"Why do you think I moved out here in the first place? Your workers were dying on the way to L.A. They needed someone here." Struck by inspiration, I stammered on.

"And I'll guarantee it. If a patient complains about my quality, I'll refund my fee and pay for them to go to any hospital they choose. Think about it."

Kaiser stood and paced in the ten by ten tent. "It does make perfect sense. Right now 25 percent of the worker's comp premium is allocated for medical and hospital expenses. Let's say we give half of that every month to you and keep the other 12.5 percent for patients transferred to LA. That amounts to…uh, about a nickel a day per worker."

Kaiser was as smart as I'd heard. I felt a surge of excitement. "And multiply five cents times five thousand workers, that's $250 a day. Enough to pay my bills and provide the best care anywhere." I wasn't about to tell him I was ready to sign on the dotted line with Chandler to keep my hospital in business and prevent the bank from taking over my father's store. I'd spent countless sleepless nights mulling over what to do. Trying to convince myself that the workers needed a good doctor and I had to do whatever it took to stay in business. Funny, how out of nowhere, things had a way of changing.

Kaiser slapped me on the back. "A nickel a day," Kaiser repeated. "Not a bad idea. I just might be able to convince Industrial Indemnity Insurance to go along."

"I don't have a lot of time," I said.

"Doctor. You're talking to a man who jumped off a train to save time. I'll have the agreement drawn up and ready to sign tomorrow." He extended his hand. "Until then, a handshake is enough for me."

We shook hands and Kaiser told Judy, "You're working for one smart doctor."

"And a good one," she said.

"Well, you two run along then. I have this bid to finish by the morning. You heard of Hoover Dam?"

"Of course," I said.

"Well, we're building a bigger one. The Grand Coulee up in Washington. Largest one in the world. I only hope we finish it before war breaks out."

"You really think we're going to war?" Judy asked.

The scent of smoke filled the tent from the cafeteria next door as they doused the cooking fires.

Kaiser nodded. "I'd bet the farm on it." He looked away and started scribbling numbers on a four-foot-long blueprint. "Come by before noon," he said.

We got up and left as Kaiser immersed himself in the blueprints.

"Car insurance," I said as we walked the dirt trail back to the hospital. Only in the desert was starlight bright enough to let you see the road ahead. "Judy, you're a genius." I felt the urge to take her hand, but resisted this time.

"It's only common sense. You know, Sid, I think it'll be exciting."

"You mean actually getting paid."

"No, silly. I mean practicing medicine where people don't have to worry about going broke to get good care."

"So do I, Judy. So do I."

We walked along in silence for a few minutes until we reached the back porch of the hospital. She hesitated for a moment and looked at me, almost as if she were waiting for a good night kiss after a date. She smiled and opened the door. "Good night, Sid."

"Night, Judy."

I strode down the hall to my office, feeling like the weight of the world had been lifted from my shoulders. Tonight—Judy, Kaiser—had been, well, perfect.

I picked up the phone and dialed my father, excited to tell him the good news. A man picked up, I wasn't sure who. "Dad?"

"Is this Sidney?"

"Yes, who's—"

"It's Maurice Abrams from next door. You're father was hoping you'd call. He's sick, Sidney. Very sick. Been taken to the hospital."

"What's wrong?"

"I'm not sure." I heard the concern in his voice. "He's sick is all. The ambulance took him to County. He wants you there. He told me. 'Get Sidney. Get my Sidney.' You'd better get there quick."

# CHAPTER 10

Los Angeles County Hospital

September 20, 1941

This couldn't be happening.

I charged outside to the ambulance, flicked on the flashing red light and took off to Los Angeles with the newly repaired siren wailing a pathetic cry against the silence of the desert.

Every word of the phone call I'd made to County replayed in my head. I'd listened in horror as Dean Keating described how my father had an intestinal obstruction and needed immediate surgery. In his prime, Keating used to be the best general surgeon in LA. But that was twenty years ago.

I raced through the desert. The high beams of an oncoming car made me squint to see the undulations of the road. I glanced down at my watch. The Timex my father had given me. Since my mother's death, he had meant so much, done so much, and now everything depended on…I let my mind go blank or else it would drive me crazy with worry and concentrated on the highway, speeding the converted hearse as fast as the engine could go. Time passed in a daze. My head was spinning; I kept hearing my mother's voice. *Pumpkin, she whispered. Everything will be fine.*

LA County hospital was in its usual state of chaos as I pulled into the ER entrance and left the ambulance in a red zone. I rushed past a startled orderly and into OR 1, Keating's private OR.

A familiar face, Donny Rand, now a staff anesthesiologist, glanced at me and shook his head. Nothing I had seen or done in medicine fully prepared me for the sight of my own father in cardiac arrest. Three surgical residents, two

OR nurses, and the bulging shape of Dean Keating surrounded him. All looking to the Dean for their next command.

"Pressure's down to sixty. Still has a pulse," Rand announced.

I worked my way around rather than through the crowd. Keating glanced up at me and then looked away, too focused to offer the slightest hint of hope. "2 cc's of epi," Keating ordered. "Dr. Garfield, your father's surgery went well, but he began losing pressure when we reversed his anesthesia."

Surgery went well? "You sure he's not bleeding internally, going into shock?"

"Positive. My hemostasis was meticulous. I ordered an electrocardiogram." He gestured to a paper tracing. "Myocardial infarction of the anterior wall. Sorry, Garfield. Unless we can get his pressure up…"

"Epi had no effect," Rand said. "Pulse thready."

I glanced at the time. If Keating had started when I'd left Desert Center, my father had been on the table for almost three hours. I closed my eyes. C'mon, Keating, show us what you're made of. Do anything as long as you save my father.

Keating kept calm, calling out orders he'd memorized, maybe even wrote in his *Textbook of Surgery*. A textbook now twenty years old.

Rand pointed to the blood pressure meter.

*This can't be my father.*

Things fell into a daze. I kept reminding myself I was in the OR.

"No pulse," Rand said softly. "He's in V-fib."

Keating slumped visibly and gazed at me with vacant blue eyes. Then he reached up his bloodied, gloved hand and pulled down his mask. "I'm sorry, Garfield. I did everything."

"Wait," I yelled. "Not everything. Not everything. Donny…pressure?"

"Maybe twenty, hard to hear without a pulse."

"Let's shock him. I've read about it in the *New England Journal*. Reverses V-fib in dogs."

"Garfield. We've had this conversation before. I don't allow experimentation in my OR."

"I don't give a shit! It's my father here and I'm not about to give up."

"Nurse, call security," Keating ordered.

The OR nurse gave me a look of recognition. Joan…one I'd worked with for years as a resident. She hesitated.

"If you want your job," Keating repeated to Joan, "you'll do as I say."

She stood there and glared, her feet fixed in place.

"Sorry, Sid," Rand said. "Keating's in charge here. As much as I wish there were something we could do…well, we can't just plug in a cord and shock him with 120 volts."

"Maybe there is."

I felt the seconds pass as my father's life faded. There was one chance. Maybe.

"Keep ventilating him. I'll run over to the psych ward. The electroconvulsive unit, it delivers DC current—"

"No," Keating protested. "Absolutely not in my OR. Get out. Now."

"Pressure's down to 0," Rand said. "I'm sorry, Sid, but it's too late."

## CHAPTER 11

Contractor's General Hospital

# December 7, 1941

The early morning sun filtered through the Venetian blinds, casting a pattern of alternating light and dark on my desk. Seven weeks had passed since my father's death. Now that he was gone, I realized how much of who I was, what I was, had been influenced by my father. After my mother had died, he'd always been there for me. Now I was completely on my own and the thought terrified me.

My office was filled with flowers in varying states of decay and on my desk was a picture of the three of us: my mother, father, and I, taken right before her death. Over the years, it had faded into a yellowish blur. Would my father's image, so clear now in my mind, fade like an old photo?

Cecil Cutting and his wife Millie had called and invited me to visit them in LA, but I'd lied and said I was doing okay. The only bright note during the three weeks had been Judy. She'd brought me food and forced me to eat when nothing tasted good. She'd single-handedly kept the hospital going and tried her hardest to cheer me up, while all I felt like doing was sitting in the dark.

I turned on my desk lamp and opened the latest *Journal of the American Medical Association*. If I didn't start using my brain again soon, it would get flabby. I read JAMA editor Morris Fishbein's rant in favor of fee-for-service medicine. He just didn't get it. Was it fair for the sick to pay for their sickness and pay more the longer and sicker they were? Why not pay doctors to keep their patients in the best health, like we were now doing? It wasn't worth the two bits I'd paid for the magazine.

A few months earlier, I'd been shooting rabbits for food. Now, my hospital was making money. Oh sure, I'd told my father it would from the start, but that had been more wishful thinking than rational accounting. Henry Kaiser had been true to his word. Starting on the day of our handshake, Industrial Indemnity paid five cents a day per worker, which was enough to pay the mortgage, the surgical supply company, the Hermans, and even a full time job for Judy.

Not having to go in with Chandler removed an enormous weight from my chest. I could breathe again without feeling like I'd sold out. No matter how I rationalized it—saving my hospital, paying off my father's loan—something in me knew it would have been wrong. Like finding money in the street and not turning it in, I'd been faced with a moral dilemma that had eaten away at me for months. Now, I felt free. Free to practice the way I thought best without a noose around my neck. I knew my father would have been proud.

The next article was more distressing. A polio outbreak in Los Angeles with another fifty cases. There had to be a way to stop the spread. Sure, there was talk of a vaccine, but that could take years. Something had to be done now, something that could stop the epidemic at the first sign of an outbreak. It was strange how dirt and poor living conditions offered some kind of immunity. It didn't make sense.

Someone knocked on the door. "Yeah, it's open."

Judy stuck her head in. Surprised to see her before breakfast, I stood up, feeling the flush that came to my face whenever she was around. Even though she was four months pregnant, she was still in great shape with only a small bulge at her middle.

"C'mon," she said. "You need to get some fresh air. You can only mope around for so long. I want to try out my new roller skates and I want you to take some pictures."

We'd taken a lot of pictures before my father died…not too much else to do when the hospital was quiet. With the aqueduct almost completed, the number of workers had been cut from five thousand to less than two thousand.

"Pregnant woman skating on the sand? That'll be fun to watch."

"I thought you were smarter than that. You're going to lower me into the concrete aqueduct. Without water, it's better than a rink."

"No way, sounds too dangerous. Remember you are pregnant."

"I'll be fine. I've been roller skating since I was five."

I ripped a check out of the checkbook and wrote in the amount I owed her for the last three months. "Well, here, just in case you don't make it out, take this."

Judy smiled and said, "I would have worked for free, you know." We stared at each other for a few seconds. Her perfume engulfed my senses. Her hand caressed my neck. "Oh, Sid," she said softly. I ran my hand tenderly over her cheek. She moved closer, our lips almost touching. I hesitated. She didn't and pulled me to her, kissing me hard. I kissed back, harder. Seconds, minutes, passed. Without a word she closed the door to my room. She untucked my shirt and slid it over my head. Then she slipped out of her dress. I'd never seen her unclothed. She was lovelier than I'd imagined—and I'd imagined her many times. Slender neck, delicate shoulders, full, but not large breasts and long supple legs.

We faced each other. Her warm lips caressed mine. Every sensation was heightened, all the more precious for the long wait. I pressed my face into the silky hollow between her shoulder and neck. We explored each other's bodies until we could no longer postpone our desire. I wanted our lovemaking to go on forever.

At last I lay on my back, her head resting gently on my chest, staring at the ceiling in disbelief at all that had happened. "I love—"

She put her finger over my lips. "Just hold me. Don't feel you have to say that."

"I'm not just saying it." That was the truth. It had just sort of spilled out of me without much forethought, but it was how I felt.

"Shhh," she whispered.

I frowned. "As corny as it may sound, I've loved you from that first day I met you. You know me, I'm not one to make quick decisions, but—"

She looked me in the eye. "You don't really know me."

"You don't tell me much, but I know you. I would have lost this hospital without your help. You are the one who has been here day after day since my father died. You're beautiful, caring, smart, funny…"

She kissed me on the cheek. "Get your camera, doctor. I'm ready to go skating."

"Like that?"

She pushed me down and kissed me hard on the lips. Then she got up, turned on her toes like a dancer and slipped on her shorts and top. "Hurry, before it gets too hot."

I grabbed the rope used to tow the ambulance when it overheated, which happened more and more lately, and we walked a few hundred feet from the back door of the hospital to where they'd just finished curing the cement channel for the aqueduct. The wind had dropped and somewhere a bird chattered.

"You're kidding, right?"

"Just watch me." She fastened her skates onto her shoes with the leather straps, grabbed the rope and careered down the side of the channel. In a month, it would be full of water, flowing from the Colorado River to Los Angeles.

"Be careful," I yelled.

She made it down the half-pipe, managing to stay on her feet, then skated down the middle with the finesse of a professional skater.

"Judy, slow down!" I snapped one photo after the other, fighting back the trickle of adrenaline that flowed as I watched her. Judy was a challenge. A mystery. She never talked about herself, her family, her past. To her there was only here and now. And keeping my thoughts on medicine…well, to be honest, anything at all around her, was becoming more and more difficult.

We'd been working together full time for three months. Up at dawn, we'd made morning rounds while the temperature outside was under one hundred. Most days were quiet. However on busy days, like after the dynamite accident near Parker Dam, when every bed was full, we worked non-stop. The perfect team. At least I thought so.

She skated up the aqueduct, waving her hands, smiling radiantly, her white shorts revealing tanned muscular legs. She was so striking, she would have made a better cover model for *Life* magazine than any woman I'd ever seen. But I hated to sound shallow, because there was a lot more to Judy than—

"Did you take it?" She yelled. "Did you get that turn?"

"Got it all. Now come back up. You're worrying me." She was everything I'd ever wanted in a nurse. Everything I'd ever wanted in a friend. And everything I'd ever wanted in a woman.

"Well, don't just stand there then," she called. "Throw me the rope."

She held on as I started to pull her up the ten-foot embankment. I was so busy staring at her, at first I didn't notice the iron rebar sticking out from the cement. "Judy, look out!"

She looked down just as her skate caught on the iron bar. She panicked. Goddamnit, she panicked and let go of the rope. She somersaulted once and fell eight feet down the side of the aqueduct, landing on her stomach with a sickening thud.

"Judy!"

She moved ever so slowly onto her back and she saw the blood streaming between her legs the same moment I did.

"Don't worry," I shouted. "I'll be right there."

She looked scared as hell, which described exactly how I felt.

I took a deep breath, letting it out slowly, trying to remind myself I was a doctor and panicking was not an option. I had the rope, I only needed something to anchor it so I could climb out with her on my back. I looked up and down the aqueduct. Both sides had been graded with only dirt and sand for hundreds of yards in every direction.

"Judy, can you move?"

"I'm freezing," she said. Freezing when it was one hundred degrees meant she was in shock.

"Try and move your legs."

She leaned forward and tried to stand, but slipped or fell in a puddle of her own blood. "Shit," she said.

"Okay, just stop. I'll come down and get you." I looked all around. There had to be something to tie the rope to. She'd slipped on the rebar, but it was too far down and too short.

"Sid, I don't…things are turning…I'm going to…" She slumped down, her head between her legs.

Desperation set in and I clawed away at the dirt at the edge of the aqueduct, thinking I could bury the rope, find a rock to tie on to, anything. Something sharp cut into my hand and I realized what it was. Rebar. The metal used to form the channel was buried just under the surface. I tied the rope onto the metal rod with the strongest surgeon's knot I could manage, placing four throws of the knot. I rappelled down the side of the aqueduct.

"Judy?" I felt her pulse. Thready. Fast. Her face the ashen gray of shock. She was in a wide lake that had to be a third of her blood. Between her legs the bleeding had slowed to a trickle. Shock and loss of blood left very little to lose. I grabbed her and placed her over my left shoulder, supporting her thighs just below the buttocks with my left arm. With my right I grabbed the rope and began to pull myself up, alternating holding the rope with my bent left arm and grabbing higher with my right. Both arms burned with the effort. The rope stretched taut and I moved upward, praying my knot would hold. Then I felt the rope moving. The rebar was too strong to bend even with both our weights, which meant my knot was slipping. There was only one chance. If I fell back and didn't get her out now, she'd bleed to death. Two feet from the top the rope slipped again.

"Dammit! Just fucking hold!" I screamed. A foot from the top, I had no choice but to push Judy up and over the edge, scraping her head and arms against the cement. I scrambled over the top, the rope still holding but down to its last simple throw, the rest of the knot untied. Judy looked even worse, her breathing shallow now, as I grabbed her and sprinted the few hundred yards to the hospital.

I kicked open the front door. Mrs. Herman was at the sink cooking.

"Mrs. Herman…it's Judy. I need your help now!"

The woman dropped her knife and looked at me with despair, the same look I'd seen on parents of sick children. "She's bleeding so badly," Mrs. Herman said. "She…she needs to go to the OR?"

I nodded. "Get it ready. I'm going to need your help."

I moved down the hall into the OR and laid her flat on the operating table, cold to the touch, her skin chalky, her pulse fast and thready. Blood soaked her shorts.

"Judy…Judy," I yelled. "Can you hear me?"

Nothing. Maybe it was only a simple miscarriage. Maybe if I hadn't been such a self-righteous schmuck and done the abortion this would have never happened. Her abdomen was as hard and pale as the knuckles of a clenched fist, which meant she was hemorrhaging internally. The fall must have ruptured her uterus.

In less than three minutes Mrs. Herman was back in her OR scrubs, an intravenous needle in her hand, ready to go.

I threaded it into a vein in front of Judy's elbow. "Normal saline, full bore," I said. "Then check her pressure." I'd taught Mrs. Herman how to assist just in case there was an emergency and Judy wasn't around to help.

"Sixty over forty," she said.

"Prep her, she needs surgery now."

Mrs. Herman nodded.

"Judy?"

No response.

"Judy?" I spoke to her anyway in case a part of her comprehended what was going on. "Breathe in the ether. Take a deep breath. You'll be asleep in a moment." Her pulse raced as her respiratory rate decreased from the anesthesia. I didn't want to even think how low her pressure might be.

Without asking, Mrs. Herman handed me the sterile drapes, and the abdomen was ready for surgery. I adjusted the overhead light, its intensity making Judy's skin even paler than before. I had to calm down. Think medically not emotionally.

"Scalpel." No time for a small suprapubic incision. I made a midline exploratory lap cut from sternum to pubis. I cut down through the skin and rectus muscles in one pass, lifted the peritoneum and snipped through with the Mayo scissors, careful to avoid damaging the underlying bowel. Her abdomen was an ocean of blood with only weak pulsations transmitted from the aorta.

"Two suctions, Mrs. Herman. Keep both going." I felt for the uterus and sponged the clots off its upper surface, looking for the source. There was a four-inch rupture, through which I could see the ghastly sight. A dead four-month-old fetus. I'd done C-sections before, but never for a ruptured uterus. The dead fetus had an anti-coagulation effect on Judy, cascading her into what was known as DIC—disseminated intravascular coagulation—and unless I removed it quickly, she'd keep bleeding and have no chance for the hemorrhage to stop.

"Retract for me…right…yes…right there." I extended the gash into a straight line and with my gloved hand scooped out the fetus and placenta and placed them in a metal bucket next to the instrument tray. She'd lost so much blood, her pressure must be close to zero. I took a deep breath. Calm down.

Just concentrate on the surgery. It should be a simple matter to sew up the uterus and stop the hemorrhage.

I loaded a three-0 catgut suture and drove the large needle into both ends of the shredded uterine muscle. It pulled through the tissue like it was made of butter. "Dammit, it's not holding." I placed another one and again instead of the suture closing the tear, it just ripped right through. I shook my head, not believing what was happening. The uterus was so badly damaged, it was like a ruptured ripe tomato. It left me no choice. I had to remove the uterus. Do a hysterectomy. Judy would never be able to have children, but at least she'd have a chance to live.

Mrs. Herman slapped a hemostat onto my extended palm. I clamped off the uterine arteries and thought there was a slight strengthening of the aortic pulse. Fifteen minutes later, the uterus was in the same bucket as the fetus and placenta.

I applied the bandage.

"Pressure?"

"One hundred over eighty," she said.

"Good, she's stabilizing. Hand me some sulfa. I don't want her going into septic shock."

Mrs. Herman removed her cloth mask and looked like she was going to pass out. "Sorry, Doctor. I need to lie down. I don't —" She rushed to the OR sink and vomited into it.

She stared at Judy and then at the dead fetus. "I go now."

A few hours ago we'd made love for the first time. Now, Judy was hanging on for her life. I grabbed her roller skates and tossed them in the trash bin with the bloody sponges. I'd bury them outside with the rest of the trash. If it weren't for those goddamn skates—

Mr. Herman's voice boomed from the kitchen over the noise of the radio turned up full volume. "Gottdamnit. Gott damn them." Since I'd known him, he'd never raised his voice.

Then I heard the radio announcer and understood. The Japanese had bombed Pearl Harbor.

# BOOK TWO

## THE WAR YEARS

# CHAPTER 12

## San Francisco

## February 16, 1942

The phone jolted me from sleep, waking me from the same dream about Judy. Things had never been the same, even after I'd nursed her back to health. I knew all about depression after my father died and it was easy to understand how she felt. I tried to snap her out of it. Talked to her, read to her. Nothing worked. She barely spoke to me, barely ate, and in the end just left me a note saying she was enlisting in the Army Nursing Corps. A goddamn note.

"Call for Dr. Garfield," said a bored operator's voice on the phone. I rubbed my eyes and sat up in bed. It was almost midnight and from my apartment window I could see the lights still glimmering in downtown Los Angeles.

"This is Dr. Garfield."

"Go ahead," the operator said.

"Dr. Garfield, this is Henry Kaiser."

Two hours later, I was on a plane from Los Angeles to San Francisco. Harold Hatch, who'd leapt off the train with Kaiser back in Desert Center, picked me up at the airport and deposited me in the lobby of the Fairmont Hotel. "Mr. Kaiser has taken over the seventh floor." Shouldn't be long and he was off to the elevator, his walk strained from his hunched back, before I could utter a word.

I straightened my khaki tie and sank back in a chair. Much had happened during the last two months since the attack on Pearl Harbor. With the war starting and the aqueduct completed, I'd sold my hospital building to a date farm in Indio to use for fruit storage. All that planning, attention to detail, and in the end it was going to be used as a storage shack. Hell, at least I'd traded in my medical equipment for a profit. All except the X-ray machine that had impressed my father. Three months since his death and I still had a hard time dealing with it. Which was why I grasped at things like that old X-ray machine, which reminded me of him.

A month ago, after Judy had left and enlisted, I'd driven to LA, winding through the desert roads for the last time, and convinced my former colleagues at Los Angeles County General Hospital to enlist with me in the same unit. If we were going to win this war, I'd told them, we'd need to keep our soldiers healthy. I meant it. After all, hadn't building the aqueduct in the middle of the Mojave been a war of survival? A real war couldn't be much worse. Our unit would be leaving in a week to Southeast Asia to keep the Burma Road open. A part of me hoped Judy would be there. But that was one dream that would likely never come true.

So what was I doing here, warming this overstuffed seat cushion? Frankly, I wondered why Kaiser wanted to see me. It didn't matter; I'd jumped at the chance. After his help in turning things around in Desert Center, I wanted to talk to him about health care after the War. It had worked in the desert and we could make it work everywhere. Affordable quality care for all was the ethical way to practice and with Kaiser's help, we could break the AMA's monopoly. We'd start in the big cities—Los Angeles, San Francisco—where large numbers of workers, even middle class professionals like teachers, couldn't afford fee-for-service medicine. We'd work with union leaders and offer voluntary enrollment for everyone from retail clerks to longshoremen. People would receive great medical care without going broke. But it would have to wait until after the War. Hell, who was I kidding? After the War? We were losing on all fronts…who knew how long that would be. Months? Years? Things might never be the same again.

I gazed around the immense lobby, reminiscent of a museum, with striking palm trees that stretched toward skylights and cherry wood tables smelling of lemon-scented oil. Men in uniforms hustled about, some with women on their arms, eager for their last fling before going overseas. Which made me wish for the thousandth time that Judy was here with me. Our relationship had finally grown into a feeling I'd never had with any other woman, as if the scales of my life had been waiting for her to put things in balance. It didn't make a bit of difference now. Judy had enlisted and was lost to me.

I glanced at my watch and rehearsed what I was going to say. I didn't want Kaiser to forget how well our system had worked. "Mr. Kaiser, thank you for all your help. I'm in the Army, but after the War…" No, that was obvious. Just a simple: "Thank you, Mr. Kaiser. Would you consider…" No, that sounded weak. "After the War, I'd like to work with you on prepaid health care." I swallowed hard. Kaiser wasn't one to mince words. I'd see what he had to say first. He'd think I was unpatriotic to even think about plans for after the War.

My legs felt stiff from sitting. I stretched and walked across the lobby to where a crowd had gathered in front of a console sized Art Deco radio and joined them in listening.

"My Fellow Americans," Franklin Delano Roosevelt said in his fatherly voice. "It is nearly two months since we were attacked at Pearl Harbor. Since then we have dispatched strong forces of our Army and Navy, several hundred thousand of them, to bases and battlefronts thousands of miles from home."

"Dr. Garfield!" Hatch yelled from the elevator. "Mr. Kaiser will see you now."

Hatch held the door open and I walked over to join him. We were the only ones in the elevator. "Does Mister Kaiser know I'm leaving for overseas in a week?"

"Yes, of course…just wait until you've talked to him. When he has his mind set on something, there's no stopping him. You'll see." On the top floor, the elevator door opened and I followed him out.

"You two have much in common, you know."

"No, I don't know. In what way?"

"He's a fanatic about medical care. Not good medical care for some. But the best possible care for everyone. Rich, worker, poor. Everyone. Isn't that what you want, too?"

"Yes…exactly."

Hatch knocked once and without waiting opened the door. Henry Kaiser smiled, shot up from the couch to greet me, and smothered my hand in his. "Great of you to come, Dr. Garfield." He let go and gestured to a smaller man in his thirties with thinning hair and a face less chiseled than Kaiser's, who nodded from across the penthouse room. "This is my son, Edgar." Kaiser adjusted the radio dial and patted the seat next to him on the couch. "Sit, the president's talking."

"Mr. Kaiser, thank you for inviting me, but—"

"Just a moment, please." Kaiser was larger than I'd remembered: heavy jawed, mouth wide and firm.

Static partially obscured FDR's voice. "We have stepped up our war production on a scale that is testing our industrial power, our engineering genius, and our economic structure to the utmost. We have had no illusions about the fact that this is a tough job—and a long one."

"Pay attention, Dr. Garfield." Kaiser tapped on the wooden radio console trying to lessen the static. "We need ships more than anything right now. That's why I sent for you."

FDR continued: "American warships are now in combat in the North and South Atlantic, in the Arctic, in the Mediterranean, in the Indian Ocean, and in the North and South Pacific. On the other side of the world, in the Far East, we have passed through a phase of serious losses. The Malayan Peninsula, the Philippines, and Singapore are in the hands of the enemy. The Japanese are pressing their northward advance against Burma with considerable power, driving toward India and China. The news in Burma tonight is not good."

Kaiser waved his hand, gesturing to Hatch to turn down the volume. "Dr. Garfield. I appreciate your coming here and I'm fully aware of your Army assignment. To win this war, we need ships…more ships than we've ever built before. I've taken over Richmond and we have thirty thousand workers with only one doctor in town."

"Thirty thousand. Are you kidding about the doctor?"

"I wish I was. It gets worse. He thinks everything can be treated with an aspirin or a pat on the back. And if that isn't enough, the local hospitals charge fee-for-service. Can you believe the bastards are trying to gouge me with a war on? Fee-for-service and they'll only take care of the white workers. We can't build ships without the best medical care possible for all workers regardless of color. That's why I called you here. I want to know how you'd organize and run it."

"How many workers when you're fully up and running?"

"A hundred thousand. From all over this country. Men, women. All races. All states of health. 4F's. Anyone who can work. And we'll do what FDR wants. We'll build ships faster than anyone thought possible."

"A hundred thousand. That will take facilities…doctors."

"Yes, yes, of course," Kaiser said. "I know that. Come on, Doctor. You can be more helpful than that."

"Okay. First, you'll need to convince the doctors. The AMA's motto is fee-for-service and the ones who aren't drafted will fight losing patients to you. You'll need to get the government to—"

"I've convinced Washington," Kaiser said, "and I'll convince the AMA. They can't argue with simple logic. We need ships to win the war. We can't build ships without men. We can't keep up our manpower without hurt and sick men being quickly returned to health. They're as much a part of shipbuilding as cranes and steel."

Edgar Kaiser opened his briefcase and pulled out a notebook. "I've already met with the Alameda County Medical Society and personally called all eighty-four members. There's a War on and they'll cooperate."

"They'd better," Henry said.

I'd thought about this night after night in the desert. Read about how they'd provided care during the First World War and figured out the way I'd want to be treated if injured on the job or the battlefield. The system of care I'd used in the desert could be scaled up to provide care to millions…well, maybe that was just a pipe dream. But it had worked for five thousand workers and it would work for a hundred thousand.

"You'll need at least a hundred doctors to take care of that many workers," I said. "If you organize the shipyards into field centers and one main hospital you could be ready in a few months."

"Now, you're talking." Henry started to laugh. "But not months. My God, we have less than two weeks. We need to be up and running in 12 days."

"Twelve days." I stared down at my watch and shook my head. "Twelve days. You'd compromise quality—"

"This isn't the time to think small," Henry said. "I need someone who can get us up and running in less than two weeks. Who would you recommend?"

"I don't know. Maybe Cecil Cutting or Ray Kay. I worked with both of them at LA County Hospital." Although I really didn't know if they could pull this off.

"This isn't time for maybes," Henry said. "I need someone who can do it. Hear me, Doctor, someone who has experience I can count on."

"Well, I could, except of course, I'm in the Army."

"You could?" Henry beamed. "Is that right? Up and running in twelve days?"

"Well, yes."

"Twelve days, no longer?"

I nodded.

"And provide good quality care?"

"Yes, if—"

"Good. That's exactly why I made a special request to the president."

Hatch handed me a letter. My eyes fixed on the signature. Franklin Delano Roosevelt, the Commander in Chief and President of the United States. Addressed to me, Sidney R. Garfield. I stared at the words, the signature. The White House letterhead. I was released from my military commission. FDR was instructing me to take charge of the Richmond shipyard medical program.

I was amazed. "You didn't even ask me about this."

"I know, I know." Henry put his hand on my shoulder. "I've known all along, you're the only one who can do it. The only one who has experience in taking care of five thousand men in the worst possible conditions."

"Twelve days to set up a hospital?" It was hard to imagine how quickly things had changed. How that phone call had changed my life.

"That's right. I don't settle for second best, Dr. Garfield. Not where my workers are concerned. Not with a war on."

A smile crept across my face. I wouldn't have to wait for the war to be over to practice the way I thought best. Henry was right: I could make a bigger contribution to the war by staying home.

"Give me the list of everyone you need," Edgar said. "Specialists, surgeons—"

"I'll have a complete plan to you tomorrow morning by six. But for sure, I'll need Cecil Cutting released from the military to be my Chief of Staff. He's the best surgeon to graduate from LA County." His wife, Millie, would kiss me for this. "And my nurse from the desert, Judy Avalon, to run the nursing service. She has already enlisted."

Edgar scrawled their names. "Consider it done."

"Dr. Garfield." Henry engulfed my right hand between both of his. "Any other questions?"

Only one came to mind. "How many ships have you ever built?"

He grinned. "None."

## CHAPTER 13

Richmond

## April 4, 1942

Monday morning, the first shift bell ringing, and nowhere in the world, except maybe in the back streets of Calcutta, could I have encountered people with health problems like the workers in Richmond. In the last two months, the small town of a few thousand across from San Francisco had grown to mammoth proportions. Marshland had been filled with dirt, creating the largest shipyard in California. Close to one hundred thousand workers crammed into every square inch; sleeping in shifts that matched their work assignments, some even "hot bunking"—taking turns using the same bed—like sailors did on submarines. Many were 4F's rejected for health reasons from the army and all of them wanted to work 24 hours a day to beat the Nazis and the Japanese.

I glanced down at my watch. "The bus with the next group of patients will be here in five minutes," I said to Cecil Cutting. A few years older than me, a half-foot taller, his hair losing ground against his forehead, Cecil had been a friend since residency and a natural as my Chief of Staff for the Richmond Field hospital.

We stood outside the main trailer and waited as the cold morning wind blew in off the Bay. The fog was rolling in like it did every day. I wasn't sure yet which I liked least, the damp cold or the scorching desert heat. "Any nurses free?"

Cecil shook his head. Edgar Kaiser had been able to get me some of the physicians and nurses I'd needed, but had no luck in finding Judy.

"We'll have to get the bus driver to help."

"Sid, when's the last time you slept?"

"Quit being a mother hen. I'm fine. You're the one who looks tired."

"Just like residency." Cecil smiled. "More than four hours a night is sleeping in."

"Well, let's hope there're no cases of pneumonia on that bus. We'll be out of beds. We need a real hospital, not this makeshift trailer."

After seventeen days of round-the-clock construction, the field hospital had been up and running. We'd connected a series of four double-wide trailers and modified them as an emergency room, exam area, OR, and ward with twenty beds to hospitalize and observe workers overnight. I'd come up with a fifty-foot-long bench to take the most efficient care of the workers. Every eight feet the table had a T-extension big enough for a worker to lie down. If a patient had an injured foot, you could lift the section up, pull out a bar and examine it. And I'd even put curtains so you could examine someone for a hernia or hemorrhoids in private.

"What's happening with finding a real hospital?" Cecil stood on the curb next to the bus stop. "If we don't get one soon—"

"I know, I know. Our whole system depends on having our own hospital. We can't send the workers off to the community—even with a war on, they won't take our Negro patients and even if they did we'd have no control over quality." A converted yellow school bus pulled up on the newly paved street in front of us.

"You're preaching to the choir," Cecil yelled over the noise and fumes of the bus. "Worrying about skin color. Where are we going to find a decent hospital for sale?"

I waited for the driver to kill the engine so I didn't have to shout. "No, there's only one and it's…well, used."

"You mean a dump?"

I nodded. "I'll have to convince Kaiser—"

"Doc…Doc!" The bus driver waved hands over head, his pants almost falling below his bulging waist. "This guy's passed out!"

Cecil and I ran to the bus, where a grease-covered Negro worker, no more than nineteen, lay on one of the benches.

"Pulse?"

"120, thready," Cecil answered. "Respiration's 25. Feels hot—probably pneumonia. The field hospital's full, you know, we'll have to try and send him out."

"Yeah, well, you know as well as I do, no one will take him. It could be Monday Morning Fever."

Cecil nodded. "Maybe."

Inside the field hospital, we placed him under the X-ray machine I'd bought from GE two years ago. I threaded in an IV and started a full bottle of Ringer's lactate.

Cecil developed the chest films and held them up. "Lungs clear. Okay, how'd you know?"

"Just a guess." I flagged down one of the nurses, doing the work of five. "Put him in the oxygen tent. I'll check back in a few minutes."

"You have that look," Cecil said.

"Yeah. Just like the bad water back at Desert Center causing abdominal cramps, or as simple as puncture wounds from nails, we're dealing with something work related. Over two hundred workers sick…young, healthy guys we can't afford to lose. We've got to figure it out and prevent it or we'll need to shut things down."

"Kaiser won't allow that," Cecil said.

"Any better ideas? We can't just let the workers get sick."

"Well, they're all welders and it's always on Monday."

"So, what's different about Monday? A new batch of solder, flux, different equipment? How many shifts are the welders working?"

"Don't know," Cecil said.

I grabbed my black bag. "Hold the fort. It's Monday and I'm getting to the bottom of this."

The hull of a Liberty Ship had to be worse than the most claustrophobic coal mine in West Virginia or Kentucky. Twenty men stuffed inside the metal tomb, each one of them only inches away from torching the guy next to them. The temperature made summer in Desert Center seem like a day in the Rockies. The metal floor was so drenched in sweat, it was hard to walk without slipping.

Mike Everett, 4F due to his history of a ruptured spleen and broken ribs, a man who appealed anyway and lost his bid to get into the Marines, was the foreman in charge of this ship. I followed close behind him, squeezing between four men welding together the two sections of the hull. The acid from the soldering flux stung my eyes and the fumes burned my lungs like a carton of cigarettes. He pointed to the temporary metal ladder used to climb up.

I shook my head. "Not yet. Do they do anything different on Mondays?"

"Same every day except Sunday, Doc. They weld. First to third shift."

"What shift did that kid you sent to the hospital today work on?"

"First…"

The hammering made it hard to hear Mike, even when he yelled next to my ear. "What?"

"He just got here an hour or so ago."

There went that idea. It would have made a lot more sense if it happened at the end of his shift after hours of breathing low oxygen, just like a diver getting the bends.

Mike pointed to the ladder again, and this time I nodded. How these guys worked down here day after day…well, it was hard to imagine. Sweat poured off me as I climbed out of the hull and into the cool air. We walked over to one of the break areas, two wooden benches, where the men sat around and smoked during their fifteen-minute morning and afternoon breaks.

"Any ideas, Doc?" Mike's hair was covered with grease, as I was sure mine was.

"None. Would make more sense if it happened on Saturday. You have any ideas?"

He shook his head. "Almost as if Sundays off made them sick…and don't you go telling Mr. Kaiser that. Otherwise he'll be having us work seven days a week."

"Oh, shit." I looked at my watch.

"What?"

"I'm meeting Kaiser in twenty minutes in Oakland. You know how he is about being late."

Mike gave me a mock salute. "Doc, you hear anything from Judy?"

"Not a word."

I'd parked the ambulance a few yards from the dock. There was only one way to get to Oakland in time: lights flashing, siren blaring and my foot heavy to the floor. I pushed it to seventy, winding my way through the fog, and made it to the old Fabiola Hospital with two minutes to spare.

Henry was already in front, along with Hatch. His hand engulfed mine as it always did. "Sid, you're supposed to be taking care of the sick workers." He smiled one of his larger than life grins. "Not building the ships yourself."

I looked at my grease-covered hand that Henry had accepted without a second glance and knew the rest of me must look just as bad.

"Show me around," he said. "I have to be in San Francisco within the hour."

"Five stories…it used to be the only hospital in Oakland," I said. "Then when they built a newer one, it closed down."

"Fabiola…know what it means?" he asked.

"Some sort of patron Saint for the injured. Husband used to beat her back in the fourth century." Henry was at the elevator, punching the button repeatedly.

"We'll have to walk. No electricity." I pointed to the stairs, littered with old food wrappers and used bandages."

"You two go ahead," Hatch said. "I'm not much with stairs."

Henry nodded. Hatch's hunchback made it difficult to climb. Although a few years ago, he'd jumped off that train. I guess we were all getting older.

We took the stairs to the top floor and walked around the old patient rooms. The walls had punched out holes and peeling paint, old mattresses had been used by rats for bedding, and a decade of dust and trash had been left undisturbed. But worst of all, Henry hadn't said a word since we'd walked up the stairs. He just looked from room to room, making mental notes in that enormous head of his.

"Let me show you the OR's." I gestured back to the stairs, and he followed me down to where six OR's that had once been clean and new were now decaying. Maybe we should have stayed on the fifth floor, where at least there was a great view. Still not a word.

"Well, I know it will need some work…but the location and the structure is perfect. We need a hospital or our whole system will break down. We're hospitalizing ten welders a week, sick from breathing fumes. The field hospital is always full, making us send our patients to community hospitals and, frankly, that's not good care. They won't take the coloreds and half the time they refuse to take the whites too. And when they do, they overcharge us, provide shoddy treatment, keep our patients hospitalized for days more than they need, and crowd them into charity wards. We have to manage our own workers or slow things down until we can. We need a hospital where Negroes and whites are treated the same…even share the same wards. Give me the okay and I'll have this hospital up and running in eight months."

Henry smiled as he put his arm around my shoulder. "What's the matter, Sid? Don't you think I have any vision?"

"Well, of course, it's just that—"

"It's just that we have an appointment with Giannini in thirty minutes. Nothing is going to slow down our shipbuilding. Hear that, Sid? Nothing. Let me drive that ambulance of yours. Hatch will meet us there."

We weren't ready to talk to A.P. Giannini, the president of Bank of America. There were no hospital remodel plans, no cost estimates, and no contractor's bids.

Henry got behind the wheel and pointed to the switch for the siren. "C'mon, Sid. Speed is my only vice…okay, maybe eating too."

"Don't we need something on paper to show Giannini?" I yelled over the siren. "Plans…figures?"

Henry shook his head. "I'll handle him, Sid. You worry too much."

I held on to the door handle as Henry sped around corners and across the bridge to San Francisco without braking once. At least it seemed that way. He pulled in front of the thirty-story Bank of America building, leaving the ambulance in the red zone. Even city cops never ticketed ambulances. The guard at the front door came to attention. "Good afternoon, Mister Kaiser."

"Hi, Walter." Henry seemed to remember everyone's name.

Once in the elevator, the attendant nodded and without asking where we were going, took us up to the top floor in less than a minute. I felt out of place with my grease-covered white coat. People were probably wondering why Henry Kaiser, master builder and industrialist, was walking around with his car mechanic.

Henry opened the door to Giannini's office and gestured for me to go first. Inside was an air-conditioned, freshly painted office…no, *office* didn't do it justice. It was more like what I imagined the palaces of the British Crown must look like. And the receptionist…well, let's just say, she made Betty Grable look plain. She smiled at Henry with a Hollywood grin and said, "Mr. Giannini is expecting you, please go right in."

The inner sanctum was an office paneled with the richest wood I'd ever seen. Giannini, who looked like he could have been Mussolini's younger brother, minus about twenty pounds, shook Henry's hand and reluctantly shook mine, which was relatively clean now. I'd rubbed off most of the grease gripping the handle on the ambulance ride.

"I'll get right to the point, A.P.," Henry said. "Dr. Garfield needs $250,000 to renovate the old Fabiola hospital. And I need it up and running to care for my men working in the shipyards."

"You're not going to give me one of your flag-waving speeches now, are you Henry? Because if you are, I have to remind you that even though I'm every bit against the Nazis as you are, I have a primary responsibility to my investors. So if you're looking for a loan without collateral, go ask the Army."

"You know that will take months. Look, Dr. Garfield has built hospitals before."

Giannini raised his brow and looked at me, really looked at me for the first time. "Is that true?"

I cleared my throat. "Yes, sir. Designed, built, financed and repaid every dollar. Made a good profit for the bank and myself."

"And just where was this hospital, young man?"

"Near Los Angeles." At least it was nearer to Los Angeles than to San Francisco, and I wasn't about to tell him it was in the middle of the desert.

"State of the art," Henry added. "Air conditioned patient rooms, X-ray machines, OR—"

"Henry, Dr. Garfield. I'm impressed, still…I won't lend you one red cent on a hospital. If something happens, there is no way our bank could foreclose. What would we do with a hospital? However, Henry, if you'll guarantee the loan, you can have the money."

Henry started to laugh. "Okay, A.P., give the Doctor his loan. Sid, you'll have that hospital."

The words yanked me backwards in time, back to the desert where my father—my wonderful father—had once said almost the exact same words: *Sidney, you'll have that hospital.*

"Dr. Garfield, they-uh's a call for you," Lucy said in her thick Alabama drawl.

"Can you take a message?" I was right in the middle of my morning rounds, with twelve more patients to go.

"Sure, Doc, but...she says it's important."

What wasn't these days? I'd finished refurbishing Fabiola hospital in three months, a task that impressed even Henry. Now, trying to oversee the staff there and at the two field hospitals...well, there wasn't ever time to call back, so might as well take it now.

"This is Dr. Garfield."

"Hi, Sid."

Judy's voice crumpled my exhausted legs onto the nearest chair.

"You okay, Doc?" Lucy asked.

I nodded.

"Sid, you there?"

"Yeah, Judy. I've been trying to—"

"I know, I'm sorry. I was so depressed. And the War, well, you understand. My commanding officer called me in. Said Henry Kaiser wanted me in his shipyards. Sid, you have anything to do with that?"

How many times had I played this conversation over in my mind, now only to find myself coming down with a bad case of dementia. "Well, yes. The words just blurted out. "We need to talk." My legs were starting to feel like they had bones again instead of jelly.

"I'm not calling about that, it's about Dwight."

"Chandler? You're calling about Chandler?" Maybe that was overreacting. Maybe he was injured in action. Even Chandler deserved some respect for serving his country. "Is he okay…I mean, has he left for Europe yet?"

"That's why I'm calling. I was hoping you could convince Mister Kaiser to pull some strings like he did for me. You know, see if he can work in Richmond with us." She sounded like I'd jump at the chance of helping good ole Dwight.

"You want me to help Chandler?" I yelled into the phone. Okay, maybe it was shallow of me, but the irony of it. My outburst had gotten Lucy's attention. She raised her brows and looked my way.

"Well, yes," she said.

"Look, Judy. I'll be honest with you. Even if I had an opening, which I don't, I wouldn't hire him. But, it's not up to me. There's a hiring freeze. The War Department won't let us be better staffed than our soldiers overseas. But we do need nurses."

"I know how close we were before the War." She sounded serious now, like she was going to tell me Chandler caught a stray bullet, but then he wouldn't need a job here. "I'm sorry, Sid, I knew how you felt. And I am grateful for everything you did. But things change. And well, now…now Dwight and I are going to be married."

I almost fell out of the chair. "Marry Chandler? Tell me you're joking. C'mon, Judy, we both know him too well. Why would you ever—"

"Please Sid, I have my reasons and I'm asking you as a friend to help. If you won't, well, then I guess I didn't know you as well as I thought."

"If you're really marrying Chandler then I guess I've never known you."

"Okay, if that's the way you feel…well, bye—"

"Wait, don't hang up. I can't do this over the phone. Come here and we'll talk."

"Thanks, Sid. It's a deal then. And thanks for speaking to Mr. Kaiser. See you soon."

Dial tone. Up too many nights in a row and not enough sleep had done me in. I wasn't sure what our deal was.

Henry Kaiser marched up to a flag-draped platform overlooking Richmond Shipyard number two and gripped the microphone with the same knuckle crunch as a Marine holding his rifle. Almost midnight, but floodlights filled the yard with the intensity of noon in July. Around us the shipyard looked like a massive assembly kit, spread out over acres of land. The entire medical staff stood at attention in freshly pressed white coats.

Henry's words blared over the loudspeakers: "Each new ship strikes a blow at the menace to the nation and for the liberty of the free people of the world. A Liberty Ship sends a message to Hitler that our president's words are not in vain. We will build a bridge of ships across the Atlantic. We will make FDR proud. Make America proud. Together we will make history. We will win this war, one ship at a time, and time, my friends is what it is all about. We are going to build a ship faster than anyone ever thought possible. Faster than ever before."

I looked around the crowd. Thousands of workers, excitement in their eyes, looked up at Henry not as a general or even a president. They respected him as a father—a father none of them would ever let down. And I realized I felt the same way. I missed my own father and in a lot of ways, Henry reminded me of him.

"We'll build that bridge across the ocean and we'll do it in less than five days." When we'd first started, building a Liberty ship a month seemed impossible. Five days was like flying to the moon.

At the stroke of midnight, Henry pressed a button to start a four-foot round classroom clock. He raised his hand and signaled to Mike Everett. A moment later, the crane's diesel engine cranked on with a sudden puff of fumes and smoke, carrying the keel into position. In the next five days a quarter million different parts would come together—43 miles of welding, 5 miles of wiring, 7 miles of piping—the whole thing equivalent to a forty-story building on its side. The 455 foot long, armed cargo ship, capable of doing 17 knots, would carry troops, ammunitions, and a half-million cubic feet of supplies to Europe and the Pacific.

"Can you do it?" Henry beamed that enormous smile of his.

Three thousand workers chorused back in unison, "Yes, we can!"

\*　\*　\*

Wandering around the shipyard, seeing the workers build the Liberty ship—nicknamed the "wonder ship"—was like watching a championship Olympic sports team. Everyone had geared up to win the home front war and had worked for months to coordinate things down to the minutest detail. Even the bow section had the ship's name, *S.S. Robert E. Peary*, painted on it before it was lifted into place.

Now, less than forty-eight hours since Henry had started the clock, the empty shipway had a full-grown hull and the two "whirlys," the slang term for the towering cranes, were lowering the third of seven huge deck sections into place. After eight p.m., enormous floodlights lit the shipyard brighter than Yankee Stadium.

Cecil ran his hand through a hairline that over the last year had lost its battle. "It's all just a publicity stunt."

"I wouldn't say that around here unless you want to get strung up on the top of that crane. You know what this is about." I picked up a stray rivet. "Hope and pride. That a group of 4F workers can help win this war."

Cecil looked me in the eyes and pointed to the large clock Henry had started forty-four hours ago. "Okay, maybe you're right. But winning the war will have to wait a few hours. We have a staff meeting. C'mon, I'll drive."

A half-hour later we were walking into Trader Vic's on San Pablo Boulevard in Oakland for our weekly chiefs of service meeting. I'd mulled over the agenda for the last two days. It was important to let everyone have their say, but at the same time, I had to keep things on track. Making this work was the most important thing on my mind. I laughed to myself—it was the *only* thing on my mind.

"Hey doc, what's so funny? You ready for a few Mai Tai's?" Trader Vic Bergeron was as far from Polynesian as an Irishman was from Sephardic. Curly blond hair, blue eyes, and a huge gut from years of eating his restaurant's fried foods, Vic was a hard man not to take an instant liking to. "Yeah," I answered. "Bring a round."

This was our version of the War Room. To my right, as always, sat Cecil Cutting, Chief of Surgery. Morris Collen, who I'd recruited from USC to be my Chief of Medicine, was Italian; dark, thin, sarcastic and a Shakespearean scholar before he'd entered med school. Paul Fitzgibbon, a former quarterback for the Green Bay Packers, who'd seen so many concussions he'd decided to become a neurologist, was now in charge of Fabiola hospital. Bob King, Ob-Gyn, cared for the women workers. He always wore baggy battle fatigues instead of a white shirt and tie like the rest of us. Independent, rebellious, he could work without sleep like no one I'd ever seen. And finally, to run the lab, Mel Friedman in pathology, with glasses so thick he could pass for Groucho Marx's twin, although I couldn't remember the last time he'd smiled.

I waited for the small talk to finish before clearing my throat and calling the meeting to order.

"The 3 by 5 cards aren't working out," Fitzgibbon started. "Can't get enough—"

"Wait a damn minute," King interrupted. "They fit in your pocket. All important patient information right there. What more—"

"More is the problem," Cecil said, even-toned. "The cards are too easy to lose and too hard to find when we need them. Paul, you can keep yours during the hospital stay. Give them to me after discharge and I'll have Millie and the girls copy them onto 8 1/2 by 11 sheets."

"Millie has the time?" I asked. Cecil's wife was in charge of the nursing staff in Richmond.

"There's a war on," Cecil quipped. "She'll get volunteers."

"Okay?" King nodded and no one objected.

"All right, on to quality issues."

"I figured out Monday morning fever," Morris said.

"You mean we did." Friedman removed his glasses and cleaned them on his napkin, like he always did when he was waiting for the applause that never came.

"We've had six cases this week, twelve last," I said. "So go on."

"It's caused by zinc poisoning."

"That doesn't make sense," King interrupted. "It would be worse on Friday after being exposed to zinc welding fumes all week, not Monday."

"Yeah," Cecil said. "It would happen on the third shift and we know it's more common with the first shifters."

"I sent off blood samples to UCSF," Friedman said. "Zinc was lowest on Monday and highest on Friday."

"That goes with Friday fevers." King spit an ice cube into his glass. "So, explain why they're on Monday."

"Tolerance," Morris said.

"Tolerance to zinc poisoning?" Fitzgibbon asked.

"That's right," Morris said. "They build up tolerance to zinc all week, so it doesn't bother them. If they're off the weekend, the levels go down and Monday they get sick when they're exposed again. Ergo…Monday morning fevers."

"It makes perfect sense," Friedman said. "Chemical and drug tolerance has been proven for lead, copper, iron—"

"Good work, you two," I interrupted. Freidman, a walking textbook of pathology would go on all night. "I'll talk to Kaiser about better ventilation and rotating the welders in shorter shifts. This is one fever we'll prevent. Now, on to budget."

"Can't we finish the fried shrimp first?" King said.

"You can eat and talk, can't you?" Friedman chewed a non-kosher morsel like he was tasting a lab specimen. "Or is it too hard for you to do two things at once?"

"Fuck you, Friedman." King snapped.

"Pipe down, will you two?" I said.

"Yeah, let's talk turkey," Morris said. "The shipyard workers are a walking pathological museum. Most are 4F-minuses when it comes to health. I have fifty in the hospital for pneumonia right now. And with no interns or residents…well, it's high time for more help."

Nods around the table.

"I know, I know." I said. "You all can do the math. We have 90% of the workers paying us seven cents a day—fifty cents a week for comprehensive coverage. That's more than $40,000 a week. More than enough to keep things going and enough to help recruit some good physicians. But it's not the money. The Alameda-Contra Costa Medical Society is barring us from becoming members, they're lobbying the—"

"I've worked that out," Cecil said. Always the diplomat, he could have negotiated peace with the Japanese if the State Department had asked him.

"How the hell'd you do that?" King asked, using his fatigues for a napkin.

Cecil shrugged. "Like everything else. For the duration."

"For the duration? God damn them," I shouted. "They're lying, you know. They want us gone now. They're holding up a white flag and stabbing us in the back. Well, I have news for them. Even if it's premature to think ahead, we're not going to close our hospitals and leave town after the War. We have ninety thousand workers here in Richmond, and another hundred thousand in the Vancouver-Portland shipyards and only a handful of physicians dedicated to group practice. We're doing it without government handouts with quality never seen before. Best mortality rates for pneumonia, least recurrence rates for hernias—"

"Sid, we know, we know." Fitzgibbon interrupted me. "We're behind you all the way. But let's talk about now. We need more docs. When are you getting us more docs?"

Trader Vic delivered another round of food. "You like the pineapple pork, Dr. Friedman?"

Friedman's face turned white. "Pork? Damn. I thought it was chicken."

Vic slapped him on the back. "Chicken? There hasn't been any chicken to buy for months. Pork will have to do."

"Sid, what about—" Fitzgibbon repeated.

"I've been calling the Federal Procurement and Assignment Board daily. After they sent me the last few doctors who drank whiskey for breakfast, I had Mr. Kaiser call. Ten new doctors will be here by the end of next week."

"The last thing we need is surgeons like Chandler," Friedman said. "Is it true he's coming? I knew him back at County. He wouldn't know a real case of appendicitis if it slapped him in the face. We should take away his scalpel before—"

"Hear, hear," Morris lifted his drink. "Enough complaining. New doctors are on their way. To Sid."

A few clinks of glass and then a giant gulp of relief.

"Funny, guys. C'mon, let's get back to the shipyards. We're missing history in the making, sitting on our duffs."

Morris stood and recited in a Shakespearian accent: "'When shall we all meet again? In thunder, lightning, or in rain? When the hurly-burly's done, when the battle's lost and won.' Macbeth. Act 1, Scene 1."

King shook his head and threw his napkin on the table. "Morris, you're so full of shit."

At precisely 3:26 on Thursday afternoon, September 10, 1942, four and a half days after starting the *S.S. Robert E. Peary*, I stood on the platform with the huge clock under an eighty-foot-tall Whirly and gazed up at the six-story scaffold that surrounded the "wonder ship." The whole scene reminded me of a sold-out football game. Ten thousand workers crowded on the concrete dock at Kaiser Shipyard Two. Hull #440 was about to slip out of its construction towers and slide down the ramp into the ocean on its way to carrying munitions to our soldiers in the Pacific. You'd think we'd won the war by the celebration, band music drowning out the sound of the newly finished ship's engine revving up for its maiden voyage.

Strange though. Henry should've been there on the viewing stand, the same one we were on when this all began. It wasn't like him to miss an event like this. Wasn't like him at all. I knew how proud he was of these workers, who'd accomplished a record that'd be hard to beat for the next hundred years. So where was he, the man they'd all—

Every shipyard horn and whistle sounded at once. An enormous blast sucked the air out of my ear canals and pounded against my eardrums. The band stopped playing. A group of soldiers marched down the road leading to the shipway, clearing the crowd for an open black limousine.

They stopped next to the viewing platform, less than ten feet away from me and for the first time in my life I saw President Roosevelt in person. Never had I felt so proud, so heart-struck with red, white, and blue American pride. FDR's smile said if we could build a ship in four days, we could win this war. Next to him in the back of the limousine, Henry signaled the Secret Servicemen to let me through.

"Mr. President," I could hear Henry's booming voice. "I'd like you to meet my doctor in charge, Sidney Garfield."

I could feel my blush of embarrassment, but managed to get the words out, "Mr. President."

"You're doing a fine job here, Doctor," FDR said. "Henry has told me all about it." FDR extended his hand and grasped mine in a firm grip. "Keep up your good work. After we win this War, we'll need doctors like you to provide the care that everyone, and I mean everyone, white, black, rich, and poor deserves." He let go of my hand and waved to the crowd as the reflection of the sun off the water caught his eyeglasses and reflected back like a beacon in an uncharted ocean.

# CHAPTER 15

## Richmond

## November 6, 1942

I dabbed at the wound, a six-inch inguinal incision, standard for a hernia repair. "Suction, there, will you?"

"How's that?" Cecil held the catheter below an oozing branch of the femoral vein as I tied it off with a silk ligature. "Can you see the sac yet?"

I held out my hand for the scrub nurse. "Mosquito." She slapped the instrument into the center of my palm. "Almost..." I teased it out with the tiny hemostat..."right...here. You know, there's gotta be a better way of doing this."

"I know. Half recur and we still do it the same way they were done twenty years ago. You have any ideas?"

The anesthesiologist, Dick Stubin, let the BP cuff deflate.

"You ever think about using plastic, you know, like a patch?"

"Plastics? Sid, where the hell would you get any? There's a war on. You going to make your own?"

I pushed the small loop of herniated bowel back into the abdomen and started suturing the sac and fascia to hold everything in place. "Yeah, maybe I will. It would work better than this. Look how flimsy the tissue is. That's why these break down. We could sew this up with steel sutures and the hernia could still work its way back out."

The OR door opened and a nurse walked in. Three p.m. on the dot, time for the shift change.

"So, plastics, huh?"

"Why not? A thin piece, solid. We cut holes around the edges and sew it in to reinforce the repair."

Cecil shook his head. "What did your Dad used to call you? Mashed potatoes…you know, that Yiddish term of his?"

"*Meshugganah*," said the nurse who'd just walked in the room.

"Right." I looked up at the eyes above the mask. Blonde eyebrows in a perfect arch. Familiar green eyes. "Judy?"

She nodded.

"Judy? Why didn't you tell me you got here? How long?"

"Dwight and I arrived yesterday."

"Oh."

"Sid? The wound's about to heal on its own."

I threw in the last few sutures and closed the skin in three layers. "Okay, Stubin, go ahead and wake him up."

I dressed the wound with a few gauze sponges and adhesive tape and the patient was as good as new. If the repair held.

Cecil snapped off his rubber gloves. "I've got to get back to Richmond. The clinic will be busting at the seams by now. Plus, you two have some catching up to do."

Judy was facing away, helping the scrub nurse by placing the used metal instruments into a washbasin. "Judy, I'd like to—"

"What?" She looked up, avoiding my eyes. She appeared uneasy, embarrassed.

"Sid, help me transfer him onto the gurney." The anesthesiologist grabbed the sheet under the patient. "On the count of three." We swung him over onto the gurney and Stubin wheeled him out to the Recovery Room.

The instruments clanked as Judy rinsed off the blood and dropped them into a clean basin for sterilization. I moved closer to her; she couldn't avoid me. "Judy what is it?"

She pulled down her mask, her face was drawn…still very attractive, but thin, like she hadn't eaten well in months. Her lips tightened. She ran her hand lightly over my unshaven cheek. "I'm sorry, Sid. I really am."

*   *   *

"What about our kids?" Mike Everett asked. "Huh, Doc? You going to start treating my kids?"

"We're talking about it." At our War Room meeting the night before, I'd brought it up. It was time to provide family coverage. The workers were just the first step in a truly comprehensive health insurance. If the AMA knew what I was planning, they'd hire themselves a U-boat and blow us out of the water. But it was the right thing to do. I'd become more convinced of that every day I saw our system in action. Families needed health care and we had the best way to provide it. "Can you pay another seven cents a day?"

"Hell, you know what they're charging us downtown? That damn doc...uh sorry, but he's so old he scares the kids, and he charges six bits for a minute and an aspirin. Believe you me, for seven cents to cover everything, you'll have a lot of takers."

"I was hoping you'd say that." Mike and I were in the middle of our morning safety rounds on the dock surrounding Ship Bay A. Below us, cranes lowered the final metal sections of a four-story-tall Liberty Ship. Workmen yelled directions up to the Whirly operator and guided the hull assembly into place like a piece of an enormous jigsaw puzzle. "Answer this for me, will you?"

Mike leaned down and picked up a handful of rivets dropped carelessly on the edge of the dock. "What the hell—"

An enormous explosion went off a few feet from us: the ripping sound of metal, a mechanical scream of tortured steel. Then the ground shook and a shock wave slammed me into the railing. I struggled to catch my breath, sliding sideways until my shoulder jammed hard against the metal chain. Then a voice in my head screamed *go go go* and I grabbed Mike and scrambled away from the edge. Smoke and the smell of burned rubber billowed from below. The shaking stopped as suddenly as it began and I let go of Mike.

"Jesus," he said. "Look at that."

Through the haze of soot I saw what had happened. One of the giant Whirly cranes lay in pieces alongside the metal hull section it was lifting. The accident had felt like minutes but had happened in the blink of an eye. Shouts came from the ship. I couldn't make out the words.

"You okay?" Mike asked.

"Yeah. Come on, let's get down there." I steadied myself on the chain handrail as we hustled down the scaffold to the metal ladder that led four stories down to the base of the shipway. I wasn't a novice at shipyard or construction accidents. Years in the desert had given me a sense of how any time you combine heavy equipment, miles of parts and a group of men and women working as hard and as fast as they can, things went wrong. And a lot had just gone wrong. At the bottom of the stairs, the twenty-foot, thousand-ton deck section had twisted into a crumpled mass of metal as unrecognizable as a ball of wrinkled paper.

"Everyone away," Mike ordered. As the supervisor on duty, he was responsible for the accident. "Anyone hurt?"

Four men, covered in black grease, scratched, some with minor cuts from flying scraps of metal, moved away, many wearing a look of shock, or maybe it was relief they were okay. A second later, I smelled it. A faint visceral odor I knew all too well, one of blood and guts. A six-foot section of the hull had splintered off the main deck and landed with the vertical metal railing post upright. "Mike!" I pointed to a woman impaled on the strut.

"Holy shit," Mike grew pale. "Is she…"

I steadied my stethoscope on her chest. She was breathing; at least the left side of her chest cavity was moving and I could hear small breaths. She was on her back, the right side of her rib cage riveted in place with the metal bar passing just below the level of her right breast. She would have been dead instantly if the same injury had happened on her left side. She was semi-conscious and going rapidly into shock.

"Lift her, help me lift her off," Mike yelled to two men standing next to us.

"No," I said. Mike and another worker grabbed her by the arms. "No!" I shouted this time.

They looked at me like I was crazy.

"Get a hacksaw, torch, whatever you can find. Cut the metal…cut the friggin' thing where it's welded to the deck. Now."

"But it will take time," Mike said. "Why not just pull her off?"

"Why? If we do it out here she'll bleed to death."

This was the same team that set the world's record in building a ship and they didn't let me down. Using a hacksaw and the largest metal sheer I'd ever seen, they had the metal free in less than five minutes.

"Put her on the stretcher. We'll carry her up." The first aid station at the shipyard had an emergency operating room designed for just this type of trauma. For a patient that wouldn't survive the transfer to Fabiola. I wish I hadn't given Cecil the day off, but it had been his and Millie's anniversary, so here I was, about to do an emergency thoracotomy and exploratory laparatomy on my own…probably stuck with a nurse who'd pass out at the sight of blood.

I kept my finger on her carotid pulse the whole way up the ramp. Thready, weak, but at least alive. Four men carried her like pallbearers, double-timing it toward the field station.

"Jesus." Mike pointed to the sheet covering the stretcher. "Look at all that blood."

"What's her name? Anyone!"

"Marlene," one of the men carrying the stretcher said. "My sister."

"Okay." I gently squeezed her shoulder. "Marlene, big breath now. Come on, big breath."

Her left chest rose slightly higher. "Okay, that's good, now…"

Chandler and Judy stood at the entrance to the field hospital, both dressed in spotless whites.

"Judy, set up for an ex-lap and I'll need a chest tube."

Her eyes met mine, a look…the same heavy look of disillusionment she'd given me the day before. I faced Chandler. "We'll leave the metal in until we can control the vessels around it."

He ran his hand through his thick, newly cut hair. "Sidney Garfield telling me what to do? C'mon Sid, give me some credit. I do remember my anatomy."

My shoulders tensed. "Sure, Dwight. Just making sure we were on the same page."

"Thanks for getting me out of the Army, Sid. But remember, I taught you how to operate."

Judy looked at her husband to be, her mouth tight, face flushed. "I'll go get the OR ready."

She rushed ahead of us into Field Station A and headed down the wood-planked hall to the OR.

Chandler shrugged and walked next to me.

I glanced at him for a moment, wondering what Judy saw in him, and then back down at Marlene. "Deep breath, Marlene. Breathe."

Chandler and I had her off the gurney and onto the OR table in less than a minute. Judy had everything—chest tube, full lap instrument tray, IV bottle—set up and ready to go. I hesitated. Judy's eyes tensed as they met mine.

"Sid?" She held out my gloves. "We have a patient to save."

# CHAPTER 16

Richmond

November 26, 1942

"How long has he been in the iron lung?"

"Two weeks and still no sign he's breathing on his own."

Since the polio outbreak had started a few months earlier in August, over six hundred children in the San Francisco area had come down with the deadly disease. I thought of Jimmy, the little boy I'd done the emergency tracheotomy on back in residency. Polio was the cruelest of all diseases. The virus invaded the spinal cord and destroyed the nerves that controlled breathing until the child suffocated to death. It reminded me of how my mother had died. No other disease tore at my gut more.

The Fabiola Polio Ward was straight out of a Jules Verne novel and made me feel even more uneasy. I wiped my hand across my forehead. I was sweating like a medical student walking into the hospital for the first time. Around me, rows of children lived inside tiny metal submarines. Hell, that was too kind. Metal coffins would be more accurate. Many would never be able to breathe on their own again. Dr. Nick Halasz pointed across the polio ward to the eight-year-old boy. Halasz was a foot or so shorter than me. His Turkish ancestry had given him his dark skin and a bushy black mustache obscured his upper lip.

"Sid," Halasz cleared his throat, "I hope I'm not keeping you awake."

"No, sorry."

The iron lungs produced a constant *whoosh whoosh*, not as loud as the shipyard, but noisy enough to make it hard to talk without raising my voice.

"Okay. Go over the mechanics for me," Halasz continued. "I make everyone—staff, resident, medical student—explain it once. Don't be insulted. That way, I'm sure you understand it."

"Sure. The whole body is enclosed in the airtight chamber, except for their head with that tight seal around the neck. For each inspiration…" I pointed to the large bellows and pump under the metal bed portion, imagining what it would feel like to be inside one of these contraptions for months without moving an arm or leg. "Uh, for each inspiration, the bellows expand, causing the pressure within the patient cabinet to be lowered, creating a vacuum that expands the chest and draws in fresh air through the patient's mouth. During expiration, the pressure equalizes and the patient exhales passively. You know, there has to be a better design for these."

"What do you mean?"

"For the nurses to take care of the patient. Now they have to pull the whole thing open, taking two nurses to yank it apart. If we put a hinge at the foot of the thing, it would open like an alligator and a single nurse could do it. It'd be a lot more comfortable for the patient."

"Not a bad idea." He finger-combed his mustache. "You should've been an engineer." The lights dimmed and the deafening sound of the eight motors powering the iron lungs came to a screeching halt. "What the hell?"

I held my breath, waiting for the back-up generator to come on. Held my breath, feeling the yearning, the starvation for oxygen after just a few seconds.

"Nurse," Halasz yelled, "call for help. We'll need eight ambu bags and at least eight nurses. And I mean now."

Not a single light came on. There were enough windows high on the wall for daylight to help us see what we were doing. "What about the back-up generator?"

"Doesn't work. Couldn't get the contractor here. Too busy at the other hospitals in town. Now, Garfield. Open the iron lungs. Now!" He slapped an ambu bag with a face mask, the kind anesthesiologists use in the OR, against my chest.

"Okay, everyone." He spoke calmly and loudly, like a general addressing his troops, but with the slightest nervous twitch at the corner of his mouth.

"There are four of us and eight of them. First, open the iron lungs or the pressure inside will stop us from breathing for them. Take two each. Five good breaths and then alternate." He clapped his hands, now more like a football coach at halftime and went to the first patient, the eight-year-old kid, and I helped him pull open the iron lung. The two nurses followed the example and together began opening the iron monsters one by one, giving each kid a few life-saving breaths.

"Dammit," Halasz said. "This one won't budge."

The five-year-old child in the iron lung couldn't cry without air in her lungs. Her lips were turning blue…that awful cadaver blue. Her eyes stared dead ahead in panic.

Sweat poured down Halasz's forehead. He pounded the latch. "Keep breathing the others."

I followed his order, giving five breaths for each of my three kids. A fourteen-year-old with "Mark Sullivan" written on his ID tag looked up at me and mouthed the name Wordsworth. It reminded me of Judy's quote: "The child is father of the man." Is that what this boy was thinking about?

"Dammit!" Halasz pounded his fist against the frozen latch. His blood covered the upper pin.

"Nick. Stop," I yelled. "Take these three. Nick?"

He looked at me, his face tight with anger. A feeling I understood too well. "Breathe for these three," I repeated.

"You can't do anything."

"Yes, I can."

I sat down on the floor and grabbed the leather bellows next to the pump between my hands. The stiff bellows weren't meant for manual compression, they were designed to be powered by a 30 amp motor. I squeezed the bellows, squeezed, giving it all I could, feeling the inside change in pressure, the lungs filling with air, the cry, the real cry, escaping from those blue lips. I relaxed, then pressed again, pressed like I was doing open heart massage, pressed over and over for twenty minutes. My face was covered in sweat; I clenched my teeth and gave it everything I had. Pressing, relaxing, pressing, relaxing, pressing, relaxing.

The lights came on with a small flicker at first, so slight I thought I'd imagined it. When they came on full force, the pump whined like a tank going uphill and the bellows expanded in my hands. I slid out from under the iron lung and in less than two minutes we had them all operational, closing the youngest and smallest first and the teenager's last.

"Wordsworth," Sullivan repeated, now easily heard. His dark hair was matted with sweat, his lips dry and chapped, but his eyes were calm as if the power going off was as routine as a fire drill at school. "Have you read him, Doc?"

"Yes," I said. "He's one of my favorites."

He looked up at me and made one of the only gestures he could. He raised both brows.

> *"And now I see with eye serene*
> *The very pulse of the machine;*
> *A being breathing thoughtful breath;'*
> *A traveler betwixt life and death."*

*Betwixt life and death.* Two weeks since the power went out and I still couldn't get those words out of my head. Courage. Something that I'd seen patients have a lot more of than some doctors.

"C'mon, Sid." Cecil Cutting rested his hand on my shoulder. "Let's get something to eat. I haven't eaten a thing since breakfast."

My stomach gurgled. "Not a bad idea. I could go for a little chowder."

"Let's go then. I'll drive."

I sank into the leather front seat of Cecil's spotless Packard and stared out the window as we passed the lineup of men waiting for the swing shift bell to sound.

"You think the war's going better?" Cecil asked.

"Who knows? The damn Nazis." I changed the subject. "You try to join the Alameda County Medical Society yet?"

Cecil shook his head. "I taught at USC. Board Certified in Surgery. And they turned me down. Closed for the War, they said. But we both know."

I nodded. "Yeah, the bastards want to shut down our hospitals and send us packing overseas. You'd think we were fighting on different sides."

"So what are you saying? We ignore them?"

"No, we fight them on a level they can't do anything about."

He looked puzzled. "Huh?"

"Quality. We show them our recovery rates are better than theirs."

"They'll never believe us."

"They'll have no choice. We'll invite them to our hospitals. Show them the charts." I stared out at the highway. "Take our pneumonia outcomes. Ten of their patients die of pneumonia versus one of ours."

"They'll never show. You'll be hitting them in a sore spot—"

"Speaking of sore spots, well, you know Chandler as well as I do."

"Chandler? What about him?"

"Judy. Why the hell would she want to marry him?"

Cecil slowed the car and gave me his best doctor-bearing-bad-news look. "Look, Sid, I'll level with you. Maybe she's a little off. Sure, she's gorgeous and all, but maybe she's the type that likes to get hurt. You've seen them. The ones that stay with their husbands even after they beat them."

"I don't know. She's too self-confident for that. Hell, I'm not that bad at reading character. When we worked together, we were like pieces of a puzzle that we both knew were a perfect fit. And now…well, shit, it's almost as if he's got something on her."

"C'mon, you've been moping around for weeks. Just talk to her already, for God's sake. Face it. Chandler doesn't need to blackmail her. He's good looking, smooth, and rich. Maybe that's what she wants. Hey, speak of the devil, isn't that Chandler there?"

Three blocks from downtown Oakland, Dwight Chandler stood on the corner next to another man.

"Isn't he on call?" Cecil asked.

"Yeah, pull over. I've had enough of this crap."

"Let me off here," I said to Cecil.

"Are you nuts? It's freezing out there."

"Just do it. I want to see what Chandler's up to."

Cecil pulled up a block away from Chandler and the other man.

"Okay, but if you come down with pneumonia, don't say I didn't warn you."

"You'll be the first to know." I slammed the door and stepped outside. The wind blew off the bay with the intensity of an Alaskan night. I had to walk. Walk off my feelings for Judy. Maybe if I'd tried harder to find her when she'd left…maybe, maybe, maybe. I never thought it was possible to lie without knowing it. I'd lied to myself for weeks that she'd break up with Chandler, that she'd come to me. And each day, the lie continued. I kept on working and she never came.

Downtown Oakland had a slew of sleazy bars and since the war broke out, they catered to every soldier's needs. Not one to drink, especially not alone, a bourbon sounded good now. It was after eleven and the streets were empty except for Chandler and the other man. They entered a bar called the Desert Inn. I slowed my pace so they wouldn't notice me and paused under the neon cactus sign which buzzed like swarming bees over the doorway. Time to quit lying to myself.

Inside was like every other bar, dark booths in the back and near the door, a long counter with a few stray women in tight skirts and even tighter sweaters.

They smiled at me as I walked in, probably hoping I was a customer. I nodded but sat three stools away from them. Chandler sat in the corner booth talking with the other man.

"What can I get you, Doc?" the bartender asked.

Shit, I hadn't bothered to take off my scrubs. I felt like an intern walking around downtown LA trying to impress everyone with the fact he was a doctor. "Bourbon, straight."

"Lose someone?" he asked.

I thought about Judy. "Yeah."

Not wanting to talk to anyone, I took the bourbon, buttoned my coat to hide my scrubs, and found an empty booth in the dark back corner next to Chandler. Up close I recognized the man sitting with him: Paul Foster. I controlled my rage and focused on the moment at hand. Since I'd last talked to him in Chandler's Palm Springs office, Foster must've been hitting the bottle. Nothing else could've been responsible for his fleshy, mottled cheeks or the pattern of purple veins that chased one another over his Aryan nose. I'd read in the paper that the former head of the Los Angeles County Medical Society was now up north as head of the California Medical Association. I turned away, my back to them, and concentrated on what they were saying.

I gulped down half the bourbon in one swallow and listened. Twenty minutes went by and all I overheard was small talk about the best places to vacation, the best cars, the best brand of cigarettes. Jesus, you'd think there wasn't a war on by the way these two talked.

An hour later, I was on my third bourbon and they were on their fourth or fifth drinks.

"Who the hell does Kaiser think he is?" Foster said with a slur. "He can't tell us how to practice."

"He's a goddamn union-loving Communist," Chandler said. "You don't think anyone will remember I worked for him?"

I'd heard enough. Even with a war on, things would always be the same. The fee-for-service way or no way.

One of the prostitutes from the bar walked toward me. She must have thought my sitting alone for an hour was an invitation. I stood up, keeping my back to Chandler and Foster and put my arm around her, pulling the smell of cigarettes, stale perfume, and cheap wine close to me. Too close.

She ground her hips into me. "Not here, honey," she said. "Let's go upstairs."

"Sure." I walked with her, arm in arm to the door.

She stroked her hand against my thigh. For a second I was tempted. We were outside the door, the neon cactus sign buzzing again in my ear. "The staircase is right there."

"Sorry, not tonight." I let go of her and walked away, my back to her and the Desert Inn.

"Hey," she yelled. "What's the matter? You a faggot?"

It was close to midnight, close to the mandatory curfew and no cabs were in sight.

I wasn't going to put it off any longer. Maybe it was the booze giving me a false sense of courage; maybe it was that constant nagging at the back of my brain that love lost was a kind of failure I couldn't live with. Whatever it was, I had to talk to Judy.

She lived in an apartment building a block or so from the field hospital. I'd convinced Henry to build it to house the nurses and help with recruitment. Judy's was on the third floor in the front, with a view of the shipyards and the bay.

I hesitated at her door, but I couldn't think straight. I knocked.

"Just a minute."

She opened the door without asking who it was and studied me up and down. "Hi, Sid." She said it as if she'd been expecting me.

She extended her arm, inviting me to come in.

I knew how I must look to her, the two-day beard, half-drunk, unkempt hair.

"It's late," she said, glancing at me again. "Why are you here?"

"I'm here," I forced myself to focus, "to apologize."

"Apologize? About?"

"That I wish things had worked out with us."

"If you wished things had worked out, why didn't you ever say anything until—?"

"I tried. So many times. Only you were my nurse and I didn't…I didn't know how to say it." I kept my eyes away from her. "I made a mistake."

She looked at me as if I'd dug myself in a hole and she wasn't going to make it easy to climb out. "Why are you here tonight, Sid?"

"To ask for another chance."

"Chance?" She wiped her eyes on her robe. "I couldn't wait to leave the country, to join the Army. Then when I was in London, I still felt so confused. I…I saw Dwight again over there. We're not perfect together, he loves money more than me; I know that. But at least I understand him. He wants to get me in bed again, but I refuse to let him until we're married." She moved a hand through her hair, pushing away the bangs that had gotten snarled in tears. "But you, I waited months to even kiss you and then…"

"I love you," I said, stepping toward her. "I'm sorry…sorry about—"

She held up her hand, keeping me from getting any closer. "It's too late, Sid. I'm marrying Dwight Chandler. Tomorrow."

I tried to read her expression. "Are you in love with him? Just tell me you are and I'll leave."

"Oh, Sid." She looked at me, her eyes wet. "You don't understand. You don't know anything about me. My parents, my family. I know you asked, but I never answered."

I said nothing.

"My father was a dreamer like you. He wanted to build a resort in the middle of the desert. Spent every penny we had. The developers came in from LA, stole his idea, and wiped us out. I watched what it did to my mother and swore I'd never let it happen to me. Promised myself that I'd never be like her. That my life would belong to no one."

"C'mon, Judy, that's not me."

She reached over and took my hand. "It's about failure. It ruined my father…don't you see? They won't let you continue after the War. All of this, your hospitals, all of your patients will be gone. They'll destroy you just like they did my family. And that's why…that's why I'm marrying Dwight."

I shook my head. "You're not making sense. What the hell are you thinking? I love you. I have since that first day in the desert. I've thought of nothing else other than marrying you. And you're talking about Dwight being safe? Just think, will you? Think about what you're doing. Work here as my nurse, get a grip on things. Give it some time. You can't marry him, you—"

"Let me finish." Her eyes, no longer moist, showed only suffering, not like a new wound, but rather a scar that had been there for years. "Don't you understand? I'm not going to make the same mistake my mother did. I care about you too much to be with you when you fail. I wouldn't do that to you or me. I want to know what I'm getting from the start. And Dwight will never change. He wants money and success and he'll get both. He's too focused to fail. I'm not going to watch them destroy you."

"How can you imagine," I snapped, "that I'd ever let them do that? Give me credit for knowing how to take care of myself." I touched her face. "Tell me one thing."

"What?"

I looked into her eyes, seeing in them the disillusionment I'd first noticed years ago. "Do you love me?"

"Oh, Sid," she murmured, "That's an unfair question."

"Why?"

"Because the answer doesn't matter."

I reached out to her, but she stopped me. "No, Sid. I don't want your pity. I made my decision. And I'm sorry…well, I'm sorry about everything. But now we'll both have to live with it."

# CHAPTER 18

## Richmond

## December 7, 1942

"Forget the damn truce," Cecil boomed into the other end of the phone. "And forget that 'for-the-duration' crap. It's just more of the same lies. Those CMA sons of bitches are claiming Kaiser and you are recruiting doctors desperately needed by the military. They've complained to the draft board and we've lost ten more doctors to the Army this week."

"What are we going to do to make them understand?" I leaned back in my chair at the Richmond field office. Cecil's skills at diplomacy were wearing thin. "We're helping to win this war by keeping our workers and their families healthy."

"Maybe that's the problem," Cecil said. "They see the writing on the wall. They see their future challenged. But if we continue to lose doctors—"

"When will they get it through their heads it's not about them or us? It's about the people we care for."

"I hate to bring up Chamberlain, but appeasement didn't keep the Brits out of the war and it's not going to work for us either."

The door opened and the floor squeaked in a familiar way. Without even looking I knew Henry Kaiser had lumbered into my office.

"Cecil, the boss is here, let me call you back."

"Tell him we need to stop those bastards."

I hung up. "Dammit."

"What is it, Sid?"

"I just got off the phone with Cutting. You know what's going on in Washington? We have one doctor here for every two thousand workers, the army has one to a hundred soldiers and they're complaining about us. Complaining. We're losing doctors to the draft and if it continues we won't have enough left to run the hospitals. The CMA has been after us from the start. Telling every doctor that works here they'll be excommunicated from the holy Church of the AMA. Hell, you call that justice?"

Henry walked over and faced me. "Do you think FDR would waste his time visiting us if we weren't just as important in winning this war? Relax, Sid. There's nothing the AMA, CMA, or County Medical Society can do to stop us. We're providing the best quality medical care anywhere, and they know it."

"Sure, but they don't give a damn about quality. It's all economics to them. We need to stop them before we lose more physicians. Stop them before they make us compromise quality and give them a real reason to shut us down."

Henry glanced at his watch. "C'mon, there's not much time."

"For what?"

"Just follow me." Henry led the way down the hallway to the rear of the Field Station. On the back loading dock, he pointed to the two ambulances, gassed and ready to take any emergencies we couldn't handle in Richmond to Fabiola Hospital in Oakland.

"Keys?" Henry asked.

"In the ignition."

He gave me a thumbs up. "Get in, I'll drive."

Not one to argue with the boss, I jumped in next to him as he powered up the engine and turned on the siren. Hanging on as he sped through the shipyard, the siren wailing, I shouted, "Where are we going?"

"Oakland." He looked around with that grin of his as he shot onto the road going close to eighty miles an hour, heading down the bay. Cars pulled to the side of the road as we shot past them. To our right, the sun glistened off the water like a million tiny diamonds. "We're meeting with the CMA. They'll listen to me; they'll have to. I'm sixty years old and people on the street spot me as if I was some movie star. I'm not kidding myself—or you. I'm riding the wave now, but I know it won't be long before it hits the rocks." He paused for a moment and then regained his smile. "But, by God, while I'm up on the crest, I'm going to get a few things done."

I nodded, then stared out the window and thought about Judy marrying Chandler the week before. Thought about how truly screwed up things were. I replayed our conversation in my mind over and over. Each time she sounded more formal, like someone reciting the rituals of another culture they didn't really understand. She started to sound like a broken record in a foreign language and I wanted to turn her off, silence my thoughts, push the OFF button and not think of her again.

Henry skidded into the ambulance area behind Fabiola Hospital. "We can walk from here," he said.

Outside, a crisp breeze blew. The morning fog had burned off hours ago.

"You in a rush?" I asked Henry.

"We have another ten minutes until our meeting, why?"

"There's a patient in the polio ward I'd like you to meet."

He gazed at me, puzzled. "Of course."

We walked across the carpeted lobby and into an open elevator. As the doors closed, three young nurses stared.

"Mr. Kaiser?" one of the nurses asked meekly.

He smiled broadly. "Good afternoon."

They giggled, and then the tallest of the three stepped closer. "Can I...well, can I hug you? I mean you've done so much for the war and all, I just—"

The elevator door opened. Henry extended his arms and hugged her the way he'd hug a niece. "My pleasure. Good day ladies. And keep up your good work. Sid, so where you taking me?"

"Follow me," I said. We walked past the pediatrics ward to the open room full of iron lungs. Twelve now. Four more since the power went out two months earlier. I'd been coming in weekly to work in the polio ward with Halasz and check on Mark Sullivan, who was making slow, very slow, progress. His mother stood next to the iron lung, feeding Mark his lunch. Mrs. Sullivan had an expressionless face, but her eyes always lit when she talked to her son. For the last month she'd worn the same clean but frayed dress.

"Hi Mark, Mrs. Sullivan. I'd like you to meet Mr. Henry Kaiser."

Henry, never one to be uncomfortable in any situation, smiled at Mark, patted the boy on the head, and shook Mrs. Sullivan's hand. "Nice to meet both of you."

"Dr. Garfield," Mark said, "I have a poem for you. And you too, Mr. Kaiser. Mom, can you hold the book for me so I can read it aloud?"

"Sure, honey."

"I Wandered Lonely as a Cloud by William Wordsworth," Mark cleared his throat.

*"I wandered lonely as a cloud*
*That floats on high o'er vales and hills,*
*When all at once I saw a crowd,*
*A host, of golden daffodils;*
*Beside the lake, beneath the trees,*
*Fluttering and dancing in the breeze.*

*Continuous as the stars that shine*
*And twinkle on the Milky Way,*
*They stretched in never-ending line*
*Along the margin of a bay;*
*Ten thousand saw I at a glance,*
*Tossing their heads in sprightly dance.*

*For oft, when on my couch I lie*

"Or here in my iron lung, if you don't mind me changing the lines," Mark said. "Well, let me finish. Mom, can you hold the book a little closer?" Henry was looking at him the way I'd seen him regard one of his own sons. Mark cleared his throat again:

*"For oft, when on my couch I lie*
*In vacant or in pensive mood,*
*They flash upon that inward eye*
*Which is the bliss of solitude;*
*And then my heart with pleasure fills,*
*And dances with the daffodils."*

Mark's mother kissed him on the forehead.

"Beautiful, just beautiful," Henry said.

I nodded. "How's the therapy coming?"

Mrs. Sullivan wiped her eyes. "He's getting better, I just know it. I couldn't afford to…well, couldn't afford it if it weren't for you, Mr. Kaiser. Before we transferred Mark here…well, you don't want to hear."

"Yes, I do," Henry said. "Please."

"My husband's in the Navy and well, I had a job, but they fired me… I mean, I had to be with Mark some days when he was…not doing as well. I sold our car, all our furniture, most of my clothes to help pay the bills. Now, there's just…" Tears began streaming down her face. Henry embraced her, tears coming down his face as well.

"Then when I got a job in the shipyard, everything changed. Seven cents a day. Even I could afford that."

He wiped his eyes. After a hug from Mrs. Sullivan and a beaming smile from Mark, we were back on the sidewalk. "You know, Henry, you've got a heart as big as your—"

He patted his stomach. "Don't say it. I get the picture."

We crossed the street to the CMA building. "C'mon," he said. "Let's show these bastards."

Inside, a matronly woman in her fifties who looked like she could be on a poster with the word *Mother* under her photo, greeted us with a warm smile. "Oh, Mr. Kaiser, please, the doctors are expecting you. Please come in."

She continued to smile and opened the door. Rising to greet us were Chandler and Foster. At the moment I didn't know who I despised more. The doctor who'd refused to help my mother or the one who'd just married Judy.

"I'm Dr. Paul Foster, head of the CMA." Foster shook Henry's hand and ignored mine. "I think you both already know Dr. Dwight Chandler, who has volunteered to head the Alameda County Medical Association…during his free time, of course, Mr. Kaiser. I know you're both busy, so I'll get right to the point." He sat and leaned back in his overstuffed leather chair. "As I'm sure you know, over the years, the AMA and CMA have raised the standards of medical education, vigorously attacked quackery, and made hospitals safer places for the sick man to go."

Henry nodded. "Yes, of course."

"Good," Chandler said. "Then you'll agree that it's an ethical crime for a medical group to come between the individual and his own doctor. A patient has a fundamental right to choose their own physician. Once the war is over, we—that is you, Mr. Kaiser and Dr. Garfield—will agree to dismantle your system of prepaid medical care. You will not go against the right of a patient—"

"Chandler," I interrupted, "there is one fundamental rule in our profession—one more important than all others—and it is not how we are paid." I found myself wagging my index finger. "It is that we must care for the sick. No matter what the circumstances, rich or poor, night or day, if someone is ill we must provide care."

"Young man, don't presume to lecture us," Foster snapped. "After all, we have charity hospitals, universities."

*"I'll get you the money," Father says.*

*"Sorry. There is the Charity Hospital." The doctor walks out.*

"Enough," Henry commanded. Foster and Chandler sat up straight in their chairs. "Don't ever tell me what I can or cannot do. When an ambulance fails to stop for the injured because they cannot pay, when a doctor refuses care based on fees, things must change. Gentlemen, you're talking about fee-for-service. Business. We should be talking about a democratic system of health care, where a patient's illness is not an asset."

I'd heard Henry deliver this lecture dozens of times and I enjoyed hearing it again. It was what I believed in the most.

"For you see, doctors, it will be group practice, Mayo Clinics for the common man, that will keep medicine in our country from going down the path of Nazi cruelty, where the sick cannot afford care. Nazi cruelty. You will not intimidate us or cheat the people out of obtaining the kind of medical and hospital care they deserve."

Henry rose. "Gentlemen, you will stop your efforts to persuade the Selective Service Board to draft our doctors and you will stop harassing everyone who joins us." Henry faced Chandler, who reflexively leaned away. "Chandler, if you're not back at the shipyards within the hour, you'll be on your way to North Africa. There's a war on, gentlemen. And we're going to win."

# BOOK THREE

## POST-WAR SURVIVAL

# CHAPTER 19

## Oakland

## January 18, 1946

I walked into Fabiola Hospital's empty polio ward and flicked on the lights. All eight silent iron lungs had been hooked up to a backup generator with a backup to the backup. The incident with Halasz three years earlier had made the need for redundancy obvious when it came to patient safety.

Polio was the worst disease I'd ever faced. A virus that viciously attacked only kids. I couldn't shake the feeling we were missing something obvious. Something simple that could make all the difference in the world.

I turned off the lights, rounded the corner, and stopped outside Mrs. Mae Rosen's room. Mrs. Rosen, a sixty-nine-year-old cancer patient, had been hospitalized for weeks after Cecil removed part of her right lung. She was one of only five inpatients in a hospital that used to be packed with over one hundred and fifty. Every day for the past month, she wrote something on a card and dangled it above her bed. Tonight it said, "The End." It wasn't written with her usual flowing, fancy letters. Just a simple eight by ten-inch card with plain lettering, the way someone might have written, "Exit on Left."

She had been in bed for nearly a month now, and even though her cancer may have been cured, her diminished lung capacity made her short of breath with the least exertion. She might never get out of bed on her own again.

"Good of you to visit me so late, Dr. Garfield." She breathed rapidly. Her bony cyanotic face contrasted sharply with the clean white pillow. "It's been so quiet lately, I was afraid you'd closed up shop and left me here on my own." Her laugh turned into a fit of coughing.

"How are you feeling tonight?" I asked.

"Oh, much better," she replied as always, and immediately changed the subject to her son—how with the war over four months ago, he'd be there to visit her any day now.

"Let me take a listen." I moved my stethoscope over her chest and listened to the gloomy chorus of wheezes, rales, and bubbles that signaled the end stage function of her lungs and heart.

"Thank you, Doctor. Thank you so much for checking on me."

Her pulse was rapid, an ominous sign of heart failure as her system worked overtime to make up for the lack of oxygen. "My pleasure, Mrs. Rosen. I'll get something to make you more comfortable. Be right back."

Alyce Chester, her dark hair tucked up in her hat, sat at the nurses' station, her back to me, a stack of charts in front of her as she wrote her progress notes. Allie, originally from Texas, was one of the best nurses I'd hired during the war and I hoped she wouldn't quit.

"Allie…uh, hi."

She turned, her eyes meeting mine, her full lips turning into a smile. "Hi, Dr. Garfield."

"Can you get some digitalis for Mrs. Rosen?"

"Sure. She's a sweet woman…wish there was more we could do for her."

I nodded. She opened the medicine cabinet and removed a glass vial of digitalis.

When we walked into the room, Mrs. Rosen said casually, "I won't be here much longer. And I wanted to thank you two for everything." Her 'The End' sign turned gently above her bed.

"Nonsense, I'll just give you a shot to strengthen your heart and you'll feel better in no time." But I was bothered by the sign and what she'd said. She'd never been pessimistic before.

"I'm not afraid," she said. "I know there's something better, I've never had doubts. I was writing this letter to my son and it made me wonder, Doctor, what was your mother's name?"

"Share-Voney," I whispered, then said louder, "Bertha."

Her eyes managed a sudden twinkle. "Bertha Garfield?"

"You knew my mother?" I asked, sitting on the side of her bed.

"Yes, we used to talk after *shul* on Saturdays. I remember the last time was before the flu…right before she passed on. It was after the service and we shared a wonderful slice of poppy seed cake. I still remember what she said to me that day."

"What, Mrs. Rosen? What did she say?" It had been so many years that all of my memories of my mother had blurred.

"She said how happy she was. How much she loved you and your father. And then do you know what she did?"

"What?"

"She knocked on wood. *Keyn aynhoreh*. Yiddish for 'no evil eye.' She would have been proud of your hospital, proud of how you care for people. But me, I don't believe in superstition, doctor. I know my end is near." She handed Allie the letter.

"I have only one fear," she continued. Her expression changed, the brave face replaced by a look of terror. She took a wheezy breath and exhaled nosily. "I don't want to suffocate. I dream of drowning, water filling my lungs, and me gasping. Please, promise you'll…not let that happen."

She stared into my eyes and I swallowed hard, knowing what she was asking.

"Let me give you this digitalis and you'll feel better, less short of breath."

She stared at me again, but her face was calm now. "Do you believe you can help me, Dr. Garfield? Please be honest with me."

"Yes, I do." I did, too, with all my heart. I'd never once given up on a patient and had never once considered 'helping things along.'

After twenty minutes, Mrs. Rosen was resting comfortably and we walked into the quiet halls of what was once a bustling, overcrowded hospital.

"You know," Allie looked up at me, "you really are a wonderful doctor."

"Thanks." My face burned with embarrassment. "I've been meaning to talk to you about staying on and becoming a nursing supervisor." I was going to offer the job to Judy, but she'd left months before to work in Chandler's San Francisco office.

Allie smiled. "I'm off shift in twenty minutes."

"Uh, would you like to get some coffee, then?"

"Sure. I'll meet you down in the cafeteria."

I finished checking on a post-op patient and rode the elevator down to the basement and empty cafeteria. Hell, the whole hospital was empty. Red, white, and blue banners still hung from every inch of the ceiling to celebrate the War's end. I sat there for a few minutes, wondering if we'd ever be busy again.

"Hi, Dr. Garfield, sorry I'm late."

"I got you some coffee." I slid her cup across the table.

"Thanks, you look tired."

"Tired and worried. With so few patients to care for, I spend most of my time worrying how to keep afloat. What about you, Allie? Are you planning on staying at the hospital, or—"

"Yes, of course, I'm staying. I've worked at some others and frankly the care here is so much better. I don't have to worry about the patients not affording—"

An announcement over the hospital PA kicked my heart into a different gear.

"*Any doctor to room 312.*"

I looked at Allie. "Mrs. Rosen."

We both ran up the stairs, where the night nurse stood over the woman. "I found her like this. She was okay less than ten minutes ago."

I stepped to the bed, slipped my stethoscope into my ears and listened. No heart beat, not a single wheeze. She was cold and rigid as if she'd been dead for hours instead of minutes and I knew there was nothing I could do.

We stood in silent respect and then Allie said, "I'm sorry, Dr. Garfield, I know how much you and Dr. Cutting cared for her."

Mrs. Rosen's face was calm, serene, as if she'd never suffered the ravages of cancer and surgery. I read for the last time the sign hanging over the bed. "The End." I had a bad feeling that if I didn't come up with a plan quickly, the words were an omen for my medical program as well.

# CHAPTER 20

Oakland

January 19, 1946

The following afternoon the Fabiola Hospital cafeteria, nicknamed Henry J's Café, smelled of grilled hamburgers and French fries. With the war over, our hospital was as empty as that first day I'd shown it to Henry. The one hundred thousand shipyard workers had been reduced to less than five thousand. Most of the drafted doctors left as soon as the war ended, leaving six of us to run the hospital. With no one on call except us, we held all of our meetings in Henry J's instead of the old "War Room" at Trader Vic's. It was day-to-day survival again, just like in the desert.

The usual chiefs of service sat on folding chairs around one of the larger tables with a chalk board next to me on an easel: Cecil Cutting, Morris Collen, Paul Fitzgibbon, Bob King, Mel Friedman, and tonight I'd asked A.B. Ordway, President of Industrial Indemnity Insurance and one of Henry's closest execs to attend.

"It's over, Sid," Mel Friedman, chief of pathology whined in his usual mournful monotone. "Time to throw in the towel."

Bob King slapped his hand on the table. "He's right. I'm tired of sleeping all night. Been three days since I delivered a baby. Three fucking days."

I gulped my coffee too fast and the hot liquid burned my throat. I tried not to cough.

"We have a great system going," Cecil said.

"Had," Morris Collen interrupted, "had 'for-the-duration.' Now that the War's over, we have layoffs."

There were groans of agreement around the table.

"Okay, listen up." This was the chance I'd thought about and planned for years. Nothing would stop me from trying. Nothing. "I'm not about to close shop like in the desert. Not this time. Our system works. You all know it does. It's the best plan for patients anywhere. Quality and affordability. For seven cents a day, we give—"

"Ah Christ," Fitzgibbon interrupted. "You're preaching to the choir here. But at the rate people are leaving, we may have no choice."

"Yeah, everyone has jumped ship," Collen said. "Okay, not funny."

"You're right," I said. "Not funny."

Pale skinned A.B. Ordway, the only one at the table wearing a suit, a man who could remember what he ate for lunch two hundred and twenty-eight days ago, pulled out a stack of papers from his briefcase. "I wanted to talk to you all about starting a new Foundation. The Permanente Foundation."

"Why the hell do we need a Foundation? Especially one named after a creek next to Kaiser's cement factory?" Collen cast a bewildered look. "We have to make money before we can donate to charity."

Ordway shook his head.

"Listen up," I said. "We're going to make a go of this. And to do so, we need a Foundation. We'll have plenty of opposition. So instead of a corporation owning our hospitals, it will be a non-profit foundation. Think about it. No one will accuse us of practicing corporate medicine. No one will be able to say Henry Kaiser pulls our strings."

Fitzgibbon thrust his chin forward as if he were ready to mow down any lineman in his way. "What hospital? If the Medical Society has its way, Fabiola will be taken over by the state and made a charity hospital."

"Absolutely not." Ordway spoke in his formidable voice. "Despite what the Alameda County Medical Society thinks, we paid off our loan for Fabiola without using one penny of government funds. Kaiser Industries owns Fabiola free and clear."

I walked over to a portable blackboard at the head of the table, picked up the chalk, and drew a large triangle in the center of it. On the bottom, I printed Foundation in large letters. "Okay, here's what I'm thinking. We have a non-profit foundation owning our hospitals and capital items like X-ray machines, ambulances, things like that."

"You mean we're a fucking charity?" King said. "Hell, without any patients, we'll need the donations to keep us going."

"Funny, Bob. Really funny." I circled the word *Foundation*. "It was Mr. Ordway's idea and frankly it's pure genius. Think, guys. All through the war we were given crap about working for Kaiser, being company docs. With a foundation owning our hospitals, and a non-profit one at that, there's no conflict of interest. No questions asked. All our money goes to patient care, not shareholders trying to make a buck. Now, let me show you the rest of the plan." I printed the words *Medical Group* on the right side of the triangle and *Health Plan* on the left. "The Medical Group will make all patient care decisions." I tapped the chalk against the board. "And I mean all. No one from the Foundation will have any say over how we treat our patients."

"What about the Health Plan," Friedman said. "I take it they'll control the money."

"Collect the money." I drew a dollar sign next to *Health Plan*. "I don't know about all of you, but I'd rather take care of patients than try to enroll new members and be a bill collector. Remember, we're going to be non-profit. Meaning all money collected goes to paying our salaries, taking care of patients, and capital improvements."

"Sounds like a pyramid scheme," Collen said, slamming his glass against the table. "Only problem, Sid, is you're not Moses and there's no patients anymore to lead around the desert. There won't be enough dues for our lease payments, let alone our salaries."

Cecil scribbled notes. "Shut up, Morris, give him a chance to finish."

"Yeah, go on," King said. "You never know, someone may actually need me tonight."

"Please then, hear me out." I drew a large circle around the entire triangle. "The minute the Alameda-Contra Costa Medical Society has a chance, they'll come after us like we're Hitler reincarnated. So we have to be up and running now. And we have to all be on the same page."

"I'll drink to that." Fitzgibbon raised his coffee cup and everyone else at the table followed suit.

"Good, then any other comments before we put it to a vote?"

"Remember this, doctors," Ordway ran his hand through his slicked back hair, "the war may be over, but Kaiser Industries is far from being obsolete. The economy in California is about to heat up and we're going to lead it. Consumer goods, aluminum, cars. The shipyards may be slowing down, but we'll have workers, gentlemen, that will need health care. And your system is the only way we want to provide it."

"How many?" King asked. "And are we talking about caring for their families?"

"Ten thousand to start plus dependents," Ordway answered. "Voluntary enrollment, of course."

I took out a handful of the Foundation and Health Plan agreements and passed them around the table. "I know ten thousand is nothing compared to what we're used to. But Mr. Ordway and Kaiser have assured me of a growing number of workers to keep us going while we enroll new patients. Well? You ready to vote?"

Everyone nodded. "All in favor?" Every hand except Friedman's went up.

"C'mon, Mel. We need you."

Freidman half-cocked his arm and finally raised it.

"*Dr. Friedman, Dr. Melvin Friedman,*" the hospital operator paged overhead.

Friedman shook his head. "What now?" He walked over to the phone.

I lifted my coffee cup, not waiting for Friedman to come back and spoil the mood. "Good, looks like we have a new Medical Group. To Permanente Medicine. And to health." My father's voice filled my head, remembering his words after I'd opened the hospital in Desert Center. *L'chaim.*

Six coffee cups clicked together in unison.

"I wouldn't celebrate yet," Friedman said. "That phone call was from one of our residents. The AMA has just declared war on us. While we're sitting here on our duffs, across the bay the AMA's annual meeting is trying to shut us down. Those assholes are outlawing everything except private practice and fee-for-service. If they pass Resolution 16, all closed panel groups like ours will be unethical."

"Okay, Mel," I said, "Then let's work on our response."

Fitzgibbon held up a letter. "Now's as good a time as any to bring this up.

Did you see what they passed out at the general session this morning?"

"No, since none of us can get in."

"One of our residents was presenting some of our research there and grabbed one of these for us. From Paul Foster, President of the CMA...blah blah, the Kaiser program is an unethical plan to cheat doctors and their patients. I can't believe this crap." He held up the second page. "Then there's a flyer asking every member of the AMA to gather evidence against Kaiser and Garfield."

I ran a hand through my hair and clenched my jaw, but couldn't calm myself. "I don't know about all of you, but this is going to end! They've declared war and we're going to fight back. We can take this to the newspapers—let the public know the AMA cares more about their money than their health."

"Sid's right," Cecil said. "Don't they see most people can't afford fee-for-service medicine? Or maybe they just don't get it? We're enrolling new members, union members who in the past have gone without care."

"Christ," Friedman said, disgusted. "This is all about business, not medicine."

Silence fell around the table.

"You're right, Mel," I said. "It's all about business and money. We're threatening their survival and they're coming after us with everything they've got. Now, it's our turn to prove to them that people want a choice. Not just business as usual."

"We're a medical group not a business," Fitzgibbon spat out, "we take care of patients. That's where ethics comes in. And that's why we have to stand on our own."

"Fitz, it's not that simple," I said. "Don't underestimate the AMA. To deal with the AMA and CMA we'll challenge them at their own meetings. Let's not bicker when our hearts are in the same place. Any of you have a better idea?"

"We need to trust Sid on this," Cecil said. "There's no other way aside from asking Kaiser for help, and we all know it. That's why we're forming the Foundation. So let's try this on our own."

I glanced at my watch. "Cecil and I have a CMA meeting tonight to go to. We'll take them on face-to-face." I waited for a reaction. No one said a thing.

"Well, anything else? Okay then, wish us luck, gentlemen."

We walked in silence to the parking lot and drove off in Cecil's Packard. "Cecil, quit being so goddamn quiet."

His hand glued to the steering wheel, he stared straight ahead. "The CMA is setting you up. You and I know it. Why go through with it?"

"Because we're *right*. I've been all around the East Bay trying to enroll new patients, convincing them our way is the best way. Comprehensive care for four bucks a month. Police, unions, the university, city workers. Anybody who'll listen. It boils down to keeping the AMA, the medical societies, and Blue Cross off our backs so people will be free to join. And if they don't join soon, we'll be out of business."

He turned into the driveway of the Jack Tar Hotel. "It's all about the bottom line. Plain and simple. The private docs are worried they're going to lose money and patients. And just how do you think you're going to convince them?"

"With the truth." I knew it sounded naïve. "Our records are open. I'll invite them to drop by. Our morbidity and mortality records speak for themselves. No one in town even comes close."

"Sid, you're a great doctor." Cecil fixed his eyes on mine. "But you're a shitty salesman. And if we're going to stay in business, that's what we need the most."

Inside the smoke-filled meeting room, Foster sat with a drink in one hand, a cigarette in their other, surrounded by a flock of admirers. Seventy, maybe eighty doctors. They glanced at us and continued talking. I started to approach Foster when Dwight Chandler stopped us.

"Sid, old boy," he extended his hand. I glared at him. "Sid," he repeated. This time I reflexively shook his hand. "Judy gives you her regards." Before I could react, he nodded to Cecil. "Cutting, glad you two could make it. We're about to eat. I'm afraid the only open table is in the back."

"Fine." I really wasn't hungry. "When do I speak?"

"Right after the Treasurer's report."

Foster rang a bell. Everyone took their seats and the waiters began serving the salads. We were the only ones at a table for eight, and farthest from the podium.

"Nice way to meet new people," I said to Cecil.

"Right. Have you decided what you're going to say?"

"Yeah, I've been working on it."

Cecil smiled, knowing me well enough to figure I'd outlined every point and gone over it fifty or so times.

Chandler, as president of the County Medical Society, made his way to the podium and slammed the gavel to call the meeting to order. The salad plates were empty. Doctors were a competitive group and no one wanted to leave a lettuce leaf behind. "We have a busy schedule tonight. I'd like to get through our business meeting quickly so we'll have time for questions and answers following our speaker, Dr. Sidney Garfield. We also invited Mr. Henry Kaiser, but he couldn't make it; apparently he was out to *launch*." There was a uniform chorus of polite laughter. "I'd also like to welcome Dr. Paul Foster, the president of the California Medical Association."

Thirty minutes later, Chandler introduced me.

"Give 'em hell," Cecil said.

I made my way up through the stares and a few polite claps. "Thank you for having me here tonight," I started. No use attempting to break the ice—a joke would have gone over like a screen door on a U-boat. "Dr. Chandler asked me to speak about our Permanente group practice, but before I do, I'd like to ask all of you a question."

Most were listening now. "How did you all learn medicine? Let me answer it for you. In a multidisciplinary medical school. In a model of group practice. Can you imagine a one-man medical school, where one doctor taught all the medical specialties?"

Cecil nodded; he knew where I was going.

"After graduation, the AMA wants medical students, all of you, taught by the finest teams of doctors, to go out and take care of thousands of illnesses as solo practitioners."

Foster, sitting in the table closest to the front with Chandler, pushed back his chair but hesitated; he remained seated, picking at his chocolate dessert.

"That's right, gentlemen, the editor of the *Journal of the American Medical Association* says that group practice is not only unethical, not only of poor quality, but also more costly than general practitioner service. Does that apply to every medical school in this country? I'm here tonight to prove to you he's wrong. I'm not here to tell you how to practice or to change the way you bill patients. I'm only here to educate you, to bring you up to date on an exciting new way of providing medical care."

Foster stood, his face red. "Dr. Garfield, I hope you're not here to insult the AMA or fee-for-service medicine. All of us have open minds here and I hope you are not so self-absorbed in your own group practice that you can't see what's best for our profession and our patients." A few claps resonated from around the room.

"I'm sorry, Dr. Foster, my intention is not to insult, but to enlighten. To talk about the rise in technology from the black bag to X-ray machines, lab analyzers, and all the sophisticated equipment needed to provide the most modern care for our patients. And with this technology and our group model, I have statistics to show how we can decrease our mortality rates from pneumonia, prevent unnecessary hospitalizations and costs, and put a stop to a variety of diseases through a comprehensive program of vaccination."

Foster smiled. "Did you read Dr. Fishbein's *whole* article in JAMA, Dr. Garfield? If you did, you'd realize he said 85% of all care can be done in the doctor's office or from the equipment in his black bag. That's the economy of care he was talking about. That's how we keep medicine affordable and at the same time allow patients to have their own private physician. The other few percent can be referred to a hospital for testing. That is true economy of care. That is the doctor-patient relationship so sacred for proper health. That is why your group will never succeed. Patients are not parts on one of Henry Kaiser's assembly lines. Patients should not be treated as commodities." Applause filled the room.

"You make an excellent point, Dr. Foster. Less than 30 years ago just about all that doctors had to offer was their personality. It was nice and comforting but how much disease did it cut short? How many lives did it save? What kind of pal to a patient can a doctor be when he X-rays that patient in the dark, when he operates on his brain, his chest or his belly under anesthesia, when he studies EKG heart tracings made by a technician? Medical science becomes more impersonal as it gets more powerful. More and more, what a patient wants to know is not that his doctor has wonderful eyes or a sympathetic personality. What patients want to know is whether a team of doctors know their X-rays, their blood chemistries and liver function tests, their anti-biotics and sulfas and the cold, advanced mechanics of urologic, neurologic, and thoracic surgery. With these modern tests come costs that most patients can't afford. That's why prepaid group practices will allow patients to have the latest in medical technology at a price they can pay. We've shown that if we take away the fee barrier and patients come in earlier for treatments, we can decrease the death rates from pneumonia by 92%. We can decrease deafness due to spinal meningitis by 80%. We can prevent tetanus and diphtheria by making sure all of our children can afford to be immunized—"

A few doctors began to leave. Chandler stood up. "Please, wait until he's done."

Foster faced the group. He shook his head. "Did you learn only numbers in medical school, Dr. Garfield? Patients are people—people who want to be cared for. Not parts to be measured, analyzed, and scrutinized."

"That's right," I answered. "It is about care. Caring enough to make the patient better. Caring enough so patients can afford to come in before their cancer has spread or their flu has turned into pneumonia. That, gentlemen, is what Permanente medicine is about. Prepayment takes away the fee as a barrier between the patient and getting the care they need."

They were talking to one another at the tables and I wondered if my words were starting to sink in. "For a small amount per month we provide the latest medical care to all. I'm not naïve, gentlemen. We all need to make money, we all want to support our families, and our salaries are competitive with yours. Only think about it. We're not basing our income on sick patients paying higher and higher fees. For us, keeping patients well keeps us in business. We're on the same side as the patient. We're a *health plan*, gentlemen, not a sick plan."

"You insult us," Paul Foster snapped. "Providing production-line medical care is not only unethical, it's poor quality. And because of that, I can assure everyone in this room that as long as I'm president of the CMA, not one Perman-ente physician will be allowed membership in our organization." The physicians in the room clapped as if Foster had just hit a home run. "Your experiment, Dr. Garfield," he continued, "may have worked in times of War when patriotic doctors were away taking care of our soldiers, but now that we're back, your days of group practice are over." He stood and left the room.

Chandler came to the podium and tapped the microphone. "Thank you, Dr. Garfield." Most of the physicians were leaving, following Foster's example. "Please everyone, stay, we have time for questions and answers." No one raised a hand.

Chandler turned to me. "Sorry, Sid."

"Thank you for inviting me," I said to Chandler and a nearly empty room.

Cecil stood and clapped as loud as he could.

# CHAPTER 21

## Oakland

## July 1, 1946

Bob King, chief of Ob-Gyn, knocked on the half-open door. "Sid, can I have a word with you?" In his crumpled, blood-splattered scrubs he looked like he'd been up for a week straight.

"Sure. C'mon in."

Bob stared at his shoes, as if contemplating how many months it had been since he'd last polished them. He finally came in my office.

"What is it, Bob? You okay?"

"No, I'm sorry, Sid. I don't know how to do this other than come right out with it. I'm quitting."

"You're kidding, right? Go get some sleep and we'll talk when you're awake."

"No, I promised myself I'd tell you today. You know how it is. Things are so slow, they may never pick up. So I went to the local Ob-Gyn Society meeting and they kicked me out. I took my wife, and not one other woman in the place would speak to her. No Permanente doctors or their wives allowed. Shit, Sid, if things go under, I need a job. I've got two kids, you know. And well, they were saying that unless I got out now, they'd never let me in the Society. Never."

"C'mon, Bob. You know we're going to make this work. Don't listen to them. Think of all we've done. How many people we've helped, cared for, made well. The babies you've delivered here in a hospital that would never have—"

"Stop it, Sid. It's bad enough without hearing one of your canned lectures.

I know all that. Your membership is down to less than 10,000. You may not even be in business next month. I'm done gambling. I don't want to be a pariah, I want to belong. Be in the society, in the CMA, in the AMA, and as long as I stay here that will never happen. In fact, they were even threatening to take away my Boards. It's about survival, Sid. Pure and simple. Survival."

Bob turned and almost bumped into my seven a.m. appointment.

Lieutenant Colonel Clifford Keene, standing at attention, was tall and rail thin, with a walrus-sized blond mustache. His khaki uniform still smelled of the rice paddies of Japan.

"Dr. Keene, the war's over. Relax. Take a seat."

"Yes, sir." He dropped stiffly into the chair.

"It's Sid. Okay, Cliff?"

"Yes, Sir."

"Did you hear what Bob King and I were just talking about?"

"Yes."

"You still interested in applying here?"

"Sir, if I skirted around a challenge, I would have never survived the War."

I paged through his application. "Four years of operating under combat conditions in the Pacific."

He nodded.

"Honors graduate from the University of Michigan."

He nodded.

"One of the first certified by the American Board of Surgery."

"Sir. I've been in a plane on and off for the last three days, so pardon my impatience. Just what are you looking for?"

"We've lost three surgeons lately. And as you saw, we just lost our chief of OB. We need someone both highly skilled and versatile. You're licensed in Michigan?"

"Yes."

"Had much experience?"

He smiled for the first time. "Four years in combat? I've done just about every kind of surgery you can imagine. Didn't deliver many babies during the War, though."

"So you do have a sense of humor. Look, Cliff, I can imagine a lot. You familiar with vascular injuries?"

He nodded.

"Neurosurgical? Orthopedics?"

"All of them."

My phone rang. "Just a second."

A frantic Morris Colleen said, "Sid, it's Bess Kaiser. An acute abdomen with malignant hypertension. My guess is a thrombosed renal artery. We're bringing her over now."

"We?" I asked, knowing the answer.

"Yes, Henry is with us. It's all I can do to keep him from picking up the scalpel."

As I hung up I looked at Keene. "Ever do an embolectomy on a renal artery?"

"Yes."

He was either exhausted or the least talkative man I'd ever met. Even old Dean Keating was garrulous compared to him. "Well, good. I haven't done one since residency and you're going to assist."

He raised a brow and seemed to regard me with new interest. "Tell me the history. Age, medical condition, symptoms."

"It's Bess Kaiser, Henry Kaiser's wife. Mid-sixties, overweight with a history of kidney and blood pressure problems. Borderline diabetes. She had the sudden onset of abdominal pain associated with hypertension."

"I can't help you, you know." He looked alert now.

"Why the hell not?"

"I'm not licensed in California."

Shit, he was right. With Cecil and his wife Millie on a weekend trip, Bob King was the closest thing to a surgeon around and he'd just quit. Which left me only one choice. "Dr. Keene, you're hired."

He looked confused. "Okay, but that still doesn't give me a license to practice."

"Consider yourself on staff as a surgery resident. No license required while you're in training."

He finger-combed his mustache. "Can you do that?"

I nodded. "We've had residents and interns rotating throughout the war. It's completely legal until you have time to apply here in California."

"Okay," Keene said. "Let's check out your instruments. Once we've started, I don't want to fumble around for something we need."

"Good. But I'm sure we'll have everything—"

"Including a Rand embolectomy forceps?"

"Well, no."

Keene shook his head. "Developed by Herb Rand back at U of M. It has a metal suction tip attached to the forceps to help remove the clot."

I called the OR and was up from my desk and at the door. "I want to be in the ER when the Kaisers arrive."

"What's her pressure?"

"240 over 120," answered Allie Chester in her Texas drawl.

"Been close to 300 on the way over." Morris tried to hide his alarm with Henry standing there.

"Quit tiptoeing around," Henry said. "I'm not a nitwit. I know how high her pressure is. Now what can we do about it?"

"Henry." Bess managed a wan smile. "Be nice to the young men."

I rubbed my hands together to warm them and then stood next to Mrs. Kaiser's gurney. "I'm going to feel your stomach, Mrs. Kaiser, tell me where it hurts the most." I pushed in on the right lower quadrant of her obese abdomen. "There?"

"Just a little."

That ruled out something simple like appendicitis. I moved to the center and she shook her head. Pushing in on the left side, she grimaced in pain. "That's where…where it hurts the worst."

"When I push, does it hurt in your back also?"

She nodded. I signaled to Keene. "This is Dr. Keene, do you mind—"

"C'mon, Sid," Henry interrupted, "quit pussyfooting around and tell me what's wrong."

Keene put one hand on her back, one over her front and pushed between them. She cried out.

Allie wiped Mrs. Kaiser's forehead with a cool cloth.

"I appreciate your kindness," Henry said, "Nurse…uh?"

"Just call me Allie, Mr. Kaiser." She gave him a warm smile. "Allie Chester."

"And Colonel," Henry turned to Keene. "What do you think is wrong?"

"It's definitely a thrombosed renal artery," Keene said.

"Mrs. Kaiser." I took her right hand between mine. "We're going to need to operate. The artery to your left kidney has a blood clot in it, causing your pain and high blood pressure. The longer we wait, the more damage to your kidney."

"Let's get going, then," Henry said.

I kicked the brakes off the gurney and pulled as Keene pushed to the elevator. "This will take about four hours."

Henry strode alongside, kissed his wife on the lips, then left just as the elevator doors closed.

It was no surprise the OR was set up perfectly as we entered. Liz, the scrub tech, was a stickler for detail. She straightened and restraightened the instrument tray. Dick Stubin, Chief of Anesthesia, had come in from home. Overweight, hypertensive, possible kidney failure—Bess Kaiser was at risk for never waking up.

Stubin looked up over the rim of his bifocals. "Systolic's over 300, you two better hurry."

Mrs. Kaiser was prepped and draped. Within five minutes we were scrubbed and ready to go. "I'll take us in," I told Keene. Liz slapped the scalpel on my gloved palm and I made a midline incision from her xyphoid to pubis. We'd need as much exposure as possible.

"Suction," I instructed Keene, as I cut through the layers of fat and finally found the abdominal rectus muscles. Small and undeveloped as in most women who didn't exercise, they easily separated in the midline to provide good exposure of her peritoneum.

"Clamps." We side-clamped the peritoneal membrane, I cut it open with Metsenbaum scissors, and we were in. Pushing aside loop upon loop of her intestines, we made our way into the depths of the abdomen where the renal artery came off the abdominal aorta.

"Liz, hold up on the Dever's."

She nodded and pulled harder on the large metal retractor to keep the bowel out of the way.

"The kidney looks pale," Keene said.

Instead of its normal brownish-purple, it was a light brown.

"Pressure's up to 310," Stubin said. "Starting to get some PVC's."

Premature Ventricular Contractures were an ominous sign. Her heart was working overtime and with her pressure so high, she could have a stroke or heart attack at any moment. I felt along the renal artery, finding a strong pulse at its branch point off the aorta. "It's a clot all right."

Keene nodded. "Less than three centimeters involved. Do you want me to do the arteriotomy?"

"You've done—"

"Yeah. Lot's of arteries are injured with shrapnel." He extended his hand to Anna. "Bulldog clamps."

He dissected around the artery, freeing it up from its paper-thin attachments to the abdomen and placed the two screw-on clamps on both sides of the clot.

Stubin listened with a stethoscope over her chest. Not one to get excited, he blurted out, "More PVC's…holy shit. She's starting to fibrillate. Still a pulse, but thready."

"Twelve blade," Keene ordered. With the pointed end of the curved scalpel, he cut through the wall of the artery, a quick squirt of blood escaping through the incision as the clot came into view. "This is where the Rand forceps would have been handy."

"Improvise," I said. "I'll hold the suction in the artery as you tease out the clot." If we left any pieces of the clot, when we released the clamp they would flow into the kidney and cause permanent damage by cutting off the circulation to the small terminal arterial branches. The purplish clot had the consistency of Jell-O and I sucked away as he removed it piece by piece.

"Still in fibrillation. You'd better hurry."

"Open the proximal clamp," Keene said.

I opened the tiny thumbscrew and blood began to flow freely out of our incision, essentially flushing things out.

"Okay, close it. I'll take the 6-0 suture." Keene's hand was steady and I could tell he was focused on one thing and one thing alone: getting that artery closed. His movements were fluid as he completed the closure in less than two minutes.

"No pulse," Stubin said. "God damn it, there's no pulse."

"Release both clamps," I ordered Keene. The obedient soldier immediately snapped them off.

"What's her pressure?" I asked Stubin.

"None, Sid. Zero."

"Undrape her chest."

"Open heart massage?" Keene asked.

I nodded, knowing the odds were small it would work. And knowing, I'd try everything. *Everything*. And that's when an article I'd read a few weeks earlier in the *New England Journal* clicked in. I clenched my fist and slammed down on the middle of her sternum.

Liz looked at me with shock, as if I had suddenly transformed into a madman.

"Take it easy, Sid," Stubin said.

Keene nodded, knowing what I was doing.

"Run an EKG strip," I ordered Stubin.

He turned on the machine and a single flat line ran across the strip of paper.

I brought my fist up again, but before I could come down, Stubin grabbed me. "Enough, stop."

"Leave him be," Keene commanded as if it were the okay to land on Normandy. "A precordial thump. It could kick-start the heart."

I slammed down on the chest.

"V fib," Stubin said. The flat line showed fine fibrillations, the heart starting to beat in an uncoordinated manner. The blood pressure cuff hissed as it deflated. "Nothing."

A bruise was beginning to form on her chest. I banged down for the third time, thinking about getting the saw and opening the ribs.

"Something…something…I'm feeling a pulse." Stubin ripped the paper out of the EKG machine. "I don't believe it. She's in normal sinus rhythm."

"Kidney's looking better," Keene said, as its blood flow returned. "But we won't know for a few weeks how much damage was permanent."

"Is the arteriotomy holding?" I asked.

"Of course," Keene answered. "Not a drip."

"Quit patting yourselves on the back," Stubin said. "I'd like to wake her up and get her to the ICU as soon as possible."

I irrigated the blood out of the abdominal cavity and closed the incisions with catgut suture. Because of her fat and the tension on the wound, I used wire retention sutures to hold the skin together.

"Dr. Garfield." Liz's eyes glistened. "That was really amazing."

I blushed and knew both Stubin and Keene were smiling under their masks.

"You two roll her to the ICU. I'll go talk to Mr. Kaiser."

Allie Chester had come up to the waiting area with him and Henry was pacing around while she leaned against the counter next to the coffeepot.

"Sid!"

"She's doing fine now. We took out the clot. We'll know more in a week or so, but for now, she's stable."

"Why do you keep saying *now*?"

I shrugged. "I wish I could predict how she'll do. She'll need some good nursing care and—"

"I'll watch her full time, if y'all like," Allie said. I studied her for the first time. Narrow face, with a sharp nose and intense, attractive dark brown eyes.

"Thank you," Henry said. "I'd like that. When can I see her?"

"A half hour or so. I'd like to check on her and make sure she's recovering from the anesthesia."

I started out the door, stopped and turned around. "Oh, one thing is for sure. She'll have a sore chest for a while."

# CHAPTER 22

## Oakland

# July 11, 1947

"Mrs. Kaiser, how are you feeling today?"

Bess Kaiser sat up in bed, her arms to her side, a rubber IV tube running from her left arm into a machine I'd never seen before. She was in a private room, the largest at Fabiola. The scent of roses overwhelmed the hospital's antiseptic smell. Every day for the past year, Henry brought her another dozen roses, and vases of flowers covered the windowsill and every open inch of the room.

"Better," she said. "Every day a little better." An optimist, just like her husband.

Allie Chester was at Mrs. Kaiser's side along with another woman, younger, with dark hair. Thin and attractive, she wore no makeup; she was a woman who didn't need to.

"Hi Dr. Garfield," Allie said. "She is doing better. Especially since we started her on dialysis yesterday. Oh, this is my sister, Victoria."

I extended my hand. "Nice to meet you, Miss Chester."

She smiled and shook my hand softly. "It's Mrs. Peterson. At least for the next few weeks; but you know, Victoria would be just fine."

"Well, nice to meet you, Victoria." Her hand hesitated in mine.

"I'm sorry," she said, letting go. "It's just... Allie's told me so much about you."

"Well, thanks. Allie's done a wonderful job taking care of Mrs. Kaiser."

Allie blushed. "Dr. Garfield, have y'all seen a dialysis machine before?"

"No." I shook my head. "Seen a diagram of one, but not in person."

145

"Henry thinks it looks like a washing machine," Mrs. Kaiser said. She was pale but smiled with what looked like pride as she spoke. "He wants to start building washing machines, you know. Everything Americans need now that the war is over. Washing machines, cars, homes, everything. He's a wonder, you know. Has enough energy for both of us. For the whole family."

I walked over to the dialysis machine. Bess Kaiser's kidneys had deteriorated over the past year and she now needed dialysis. "Where'd he get this?" I asked Allie.

"Flew it in from London. First one in the U.S. Uses cellophane to filter the blood clean."

"You know, Sid," Victoria interrupted. "Oh, do you mind if I call you Sid?"

"No…uh, it's fine." Her eyes, brown with flecks of gold, had a mischievous quality—or maybe it was her smile. No, it was her eyes. For a soon-to-be-divorced married woman, she certainly was…well, the opposite of her sister, who was all business when it came to her patients. Not to say cold, for Allie was caring and warm, but definitely not flirtatious.

"If I understand it right," Victoria smiled again, "we're using a washing machine to clean Mrs. Kaiser's blood."

I shrugged. "Yeah, putting it simply, you're right."

She pouted. "Simple?"

I looked down at my watch: late as usual. "Excuse me. Nice to meet you, Victoria." I wished Mrs. Kaiser well and closed the door behind me.

I'd packed a picnic lunch and was ready for a day in the park. I needed to get my mind off work, off everything. The truth of it was, I missed being part of a family…or at least seeing how a real family acted. Maybe a picnic with the Cuttings would help with my growing loneliness.

The doorbell rang, followed by a knocking. The knock grew louder, impatient. "Western Union, Dr. Garfield."

A ruddy-faced man handed me a telegram. "Sign here, Doc."

I complied and he left. The war hadn't been over long enough to not associate telegrams with death. I turned it over in my hand.

Cecil arrived. "What was that about?"

"A telegram. Maybe it's good news."

"When was the last time a telegram had good—"

"There's always a first time, you know." I slid my finger under the yellow envelope's sealed edge and the paper sliced through my skin like a scalpel. Just what I needed, a paper cut on my operating hand. If I were superstitious and believed in omens, this would definitely mean bad news. But I was a physician; all that luck crap didn't mean a thing. Then I thought of Mrs. Rosen and her Yiddish term about the evil eye.

"Who's it from?" Cecil looked over my shoulder.

I read the telegram, mouthing each word. "California Medical Board. I don't believe this. I don't…they can't do this!"

"What? Do what?"

"The bastards are accusing me of unprofessional conduct and charging the Foundation with fraud. They're trying to strip me of my license and shut down the group at the same time." I read the telegram a second time, then a third. "If it's a fight they want," I crumpled the telegram in my fist, "that's exactly what they'll get."

Cecil handed me the phone. "Call Kaiser, see what he can do."

I nodded and dialed. "Henry? It's Sid. Can you talk?" Henry was in Washington, meeting with Truman and some high-ranking senators trying to push through his post-war industrial plans and stop the AMA from its organized campaign against group medicine.

Henry sighed. "As long as I'm breathing, I can always talk."

"Good, are you sitting down?"

"Sid, I don't need to be sitting to hear bad news. Is Bess okay?"

"Yes. It's about me."

"What have they done now?"

"The Medical Association has accused me of unprofessional behavior and the Foundation of fraud. They're claiming the Foundation is making money under the cover of charity."

"You know how hard I've tried to get along with them." Henry spoke calmly. "I do not believe that wars are necessary either among nations or doctors. Physicians should be using their energies to save human life, not fight each other. But they've gone too far. They've left us no choice, just as the Japanese left FDR no choice when they bombed Pearl Harbor. We'll declare war on those bastards. If the AMA wants a fight, then I'll damn well give them one. Tell me the specifics."

"You understand that residents and interns don't have licenses during their first two years of training, right?"

"Yes, of course."

"Well, the Alameda County Medical Association cooked up these charges against me for hiring Clifford Keene on as a resident until he got his California license. Bess wouldn't be alive if he hadn't been there to help. He's licensed in Michigan and a member of the American College of Surgeons, for God's sake. And we're an accredited residency program and I can hire whom I please. You know his war record. They've also accused us of preventing patients from having free choice of physicians, our medical care understaffed and substandard, and the Foundation unlawfully making a profit."

"Okay, that's it. I'm calling Senator Wagner from New York…maybe even Truman. This is a violation of the Sherman Act. A conspiracy to restrain the practice of medicine. Pure and simple. We'll have ten of my lawyers against every one of theirs. They're going to find themselves under investigation."

"I hate to sound desperate, Henry, but we are. We're losing members, I can't recruit good physicians and if they get their way I won't be able to practice."

"Sid…Sid." Henry's voice changed from indignation to calm, fatherly. I knew if I could look across the phone lines, he'd have that grin on his face. The one he wore before taking on a new challenge. "Let's go to work on these bastards."

# CHAPTER 23

## Oakland

## August 1, 1947

It had to be over a hundred. A summer heat wave had hit Oakland, burning off even the slightest trace of fog by first light. I drove through downtown Oakland, the asphalt so hot that mirages rose off its baking surface. When I rolled down the car window the blast of heat made me think of the Depression and the hospital at Desert Center. Now that I knew how well prepaid medicine worked, that it could help so many people, there was no going back. And the only way to make it succeed was to explain it to people. Blue Cross advertised in the newspapers and over the radio and no one batted an eye. Because it was supposedly for all doctors. But for Permanente to advertise or solicit business for a multi-specialty group like ours was a crime, one that put my medical license at risk.

Unless I could explain things to the public. As Cecil often reminded me, I was a shitty salesman. However, I did have Henry Kaiser on my side. There was talk of him running for president. What we needed was good public relations. But how could a PR expert help us without advertising?

Not one to drink alone, I pulled into Trader Vic's. I felt like my head was unscrewed and drenched in sweat by the time I made it to the bar.

Vic greeted me with a hug, and then held onto my shoulders. "Doc, you okay?"

I thought about it for a moment. "You remember that Mai Tai—"

"Doc, one double Mai Tai, on the house." He went behind the counter. Three p.m., prior to the dinner rush, the bar was quiet.

"You want to talk," Vic asked, "or just sip?"

"Nice of you to offer, but I'd just like to sip."

"Okay, Doc, one Mai Tai coming up."

"Make that two, please," a woman's voice said.

Victoria Peterson, Allie Chester's sister, walked up behind me. Dressed in a dark blue suit, her dour expression matched mine.

"Just got back from meeting with my divorce attorney. Mind if I join you?" That mischievous look she'd had the other day, was replaced with a flat coat of paint.

"I may not be much company."

"That's fine, neither am I."

Vic placed the two drinks on paper napkins in front of us. I removed the umbrella and chewed on the pineapple garnish. I felt uncomfortable not saying anything. "You try one of these before?"

"Please, Sid, I'm fine just sitting here drinking. Really I am."

I looked over at her and she smiled. Nothing behind it, just a friendly smile, as when we'd first met. Small straight nose, dark hair falling across flawless skin. She sipped her drink and I stopped staring.

"What is it?"

"I'm sorry." I gulped my drink.

After a few minutes of silence, she turned, shaking her head. "You know much about polio?"

"Horrible disease. I'm sorry, didn't you say your husband has—"

"Had. Now that he's recovered, the bastard wants a divorce. Waited for me to care for him, and I mean *care*. Feeding, bathing, everything for months and now he's taking off with his secretary. I'm just…just too much like a sister, he says. Can you imagine? The sonofabitch thinks I took care of him because…I'm sorry. I didn't mean to go off like that. How about another drink?"

I couldn't remember the last time I'd had more than one mixed drink, and I would have said no, but didn't want to sound impolite. Who was I kidding? I was ready to try and forget. "Sure, sounds good."

She crossed her legs—a soft hum of nylon against nylon—and straightened herself in her seat. "What about you, Sid. How come you're not married?"

I laughed. "Timing," I answered. "Life's about timing. The one woman I fell in love with went off and married my worst enemy."

She shook her head. "There's always something."

"You're right there. So why did you get married?"

"All the usual reasons. I was attracted as hell to him. Well to do, handsome, everyone said we were the perfect couple. And I thought we were…at least until the polio. Then things changed. I took care of him when he was helpless and he can't…he just can't seem to look at me the same."

I don't know why, but I told her about Judy, about Chandler, about… everything. She listened intently, then said, "You're not here because of Judy. I'm a good listener. Maybe talking about it will help."

I finished what was left of my Mai Tai. "Unless you're a public relations expert, I don't think there's much you can do."

"Try me."

"Well, the Medical Board just sent me a letter threatening to revoke my license. Now the AMA, CMA, just about every doctor in town wants to shut us down. If they could, they'd tar and feather us and dump us in the Pacific with the remains of the Japanese Navy. Now they're doing everything they can to make me look incompetent. I can't advertise Permanente medicine because it's unethical and yet everyone else can do their best to smear us."

"You ever read Paul de Kruif, the medical writer for *Reader's Digest*?" she asked.

"Sure, who hasn't? He's the most popular medical writer around. Why?"

"How many people do you think see *Reader's Digest* every month?"

"Millions?"

"I may just have your PR campaign. Paul de Kruif is my uncle."

Before I could react, Vic was signaling me from behind the bar. "Phone for you."

"Dr. Garfield," I said into the phone.

Cecil sounded excited. "Sid, Kaiser's looking all over for you."

"What is it? Bess okay?"

"Yeah, holding her own on dialysis. But that's not why I'm calling. We need to call a War Room meeting today."

"What about?"

"Kaiser made a deal with the AFL-CIO. If we can hire enough good physicians and find enough office space, we'll have 40,000 Union members starting next month."

# CHAPTER 24

## Oakland

## August 27, 1947

Henry looked drawn and helpless as he paced around the makeshift office he'd set up to stay close to Bess. They had mansions in both Oakland and Lake Tahoe, but they were too far away, so he'd bought the apartment building across the street from the hospital. "What can you do for her, Sid? She's getting worse every day."

"I'd hoped her kidneys would recover, and the dialysis would only be temporary." I swallowed hard, knowing the old reassuring doctor clichés would sound empty. "She's just not...her kidneys aren't working."

He ran his palm over his forehead. "How much longer can she go on like this?"

I shook my head, not wanting to answer, to take the fifth like on one of those radio shows.

"Sid, Sid." He put his arm around me. "We know each other too well for you to hold out on me. I want the truth. Plain and simple."

"Okay, then. The blood clot caused permanent damage to her kidneys. With her diabetes and hypertension, there's little chance she'll ever get any function back."

He removed his arm and faced me. "Don't tell me there's nothing you can do."

"We can increase her time on dialysis—"

"No, no." He shook his head. "She hates being hooked up to the machine all day. Come on, think, man. Think of something."

"There is, but…there's no way she'd—"

"She'd what? C'mon, Sid, quit hedging, just tell me."

"You ever hear of a kidney transplant?"

He nodded. "There was that article Paul deKruif wrote last month in *Reader's Digest*. Only he said they didn't work. Resistance, like the body fighting bacteria—"

"Rejection. There's a good chance of rejection."

"If she had an identical twin, maybe even a brother or sister."

Henry shook his head. "Only child. What about my kidney? I have two, don't I?"

"Too risky for both of you." I knew he would do anything for her, but the chances of him surviving a kidney removal with his enormous weight were slim. Plus rejection.

"I don't give a damn how risky. If it can be done, do it."

I stepped back. "This isn't like building a ship. You can't borrow parts or rush production. There's just too much to lose, for both of you."

The door opened without a knock and Allie walked in, wearing her nursing uniform, a radiant smile on her face. "Oh, I'm sorry Mr. Kaiser, I thought you were alone. Hello, Dr. Garfield."

"Hi Allie, how's Mrs. Kaiser?"

"She had a very good day." Allie smiled. "I haven't seen her so hopeful in months."

"Good," Henry said. "Attitude is everything."

I leaned back in the most comfortable leather seat I'd ever sat in and looked over at Henry, who was in a chipper mood. I could get used to first class. Too bad the trip from San Francisco to AMA headquarters in Chicago on Pan Am Flight 207 would take less than eight hours.

"Sid, I hope you don't mind me asking, but what's going on with your life?"

"My appeal is set for next month."

"Not your medical license, I mean your *life*. We've known each other for years, and I've never once heard you talk about a family, settling down. I can't tell you how much Bess and the boys have meant to my life."

"What are you getting at?" I couldn't help but laugh. "You think I need to get married?"

Henry eyed me seriously. "What are you laughing at? You must have thought about it. You'd probably be married now if Chandler hadn't stolen that nurse of yours…what was her name?"

How many times had I thought about that? A thousand? Seemed like a million. He was right, I would have asked Judy to marry me and couldn't shake the feeling I'd blown the one chance in my life to truly be happy.

"Sid, you listening?"

"Judy. Her name was Judy. Why do you ask?"

"Why? Because you've been moping around, worried about the medical group. You need something in your life other than medicine. I know you and you're not that shallow. You should get married."

I laughed again. "Who do you have in mind?"

Henry settled back in his chair. "You're seeing Allie's sister, Victoria aren't you?"

"Seeing? No, I wouldn't call it seeing her. I've talked to her a few times."

"She's a beautiful woman; Allie and her both are. In fact, I've noticed she causes a few men to fall off their seats when she walks in the room. Her divorce is final now and from what Allie tells me she's intelligent, fun, and even a great cook."

"You're serious about this. If I didn't know better, I'd say someone put you up to it."

Henry put on a saintly look. "Okay, I'll come clean. Bess did. She's worried about you, Sid. Admittedly, caution is a virtue, but in your case you carry it too far. Look at how you approach things at work. Always step by step instead of just…"

"So, you're saying I'm just plain dull and boring?"

"Now, come on, I didn't say that. I know you have a lot on your mind with the suspension, the AMA and all, but to put it in your terms, there's only one cure."

"Getting married?"

He cast me a look of fatherly affection. "That's right. You're going to start taking a salary whether you like it or not, and I mean one worthy of a Medical

Director. You're going to start a family."

"It's not that easy—"

He grabbed me around the shoulder. "It is that easy. Even I can see you've never gotten over Judy. Stop wasting your life. Ask Victoria out. I know from Allie she's enamored with you. You can do it. You can."

My heart quickened. Victoria enamored with me? I sank back into the thick leather seat. Maybe Henry was right. It was time to get over Judy.

# CHAPTER 25

Oakland

August 28, 1947

Morris Fishbein had been the editor of the *Journal of the American Medical Association* and the most powerful doctor in the AMA for over twenty years. He was also the most outspoken critic of prepaid health plans in the country, especially Kaiser Permanente, and was leading the war to stop us with Resolution 16. His editorials in JAMA were read weekly by most doctors and he had the power to sway their opinion in any direction he wanted. Without his cooperation, we'd get nowhere.

His secretary showed us into his office, a small room compared to the office of a corporate executive, every inch covered in shelves jammed with journals and books. Dust filled the room and it smelled ancient, not of mold, more of decay. Fishbein, a small man in his late fifties, stood and extended his thin, manicured hand to Henry.

"A pleasure to meet you, Mr. Kaiser." He glanced in my direction. "And Dr. Garfield. Please take off your hats and have a seat."

We dropped our hats on a small coffee table.

"Thank you for seeing us, Dr. Fishbein, we're here—"

"You know why we're here," Henry interrupted me. We had agreed this was to be a doctor-to-doctor discussion, at least to begin with. But as usual, Henry had a plan of his own. "Let's get right to the point. I've fought socialized medicine since FDR first proposed the idea. Free enterprise, freedom to choose. You agree, Dr. Fishbein?"

"Yes, of course, Mr. Kaiser. But that's the problem isn't it? Your patients can't choose their own physicians, can they?"

"Within our group," I answered, "they can have—"

"Voluntary health care," Henry interrupted. "No one is forced to choose Kaiser Permanente. They do so on their own."

Fishbein held up a document. "I'm afraid that's not true. I have patient testimonial that their union was forced to join your Health Plan or—"

"No one is forced to join us," Henry snapped.

"Mr. Kaiser, let's be honest here. You know as well as I do the only reason people sign up for your Health Plan is they have no choice."

Fishbein sounded condescending, a big mistake around Henry. I waited for him to explode.

Fishbein continued. "Why in the world would they ever consider signing up for a program where they cannot have their own doctor?"

"They can choose any doctor in our group," I said.

"Patients should be able to choose *any* doctor they want. The AMA has done a survey that has shown—"

"You're wasting our time," Henry said. "We know all this. What we want is for people to be able to afford their doctor. Do you disagree, Dr. Fishbein?"

"Of course not," he said. "But the key words are *their own doctor*. One of their own choosing."

"You're not that naïve, are you Dr. Fishbein? The only choice the AMA is giving people is to go bankrupt when they get sick." Henry stood, grabbed the closest hat and rammed it on his head. Only it was my hat, a couple sizes too small. "I can see we're wasting each other's time."

I needed to calm things down. "When was the last time you treated a patient, Dr. Fishbein?"

"Your point? I talk to my colleagues every day. I know what's going on. How you're trying to use big business to drive the solo practitioner out of his practice."

Henry was oblivious to my small hat on his head. "If you and the AMA are not willing to listen, there are politicians in Washington who are. Don't forget who votes them in. It's the average Joe who can't afford to lose his shirt every time he gets sick. If you want to sit here in your Ivory Tower and pretend things will never change, than I'm afraid you're going to need a new job."

Fishbein leaned back in his chair and glared at Henry. "Okay, Mr. Kaiser. Have it your way. The AMA will not be bullied, even by the likes of you."

"If the government proceeds against you for restraint of trade, one of two things will happen to the AMA. You'll be dissolved or bankrupt." Henry held up the AMA's book of principles. "According to this the AMA stands for quality health care for everyone in America. There's nothing in here about health care only for those who can afford to pay."

"Of course not." Fishbein hesitated. "But a person's right to choose their doctor is a basic right of the doctor-patient relationship."

"Do you really mean that?" I rose from my chair. "Because if you do, I want you to think for a moment. Think like a patient. How many patients can afford to pay their surgeon a hundred dollars to remove their appendix or two hundred dollars to have a baby? Are they all supposed to go to charity hospitals when an alternative is available, one that allows patients the right to *voluntarily* enroll? Where for $6.95 a month an entire family is fully covered for whatever unforeseen health problem—"

"I've heard this before," Fishbein said. "But I read journals, not *Reader's Digest*."

"Let's stop the pat remarks and discuss this intelligently," I said. "I know a group like ours is not for everyone. Many will want to continue with their fee-for-service doctor. What we're asking for is the same right you're saying that patients should have. They should have the right to choose their type of care, group or solo practitioner, prepaid or fee-for-service. Simple freedom of choice. How can you argue with that?"

Fishbein stood and ran his hand through his wisps of hair. "I'm not about to argue. You and your prepaid medicine are like a cancer. We must stop you before you spread any further. Good day, gentlemen."

In the hallway Henry broke out in laughter seeing his large hat on my head. I took it off and handed it to him. "Here, Henry, it looks better on you."

"See, Sidney, you do have a sense of humor. Our talk on the plane wasn't wasted. You know, it's far from over."

"No, what do you mean?"

"Like a cancer? What poppycock. Fishbein just declared war and it's one he won't win."

"What are you getting at?"

"We're buying time. The larger and faster we grow, the harder it will be for them to fight us. It's a matter of size, Sid. A numbers game, pure and simple."

The receptionist stopped us at the front door. "Mr. Kaiser, your son's on the phone. He says it's urgent." She handed him the phone.

"Edgar?" Henry's face sagged. "Bess has gone into a coma," he said.

I took the phone. "Edgar, who's with her?"

"Dr. Cutting and Allie," he said. "She's," his voice broke, "she's not going to—"

"Give me Dr. Cutting."

"Sid, Mrs. Kaiser developed pneumonia last night." Cecil sounded exhausted, as if he hadn't slept. "Every system shut down today. There's nothing more—"

Henry grabbed the phone. "Don't you give up on my Bess. Put her on the phone."

I could imagine what Cecil was saying.

"I don't care, after forty-four years, she'll recognize me. Put the phone next to her ear. Just hold it there. Now! You hear me?"

Tears streamed down Henry's face as he whispered into the phone. I couldn't make out the words.

Then he began to shout. "Don't you leave me. Hear me, Bess? Don't you...hello? Edgar? No...no...no...she...my Bess, my Bess." He dropped the phone.

# CHAPTER 26

## Oakland

## September 7, 1947

After Bess Kaiser's funeral, Henry went into seclusion. I knew how I felt after my father's death and did my best to call or go by and see him. But Henry, who often spent twenty hours a day on the phone, was refusing to talk to anyone.

I glanced at the wall clock: noon. I took a bite of Trader Vic's specialty, sesame chicken, and washed it down with iced tea. Victoria and her Uncle, Paul de Kruif, were due any moment. Maybe I couldn't advertise, but if things went well, I wouldn't need to.

"Hi, Sid."

I stood up. "Hi, Victoria."

"Dr. Garfield. Meet my Uncle, Paul de Kruif."

"It's an honor, sir," I said as I shook his hand. De Kruif, in his sixties, wore a French beret and looked as if he could hold his own in an eating contest with Henry Kaiser.

"Please, Dr. Garfield, if only half what my niece has told me about you is true, the honor is mine."

"Call me Sid."

"Okay, Sid, you can just call me De Kruif."

"Funny," Victoria said. "Isn't he cute?" She playfully stroked her uncle's cheek.

"Flattery will get you everywhere. Now, Sid, tell me in a sentence or two how I can hook my readers with your story."

"It's simple. So simple, you're going to wonder why it hasn't always been this way."

He took out a fountain pen and held it over a blank sheet of paper. "Go ahead, then. Give me the headline."

"What would you rather do, De Kruif, pay your doctor for keeping you sick or making you well? That's it. Period. End of story."

Victoria smiled and moved closer. "I vote for keeping me well."

"So do I," DeKruif said, jotting down a few notes. "Tell me more."

"Okay, for a few cents a day, our doctors guarantee to keep you well, provide everything you need if you get sick and do everything we can to prevent you from *getting* sick. Fee-for-service doctors make more money every time you visit. The sicker you get, the more they make."

"Of course, you're not implying they would deliberately keep you sick."

"No, I'd say most have their hearts in the right place. But some—"

"I like your thinking, Sid."

"And he is kind of cute," Victoria added.

DeKruif fussed with his beret. "That's it, Victoria. That's how we'll start it. I'll describe Sid, make every woman in America want to meet him. Let's see. How does this sound: Sidney Garfield, a man of mystery. His finely tailored clothes remained unwrinkled because of the economy and careful precision of the way he moves about. He seems not medical and even a bit Hollywoodish in his elegance, but beneath that he was wiry and gave one the feeling that one had better not get funny with him. His face had high cheekbones, chiseled in clean lines, photogenic. His hair, cut close, was curly reddish-gold, his skin deeply tanned. His gray-green eyes told little because they were usually peering through narrow slits, especially when he smiled—"

"Hold on!" I waved my hands. "Are you kidding? Who are you talking about?"

"That's you, Sid," Victoria said. "I love it. Uncle Paul, you're a genius."

"Now that we have them hooked." De Kruif scribbled some more notes. "More on your medical care. Anyone else doing prepaid?"

"A few—"

"No, we'll say you're unique. Sid Garfield stands alone, like most of the other medical mavericks. He stands alone, nationally unknown and neglected.

The forces now battling for power over the medical fate of the people act as if Garfield did not exist."

"Beautiful," Victoria said. "Just beautiful."

De Kruif smiled, obviously enjoying Victoria's praise. "I'll call the article 'What Sid Did.' You're having people prepay. Are you making a profit? Keeping things going?"

"Yes, enough to build our own hospitals. Without a cent of government money."

"Good, people like that. After the Depression, no one wants to hear about handouts. How's this sound?" He scribbled as he read aloud. "So here was what Sid did: he built a pilot plant for good medical care within the means of the ordinary citizen, paying its own way without charity or government socialization. He made prepayment profitable and revolutionized the practice of medicine."

"That's good, but I really wanted to stress preventive care, keeping people well instead of sick."

"Okay, I was coming to that. To get people to read this and to get *Reader's Digest* to publish it, we can't hit them over the head with facts. It's embellishment that makes it interesting. Here's what I'll write. "The fee-for-service practicing doctor makes more money, the longer and the more seriously each of his patients is sick—to the possible financial ruin of that patient. But under Sid's new system, the treatment of the sick will inevitably become a vanishing economy. It pays the doctors most to keep all possible patients in the best health…How much a week we talking here? I'm sure you made it affordable."

"Seven cents a day," Victoria chimed in. "Allie's told me all about that."

"Good," De Kruif said. "No, great." He scrawled some more words. "A small prepayment of so many cents a day, which is within the means of the working citizens of the nation. Now…" he paused. "We need bad guys. Big government? The AMA? Who's against…don't answer. It's obvious. The AMA has to hate prepayment."

I nodded. "More than the worst plague."

"Hold on a minute. I've got some inspiration here." He quickly wrote another paragraph. "The boys in the AMA powerhouse and in the local county and state AMA powerhouses are against prepayment. Can you imagine? They are against keeping patients well. The smears of those doctors against Sid are comical—provided that you avoid thinking of the hundreds of thousands who would be sick and might die if AMA plots like this one against Sid are successful."

He paused, removed his beret and ran his hand over his bald scalp. "Now, we'll end with simple ethics no one can argue with. What Sid's plan means is that, when there is no money consideration between doctors and their patients, there is the chance for simple Christianity to come in. I know, you're Jewish… still that doesn't matter here, it's all the same. Now, we need to end with a catchy phrase. Sid, you have any ideas?"

"I'm not really good at that," I said.

"I'd end with God," Victoria said. "After all, most of you doctors think you're God."

"Funny."

"No, I think she's got it there," De Kruif said. "*Reader's Digest* will eat this up. We won't let the boys in the AMA win. We'll put this right on the cover: 'Exit dollars—enter God.' Now tell me how anyone, even the AMA, can argue with God."

There was a curious thing about attraction. The first time I met Judy, I thought the wind had been knocked out of me, like I was breathing through a tiny straw. I'd fallen for her so completely that her rejection fortified my defenses around other women. I wasn't about to allow myself to become that smitten with Victoria; at least I told myself I wouldn't.

"I'll get that." I opened the back door of Cecil's spotless Packard and Victoria scooted into the rear seat behind Cecil and Millie. I'd been around many during the last few years. Only, none of them—until Victoria—had that charm I found irresistible. And it made me nervous as hell.

I slid in the back beside Victoria. She smiled warmly at me, "I'm looking forward to tonight."

I'd done my best to put Judy out of my mind, and looking at Victoria confirmed how truly opposite these two women were. Not just in looks— blonde vs. brunette, tall vs. short—but in personality: Judy closed and secretive, Victoria outgoing, open and genuine. Why was I feeling pangs of guilt for finding her so attractive? Judy had made her decision. For God's sake, it was time to move on with my life.

The setting sun cast its radiance against the bay as we drove to Trader Vic's for dinner. Victoria sat close to me. Her hair brushed my cheek and I breathed in expensive perfume. She took my hand as if it was the most natural thing to do. As if she'd held it a thousand times before.

Trader Vic's was already crowded, even before six. I looked around for an empty table. "Busy tonight."

"Doctors!" Vic Bergeron bear-hugged us. "And your beautiful dates." He kissed both of their hands.

"Great food, great service," he beamed. "And of course, cheap drinks. Congratulate me. I'm expanding. Two new Trader Vic's. One in Beverly Hills and one in San Francisco. Starting in a month, I'll be spending my time on the road."

"Congratulations, Vic," I said. "I'm sure they'll both be hits."

"We're in a little bit of a hurry tonight," Cecil said. "UCSF residency awards and dancing at the Fairmont."

"Appetizers and drinks, then?" Vic asked. "Come on over to the bar, I'll find you some chairs."

Once we were seated, Vic went behind the bar. "I have a new concoction I'd like to try on you. On the house. It's called a volcano. You'll see why."

He poured vodka, Southern Comfort, pineapple juice, and Amaretto into a glass, stirred and added an umbrella with a cherry. It looked like the name, ready to erupt.

I closed my eyes and indulged. The liquid fizzled in my mouth then went down with a pleasant bite. "Genius. Vic, you're a genius."

The first volcano tasted great and helped to calm my nerves, so I sipped on a second while we made small talk about the hospital and some of our patients. I found it increasingly difficult to concentrate.

"Sid," Cecil said, "There's one of Millie's friends. Be right back." Cecil and Millie left us to a corner booth and scooted in next to two women.

My eyes focused on Victoria's hair catching the colored flickering of the tiki lights and I blurted out, "When was the first time you fell in love?"

She looked at me with surprise.

"I'm sorry, I don't have any right to ask." One volcano and I'd lost all common sense.

"That's okay," she said. "I was a late bloomer. You know, too busy getting good grades to worry about boys in high school. So in my first year in college… well, my biology professor. God, just looking at him. Frank Wellington."

"Did anything happen?"

"Maybe."

"Isn't there a rule against that? You could've been thrown out of college."

"It isn't the worst thing in the world. Some of the smartest people drop out and then go on to become millionaires. Henry Kaiser never went to college, you know. Not that I want to be a millionaire, mind you. I mean, sure, it would be great. But, I've always wanted to be a mother, to have a large family."

"Yeah. I've always thought about a family." Which was at least partly true. I'd thought about it years ago with Judy. "So what happened to the professor?" I asked.

She shook her head. "After I learned biology…it just wasn't the same. What about you, Sid? Tell me why you were so in love."

"Well…"

I was surprised when Cecil pulled on my arm. I hadn't noticed they'd returned. Two volcanoes and I'd forgotten where I was.

"We'd best be going," he said.

Back in the car, I put my arm around Victoria. Her perfume and the warmth of her cheek against mine were intoxicating. She turned to face me and my lips touched hers. A gentle kiss—soft lips and warm breath and her fingertips light on the back of my neck. I pulled her closer. She ran the tip of her tongue along my lips, top and bottom, then opened her mouth to my tongue. "I could fall in love with you in about two minutes," she whispered.

I stared at her, seeing in her eyes the same desire I felt. My face flushed and I couldn't think of an answer. Like a high school kid I said nothing, pulling her to me and kissing her until the valet at the Fairmont opened the door. I didn't want to stop. The valet cleared his throat and I slid over and extended my hand to help her. Victoria leaned into me as we entered the hotel.

Inside the ballroom, a big band played while a crowd of starched shirted men and gowned women clamored on at their tables. Out on the dance floor a few couples showed off the latest steps. Victoria and I joined them.

As we hit the polished hardwood floor, I found I had somehow become an expert at swing dancing. I spun Victoria around, whirling her effortlessly, at least in my compromised opinion. Looking into her lovely green eyes, twirling her in my arms, her words ran through my head: *I could fall in love with you.* I'd felt that way with Judy the first time we'd met and wasn't sure yet how I felt about Victoria. It didn't take a doctor to recommend what to do next. I should just stop analyzing everything, stop worrying about every detail, and let things develop.

When the music turned slow, Victoria fell into my arms.

A hand grabbed my shoulder and broke the moment. "Sid!" Nick Halasz smiled from under his bushy mustache. "Great to see you."

"Hi, Nick."

"So, is it true?"

"Huh?"

"Kaiser told the AMA to go to…" He shook his head.

"Yeah, but—"

"Hey, I couldn't agree more." He leaned close. "Watch your back tonight, my friend." He hurried off.

Victoria gave me an odd look. "I need some air."

"Yeah, I know what you mean."

I put my arm around her and headed for the door. Behind us, a familiar voice said, "Hi, Sid."

My whole body froze when I saw Judy. A spontaneous smile had half-formed on her face, the look of both surprise and gladness to see me. Then her smile vanished, replaced by a look that was just plain neutral. Next to her Dwight Chandler talked to Paul Foster and a dowdy, overdressed woman wrapped in a mink stole.

I couldn't speak for a moment. Judy's neutral look was somehow more painful following that glimpse of emotion, that remnant of how we once felt. Victoria took my hand and leaned closer as if she sensed what I was feeling. Before I could utter a word, Foster's wife said, "Let's go. I will not be anywhere near these people."

I wasn't sure I'd heard her right. "Excuse me?"

She went on: "They shouldn't allow your kind in here. You're a disgrace! We're not going to let you Communists ruin our American doctors."

Victoria glared at her. Judy's look was equally cold. "Anne, apologize."

"What…" Mrs. Foster seemed too dazed to talk. Judy coming to my defense must have shocked her.

"You need to apologize," Judy repeated.

Mrs. Foster tightened her lips, "Why, I never!"

"What's gotten into you?" Chandler snapped at his wife.

Judy's expression softened. "Please, Anne, you know what you said is wrong. And at the least it was rude."

"Very well," Mrs. Foster said. "I'm…sorry."

She nodded brusquely and the four of them moved away. Judy's voice, still somewhere in my head, was falling away, farther and farther into background static. Time to get over her. Finally and forever. Time to get over a schoolboy crush and get on with life. Only I couldn't stop watching her every step as she walked away.

"Sid?" Victoria stood next to me, her shoulders hunched, staring down at her hands with a stricken look on her face. All of a sudden, I realized how transparent I'd been. I felt like I should have been on trial in Nuremberg.

"This may not be the right time…no it is the right time." Victoria's eyes flicked from side to side, not meeting mine. "I can see now where your heart is. I won't settle for second best. Not again. Good-bye, Sid." She kissed me on the cheek, turned and walked away, her high heels clicking on the dance floor.

"Victoria, wait!" She kept walking.

# BOOK FOUR

## THE COURAGE TO SUCCEED

Cecil Cutting shoved the paper back in my face. "What the hell is this? You're quitting the medical group? *Your* medical group? Is this some type of sick joke?"

It was mid-afternoon, close to ninety degrees, and we sat outside on his back patio in Pleasanton, overlooking a canyon where water flowed most of the winter. "Think about it. It makes perfect sense. As soon as Garfield and Associates ceases to exist, the AMA has no one to attack. Going after fifty doctors is a different sort of deal compared to attacking one. Besides, I'm not quitting, I'm just no longer going to be sole proprietor."

Cecil picked up a hose and began to water a group of red-flowered azaleas on the edge of his deck. "Sid, I know what you're doing, God damn it, and it just isn't fair."

"Fair? Why not? We form The Permanente Medical Group instead of Garfield and Associates and I'm just one of many partners. There's no single controlling partner to go after. Hell, we're better than any other group around. Let them try and stop us."

"Like the old West, huh?" He brought up the hose as if he were drawing a gun and soaked my shirt.

"You think that's funny?" I stepped on the hose and made a grab for it. We wrestled for the nozzle, the water soaking us both, running over my face and streaming down my shirt.

Millie Cutting yelled from the kitchen window, "Dinner's ready."

I turned to Cecil and began to laugh. "Consider Garfield and Associates all washed up."

"Bad joke, Sid. Just plain bad."

"Red or dead!" Fifty longshoreman union members around us chanted, "Red or dead, red or dead!"

Cigarette smoke filled the cavernous meeting hall with a silver mist. I looked through the haze at Morris Collen and Cecil. "We'd better get the hell out of here."

The ULFW workers were on their feet, raising their fists and yelling. A camera flashed. Too late to duck. One picture of the three of us here would bring McCarthy to the front door of our hospital.

I'd parked my "Henry J" sedan—one of the first off the production line, and one of the bonuses Kaiser now gave the physicians—right outside. I looked over my shoulder, hoping the newspaperman with the camera was still inside. Didn't matter; the fog was so thick that the picture would have been a blur. I slumped down behind the steering wheel, Cecil next to me, Morris in the back. Both were silent as I headed into the soup.

"Hope you put those 'McCarthy for President' stickers on my bumper," I kidded.

Cecil laughed.

"I know," Morris said, "it scared the hell out of me, too. It was supposed to be a way for us to reach out to the community. You know, meet and attract new patients. I didn't know it would be a commie rally."

I squinted, trying to see the white line in the middle of the road. "Kaiser will go nuts if our pictures end up on the front of the *Tribune*."

"Good, serves him right. You talk to him about splitting up the medical group and trying to take control?"

"He's paying our salaries again, isn't he?"

"You're not answering," Morris said.

"He doesn't get it. To him, we should all be honored that he's the boss and we're Kaiser doctors. Kaiser Steel. Kaiser Aluminum. Kaiser cars…why not Kaiser docs? Well, we've got to convince him we make all the medical decisions, or frankly, I don't see how we can continue."

"Okay, convince him," Morris said. "He'll listen to you."

"Easier said than done." I knew it sounded clichéd but with Henry it was reality. We both wanted to enroll more and more people to benefit from prepaid care, but we differed dramatically on how to do it. He thought like a banker, wanting the patients first to put up as collateral for more doctors and hospitals. I wanted the doctors and hospitals first so we would be ready to provide the care as patients joined the plan. With Henry it was always a game of catch-up and in the end that could prove disastrous.

"Jesus, Sid, slow down," Cecil said. "You can't see two feet in front of you."

Morris said. "You've got to talk to him, Sid. Kaiser's out of control. Now, he's even having the FBI do security checks on all new hires. Can you believe this shit? Are they going to start blacklisting us like in Hollywood?"

"The AMA's been branding our group as Communist for years." I eased on the brakes, heading east to get away from the fog. "With the witch hunt in Washington going on and with 160,000 members in the north, and 90,000 members in LA, well—"

"I know," Cecil said. "We can't afford scandal."

"You got it." The fog cleared enough that I could see the street ahead of us.

"Good," Morris said. "Then you fire Lipscomb."

"Why? He's as good an intern as any." I'd hired Wendell Lipscomb last July. A decorated WWII Tuskegee airman, he'd graduated from UC Berkeley medical school, the only Negro student in his class. He'd purposely applied without submitting a picture, but I would have accepted him anyway.

"Did you know he was in Prague a few years ago attending the World Federation of Democratic Youth?" Morris said. "The one to foster socialism and communism in the world?"

I stared into the fog. "Shit."

"Scalpel." The nurse slapped the handle of a ten blade on my palm. With even downward pressure, I sliced through the skin and muscle layers with the standard right upper quadrant incision for gallstones. We were operating on Ida Washington, a fifty-eight-year-old woman who'd been the Kaiser family nanny and maid for over thirty years.

I gazed at the blood seeping from the edges of the wound. Even though my medical license was suspended, Henry and Ida wanted me to do the surgery. I'd known her for years and couldn't refuse.

"Lipscomb?" I said. The intern appeared to be staring at the floor. "You paying attention?"

"Yes, Sir. I'm sorry. It's just...well, I wasn't *cut out* to be a surgeon."

"Funny, Lipscomb. What is it you want to do?" I clamped and tied a superficial vein to stop the blood from oozing into the field.

"Psych, Sir. It's one of the few specialties I can do and make a difference."

"What do you mean?"

"I wanted to be a pilot first, you know."

I nodded, my eyes on the wound.

"But no airline would hire me, even though I'd flown more hours than any white pilot applying. You know, one of my OB professors actually said to my class "It's good to see a Negro here because they make such wonderful experimental subjects.""

Sounded like something Dean Keating might have said. "Four by four." The nurse handed me a sponge and I used it to tamponade a bleeder. "So why psychiatry?"

"You help the mind, you help the body. I really believe that."

"Hold this." I handed him the Deaver retractor. "Pull up on the ribs. Harder. Okay."

"Dr. Garfield, you know how many Negroes live in Oakland?"

I shook my head.

"One-hundred and twenty thousand. And you know how many Negro doctors there are?"

"No."

"Three, including me."

"That still doesn't answer, why psych?" I dissected the tiny blood vessels surrounding the gallbladder. "Hemostat."

"Because I want to be able to treat people who have been oppressed. Black, white, yellow, I don't care. I'll help them overcome, at least mentally, the obstacles they've been forced to face."

"Cut the suture...there. Okay, so you—"

"Psychiatry is where I can help the most. Any doctor can treat a cold or flu, or, pardon me for saying this, take out a gallbladder. But you've had to experience it first-hand to help people who have been put down and degraded their entire lives."

I glanced up at his dark, penetrating eyes.

"Think about what my OB professor said. I'm an experiment. That's all. No white person likes it when I examine them and I'm not allowed to deliver white women."

"Kelly clamp." The nurse handed me the long hemostat to tie off the pedicle to the gallbladder. "I never said you couldn't deliver. Where'd you... who told you that?"

"No one, it's the look of the husband when I walk in the room. Right or wrong, I'm not about to...let's just end it with that."

I faced him again. "Take a feel of this." I handed him the gallbladder.

"Like a bag of marbles," he said.

I nodded. "Some very painful ones. You want to close?"

"Sure. 3-0 catgut?"

"That's right, muscle, then sub-q. Close the skin with 2-0 silk. And do a good job or she'll be showing her scar to Kaiser and we'll never hear the end of it."

Henry leaned back in a chair in his office on the top floor of the Kaiser Industries building in Oakland. Two months after Bess' death and he was back in full gear. I'd never seen as many phones in one room. If ever there was a company town, Oakland had become one. They even named the street Kaiser Place.

"Henry, I can't fire Lipscomb. He's a good doctor."

"He was a member of the Red Church," Henry retorted. "I'm as sorry as you are, but it comes down to the program or one man. How's Ida doing?"

"She's fine—and don't change the subject. Didn't we start this so we could take care of everyone? Not discriminate? Now, you're telling me—"

"Sid, you're preaching to the choir here. You have a plan in mind, just get to it."

I ran my finger over the polished surface of his mahogany desk and considered my next argument. "You know how many ILWU dockworkers we have as members? Here and in Southern California?"

"Of course, ten thousand give or take a few."

"Well, apparently, word leaked about Dr. Lipscomb. He's talked to them and the San Francisco chapter of the NAACP. We'll have the Urban League, maybe even the *Tribune*—"

"Sid, get to the point. I've got Senator McCarthy on my back. Can you imagine? That pompous asshole, accusing me, Henry Kaiser, of sympathizing with Communists? Where the hell was he when we were turning out the ships that won the war?"

"I like Lipscomb. He's been up front about being an idealist. Hell, after the discrimination he's lived through, it's hard to believe he still has a positive attitude. He wanted to intern with us because he thought we practiced medicine for everyone—not just the rich who could afford fee for service."

Henry folded his hands across his enormous stomach, signaling me to get on with it.

"Let him finish his internship. It's only another two weeks. He's interested in psychiatry and we don't have a residency program for that. We'll all part friendly. No union strikes, no bad press—"

"Bad press? If we don't get hit with discrimination, we'll be called Communists. Which is worse?"

I fell silent for a moment. "'Always go with the truth.' Didn't you tell me that once?" I knew he hadn't but he might buy it. "If we fire Lipscomb it will be discrimination. If we keep him on, even if he was Stalin himself, it still doesn't make the rest of us Communists."

He nodded. "Sid, I taught you well."

"There's another issue. You have to stop trying to run the medical group. You can't divide us up into separate groups. Henry, this isn't one of your other companies. Doctors need to be in charge or we'll have an open revolt on our hands. The doctors don't like it and in the end it will decrease quality and service."

"You're wrong, Sid. Smaller groups will compete with each other and improve quality. Find me a doctor that doesn't want to show he's the best around. You ever met one? I sure haven't. We'll have each group at every hospital competing with the other. Quality will soar." He looked at his watch. "I'm meeting with Giannini at the B of A in ten minutes. Oh, that reminds me. Allie's having a dinner party this Saturday. You free?"

For the last month, Henry had been seeing more and more of Victoria's sister. "I'll be there. But, Henry…"

He looked at me impatiently.

"You can't be the boss of everything."

"Yes, I can, Sid." The door slammed as he rushed out.

# CHAPTER 28

California Highway 1

November 6, 1948

"Sid, watch it!"

I swerved to the right, just missing a truck hauling tomatoes. The car slid sideways, jamming my left shoulder hard against the doorframe. I regained control and dropped the speed to fifty.

"Jesus, Sid," Cecil said, "if you can't concentrate, pull over and let me drive. Being run over by a tomato truck is not the way I want to go."

"I'm okay." Of course, I wasn't. I wound my window all the way down and let the cool ocean air rush in. "Read this." I shoved an envelope over to him on the seat. I was nearly forty years old now. Old enough to know when reality slapped me in the face. I recalled when I'd opened the envelope the night before. I'd slipped my finger under the seal and absently opened the brown envelope. It had cut my finger. Just like the envelope threatening my medical license had done years before. I stared in disbelief at the letter in front of me. I was being ordered to report for a physical. I re-read the letter, not believing this could ever happen. The AMA had found another way to get to me and the group. The local selective service board was drafting me for duty, claiming I never served during the war. With my license to practice medicine still at risk, I felt like I'd walked out on a movie before the ending.

Cecil opened the envelope and stared straight ahead. "We can't let them get away with this."

I said nothing.

He shook his head. "Sid, they can't do this to you."

"Well, they did. Can you imagine drafting me? I'm thirty-seven years old, for God's sake."

He shook his head again. "No. But you'd better slow down or we'll end up like Hearst."

We were passing through the picture perfect coastal town of San Simeon with Hearst's Castle towering over the mountains on our left. At least it was his castle until he'd died the year before from a ruptured abdominal aneurysm. Seagulls cawed, the sun felt warm, and the smell of sea salt filled the air.

Cecil waited for me to say something.

"I screwed up just about everything."

"What the hell you talking about? You're not going nuts on me, are you? Because if you are, maybe you'd better turn around. We're meeting with two union leaders in LA who will give us our first big break in Southern California. They don't want you—"

"I'm talking about my life. The appeals over my medical license have dragged on for years. I'm a drain on our medical group." I thought of that plane ride to Chicago with Henry when he'd tried to convince me to settle down. "Look at you Cecil. Happily married, two kids, the best surgeon I've ever operated with. Then look at me. Nothing. No wife, no kids, the group threatening mutiny, some ready to quit—what's it all for?"

The wind buffeted the car again and I gripped the steering wheel tighter to keep us from swerving into oncoming traffic.

"What happened to you and Victoria?" he asked.

"She saw the way I looked at Judy and well, that was that."

"Sid, we've talked about this a thousand times. For God's sake, forget Judy and call Victoria back. Hell, think about what you've accomplished. You're the best thing to happen to medicine since Hippocrates."

I turned to see if he was smiling. But he was tight lipped and serious.

"Your little Health Plan is about to go statewide in a big way. It must mean something to you to be back in LA. Imagine what Dean Keating would have said."

"Yeah. That shorthand speech of his. '*Garfield, there's only one-way to practice medicine. My way. I won't stand for change. I won't allow it.*'"

I gazed at the ocean on my right as we passed through Cambria, a charming town that resembled an old English village.

"Keating must be turning over in his grave. So what are you going to tell Ray Kay? With Kaiser trying to take control of the medical group, he's been talking about setting up his own group in Southern California."

Cecil, Ray, and I had been friends since the days at LA County. I'd talked Ray out of his teaching job at County to join us as Medical Director of the Fontana Hospital, which served the workers at Kaiser's steel mill. The one that had made the steel for the ships built in Richmond. Fontana, only twenty minutes from downtown LA, was close enough for Ray to want to expand into the city. I had to make Ray understand he still worked for me and was still part of The Permanente Medical Group. No matter what his worries were about Kaiser trying to be the boss and running the group, I'd make him understand that I was still in control of all medical decisions.

"Sid, you listening? Or daydreaming again?"

"Yeah, I hear you. You know Ray as well as I do, what do you think he's up to?"

"It doesn't matter what I think."

"Since when? But I guess we'll just have to wait and see."

After three hours of driving, we exited the highway about ten miles south of downtown Los Angeles. "Okay, I'm lost."

"Well, find a gas station and let's ask directions."

"C'mon, Cecil, you can read a map. How hard can it be to find Harbor City? It has to be right next to the harbor, right?"

"You find it, then. All I've seen for the last half-hour are oil wells and dirt."

I looked at the dash clock. "What time is the groundbreaking?"

"About twenty minutes ago."

"Shit, Ray's going to kill us. I'll pull over. You ask." About a half mile up, I turned into a Union 76 station, the modern kind with the rotating orange and blue ball. According to the attendant we were a good five miles away.

Cecil glanced right and shook his head. "The leaders of the two largest unions in the state are at the groundbreaking ceremony for the new Kaiser Hospital and we're going to be late. What would 'Hurry up Henry' say about this?"

"I'm not going to tell him. Are you?"

Cecil shook his head. "You know what he'd say though. The story about jumping off the train—"

I held up my hand. "Stop, don't. I've heard it a thousand times." I followed the attendant's directions and found the empty lot and large billboard: "Future Home of Kaiser Permanente Hospital." The Harbor City hospital would be the biggest in Southern California. I pulled up to the curb.

Next to short-statured Ray Kay stood a guy in a dark suit that had clearly come from a big-and-tall store and was probably the largest size it offered. He held a shovel in his hand and had to be the head of the Longshoreman's Union. Waving the shovel at us, he—luckily—wore what appeared to be a genuine smile. Which was more than I could say for Ray, who glared at me like he was ready to cut out my appendix without anesthesia. Okay, that was being too nice. Ray wanted to cut off my balls.

"Sid, right on time," he said, sarcastically.

"Hi, Ray," Cecil answered for me.

I extended my hand to the big guy with the shovel. "Sid Garfield, nice to meet you."

He gripped it hard in a knuckle breaker. "Harry Bridges. Good to meet you, Doc. I thought all you Kaiser docs would be on time like your boss."

"We're not Kaiser docs," Ray interrupted. "We don't work for—"

"That's right," Cecil interrupted. "We work for Sidney Garfield."

"I'm sure you wouldn't want Henry Kaiser making medical decisions," I said. "Any more than you'd want me unloading ships."

A man about my age, thickset and dark, who looked like everyone's friendly next door neighbor, rushed through the dusty lot and joined us. "Sorry I'm late. Maury Landman. Head of the Retail Clerks Union."

"Thanks for coming." Ray enthusiastically shook Maury's hand.

"Wouldn't miss it," he said, smiling. "We're taking a big gamble on you guys. No hospital yet and every doctor in town tells me I'm making a mistake."

"You won't regret it," Ray said. "We'll have the hospital up in six months—"

"What kind of care do your workers get now?" I couldn't help interrupting again.

"Well, none," Maury said. "Too expensive to reimburse them for every bill from hundreds of doctors."

"That's where we come in," I said. "We call it value. Highest quality care and it won't bankrupt you or your workers."

"Should we start, gentlemen?" Ray said. "The press is here."

After a few shovel-fulls of dirt, a couple flashes of the cameras, and hand-shakes with the Union leaders, we climbed into my car.

"You almost blew it by being late," Ray said.

"Me? You were the one carrying on about not being Kaiser docs."

"Okay, okay, you're right. I liked the line about value. You know, Kaiser was down the other night. We met at the Bel Air Hotel until three in the morning and didn't agree on one thing. He kept saying if we don't want to work for him, buy the hospitals. And I kept bluffing that we might just do that. You know how bad things are?"

"Tell me," I said.

Ray ran his hand through his short-cropped hair. "Kaiser keeps signing up new members without asking us. You heard those Union guys today. They're joining, but skeptical. We need the hospitals and doctors in place *before* we grow, not after. Is Henry Kaiser asking us what we think? Hell no. It's hurry and catch up and to me that's just plain not good medicine."

"I know, I've been talking to Henry and getting nowhere."

"Maybe that's the problem," Ray said. "Maybe you're too close to him."

I felt my face flush. "Maybe you're right. That's why I talked him into meeting with all of us. Morris and Cecil representing the north. You the south. Henry will have Edgar and an attorney representing the Kaiser Health Plan and Board."

"And you think they'll listen? I talked to Kaiser for hours and I swear he didn't hear a thing I said."

"You have a better idea?" Cecil said.

Ray nodded. "As a matter of fact, I do. The best thing for all would be a separate group in the south with our own Health Plan. You know, you two can't just drive up and down the state every day."

I'd expected this. "Why not? It was a nice drive, wasn't it, Cecil?"

"Yeah, it was. I could get used to it."

"You guys are regular comedians," Ray said.

"Am I hearing you right Ray?"

"Yes. Two medical groups and two Health Plans. One in the north and one in the south."

"And just why would we want that?"

"Because…" Ray paused. "Because to prosper and grow we need to make our own decisions. We can't call up to Oakland for every little thing."

"But size matters," Cecil said. "Too small and you'll be inefficient and costly. Too large and you'll be inefficient and costly. That's exactly what the Health Plan wants, to splinter us into smaller groups so they can control us. One thing's for sure, they'll never agree to more than one Health Plan."

"Size matters, huh?" Ray said. "I'll show you what happens when the Health Plan is in control. One word. Chaos. Excuse my French, but it's fucking chaos."

# CHAPTER 29

Hollywood

November 6, 1948

Ray pointed to an empty spot along Sunset Boulevard in the heart of Hollywood. "Park over there."

"I thought the clinic was four blocks from here," Cecil said.

"It is. We're lucky to park this close."

I opened the door and got out of my air conditioned Kaiser Fraser sedan. It was like stepping into a furnace. "How hot is it? Feels like over a hundred."

"Heat wave," Ray said. "A Santa Ana. It's been hot and windy. Take a look up there." He gestured to the hills in the distance where a huge lettered sign spelled 'OLLYWOOD.' "So windy, the 'H' in the Hollywood sign blew over yesterday. Things are falling apart around here…but that's nothing compared to what you're about to see."

"C'mon," I said. "It can't be all that bad."

"Kids just got out of school a few weeks ago and every one of them is swimming in a community pool." Ray wiped his forehead with a handkerchief. "Four polio cases yesterday. All under ten. It's that bad."

"Are all these cars from clinic patients?" Cecil asked. There wasn't a parking space on either side of Sunset Boulevard.

"It's worse during the week," Ray said. "You should see it when people are working at those office buildings across the street. And there're a lot of patients that take the bus."

I thought Ray was exaggerating until I saw a line of people standing in front of the two-story brick-fronted clinic.

He shook his head. "We had to convert the waiting area to exam rooms. You'll see."

We walked past the line of patients and entered a scene that reminded me of my busiest day at LA County. Babies crying, children fidgeting, adults sweating. The room smelled of soiled diapers and antiseptic. Every inch of space was packed with people waiting to be seen or sprawled on gurneys.

"How many staff working?" Cecil asked.

"Three doctors, four nurses, a lab runner, and a scared intern." Ray's eyes met mine. "That's all I've been able to hire."

I glanced around the room. "Well, you have six doctors, now."

"Dr. Kay, we've been trying to reach you," the nurse said. "I think it's a heart attack."

"Get the lab runner. I want an EKG now!" He turned to us. "You two make yourselves useful."

"I'll take the GI problem in there," Cecil said. "I can smell it from here." As surgeons that was one thing we were used to treating.

"Doctor," another nurse said, "a child in room 4 is having trouble breathing."

I knocked on the door and went inside. For a second I thought I was seeing double. Two girls, about seven, obviously identical twins, lay on the exam table next to each other, their mother standing behind them, her face twisted with concern.

"Hi, Mrs...." I glanced down at the clipboard with the vital signs. "Lake, I'm Dr. Garfield." I gently felt the foreheads of the girls. "Which one of you is Leslie and which is Laura?"

"I'm Leslie." One of the girls propped herself up on an elbow and managed a slight smile. Both were blonde, blue eyed, skinny as rails, and chalky white.

"And you must be Laura." The other girl lay still, looking scared to death.

"I told my sister not to take the girls to the pool," Mrs. Lake said. "I told her." She clenched her fists so hard, her knuckles turned white.

"They were both at the same pool?"

"Yes, a week ago," she said. "Heavens, you'd think she didn't have a brain in her head. I don't know why I let her talk me into it. She just loves the girls, but she lives...well, not in the best part of town."

"She took us to the nice pool, Mama," Leslie said. "Not the dirty one."

"Well, let me take a look at Laura. Open your mouth for me, will you sweetie?" She didn't cry as I pushed her tongue down with a wooden blade and aimed the flashlight at the back of her throat. Her tonsils were normal, no swelling or redness. I felt her neck for enlarged lymph nodes and listened to her chest. Both normal. Nothing to explain her labored breathing. "Okay, Laura, squeeze my fingers." She gripped my fingers with both hands, maybe a little weak, but all right. "Now lift your legs." She didn't move.

"Laura," Mrs. Lake said, "listen to the doctor. Lift your legs, honey."

"I can't." I could see the terror in her face. Even at seven, she understood perfectly well what polio was. Over 58,000 kids in the U.S. had come down with polio this year and a third were paralyzed. Visions of a wheelchair, never walking again, living inside one of those monster iron lung machines. She knew.

"Mrs. Lake, I need to do a spinal tap to find out what's wrong."

"Is it…you know, is it?"

She didn't want to scare the girls by saying the word *polio*. "I'll be right back with one of the nurses to help."

Outside the room, the line had grown longer. People coughing, wheezing, more babies crying. "Hey, Sid, can you lend me a hand in here?" It was Cecil with the GI bleeder in the next room. Even from twenty feet away there was the unmistakable smell of blood and vomit. The man's face was the blue-gray of shock. He was sitting up in bed, holding a large metal basin full of bright red blood and clots. "Get me the largest nasogastric tube you can find and plenty of ice," Cecil said.

With the help of a nurse that looked as if she hadn't slept in a month, I found a large bore rubber tube and filled a bucket with ice.

I handed him the rubber tube. "Mr. Pillsbury, I'm going to need you to swallow this," Cecil said. The man's eyes widened at the sight of the long hose. "It'll make you want to gag, but it will help me stop the bleeding. Now open your mouth wide." Cecil pushed the tube into his mouth and with his bare fingers guided it down the back of his throat into the esophagus. He wretched and gagged, spitting blood onto my clothes and face.

When the twenty-four inch mark was even with the patient's front teeth, Cecil stopped.

"Okay, you hold it, I'll irrigate." I filled a glass syringe with ice water and pumped it into his stomach. I aspirated serum and clots into the syringe, expelled the blood into the basin, filled the syringe again with ice water and repeated the lavage, this time the blood turning pinker and free of clots.

"It's working, Mr. Pillsbury," I reassured him after the fifth lavage, the syringe bringing back only small traces of blood. "You're going to be fine."

"Thanks, Sid," Cecil said. "I'll stay and watch him."

Blood covered my white shirt and coat as I went back into the hallway, looking for a nurse. "LP tray? Where's the—" She pointed to a cabinet and rushed to another room.

I grabbed the lumbar puncture tray and returned to room 4. Inside, Laura was having a harder time breathing. "Mrs. Lake, I'm going to need you to hold her on her side for me."

With Laura positioned that way, her back flexed, I counted the bony protuberances of her backbone to find the space between L4 and 5, the intervertebral place to insert the spinal needle. "Okay, you'll feel a little sting," I said as I injected the Novocain to numb the skin. I guided the four-inch-long needle between the vertebrae and felt the slight pop of the membrane as it entered the spinal canal. Lauren trembled but didn't utter the slightest whimper. I aspirated back on the syringe. Dammit. Instead of the normal water-clear spinal fluid, it emerged the milky color of infection. Polio.

Mrs. Lake must have read my expression, I'd never perfected a poker face either in cards or around my patients. She turned and wiped her eyes.

"I'll be right back after I run some tests."

I found Ray reading an EKG strip of paper and held up the test tube. "Where's the lab?"

"It's—"

One of the physicians on duty, dressed in filthy scrubs, his name tag identifying, Michael Palmer, MD, slammed a clipboard against the table. "I quit," he yelled over a crying baby nearby. "I haven't had a break in two days. This prepaid system of yours is failing fast. I didn't sign up for this shit." He turned on his heels and slammed the front door behind him.

"Dr. Kay," the nurse said. "Dr. Palmer didn't finish…there's a man with a scalp wound and it's bleeding pretty bad."

"I'll do it," I said.

"Let me see that test tube." Ray held it up to the light. "Shit, another kid with polio."

I nodded. "This is a strange one, though. Identical twins. Only one is sick and both were in the same pool."

"There was an article on that," Ray said, "God, I can't remember where. Take care of the scalp. It'll come to me."

I picked up the clipboard and walked in the room. "Mr. Patterson, I'm Dr. Garfield."

He held an ice pack on his head, blood running down his neck. "What kind of a place is this?" he asked. "That last doctor started cussing at me and ran out of here. Christ, this is the last place I want to be. Now, are you going to help me or —"

"Yes, yes, of course. Sorry about that." I sutured up the scalp wound in less than five minutes. Part of me was angry at Palmer for walking out on us, the other part relieved that a doctor who could abandon his patient was no longer part of our group.

"*JAMA*, last week," Ray said in the hall.

"What?"

"The article on polio I was telling you about. By a Dr. Jonas Salk. Talked about developing a vaccine using antibodies from people who recovered from polio."

"People immune…you thinking what I'm thinking? Huh, Ray?"

He nodded. "You sure they're identical twins?"

"They're identical all right."

"You realize some might call this experimenting."

I thought of Mike and how he wouldn't have made it if I'd listened to Dean Keating. And I thought of Mark Sullivan and how he'd lived in an iron lung for months. "C'mon, Ray. Doctors are spraying worthless crap up kids' noses, thinking it will stop them from getting polio and half of them lose their sense of smell and still get it. Without trying, she'll have little hope."

"Okay, but we'll do this right. We'll draw serum samples from both sisters every twelve hours, freeze them and send them off for study."

"That's the only way I'd do it." I gripped the test tube in my hand. "Maybe we'll finally be able to make a difference."

Ray and I grabbed a rack of test tubes and two twenty cc syringes. I knocked on the door again and asked Mrs. Lake to step outside, leaving the door open so we could watch and make sure Laura was stable. "This is Dr. Kay, Mrs. Lake. I'm sorry, but we're both sure that Laura has polio."

She squeezed her eyes tight as if wishing she could disappear. "Is there anything you can do?"

"Maybe," I said. "But it's something that's never been tried before." I explained to her briefly about how polio is caused by a virus and how the body makes antibodies to kill viruses. "Leslie must have antibodies in her system… that's the only way to explain why she isn't sick."

"I don't understand."

Ray put down the test tubes on a small table next to the girls. "We can use Leslie's serum, her blood, to transfer antibodies to Laura. Like a blood transfusion."

"Can it make Leslie sick?" Mrs. Lake asked.

"No, maybe just a little weak for a day or so. But it can't hurt her. And if we're right, Laura could get better."

"Yes, please. Please doctors. Try it, try anything. But—"

"You have a question?" I asked.

"I can't pay right now," she said.

"It's all covered," Ray said. "You owe us nothing."

*"Doctor, I can't pay you now, but I promise—" My father begs.*

*"Sorry. There is the Charity Hospital." Foster slams the door.*

Both girls were brave, neither crying as we withdrew Leslie's blood and injected it into Laura.

"Should we transfer her to the hospital?" Ray asked.

I looked outside at the line of patients still waiting to be seen. "Why don't we watch her for a while?" I said. "Looks like we could be here all night."

At two a.m., we were down to our last patient. Exhausted, I peeked through the door to exam room 4. One of the girls was fast asleep, the other sitting up, dangling her legs over the edge of the table. Mrs. Lake had tears streaming down her face. I did a double take to make sure the girl was sleeping. She was. Breathing soft and smooth. "Leslie," I said to the girl sitting up, "you did a brave thing to help your sister."

The girl smiled—a radiant smile even without her two permanent front teeth. "I'm not Leslie," she said. "I'm Laura."

It was the miracles in medicine that made everything else—the hours, the politics, the backstabbing—worth it. Ray appeared at the door. "Sid, you okay?"

"You have that article from *JAMA*?"

"Yeah, why?"

"I'd like to put in a call to Dr. Salk. Look at Laura."

"Amazing," Ray said. "No, it's unbelievable."

I nodded. "It means serum antibodies can immediately kill the polio virus and stop paralysis before it has a chance to take hold. We have some valuable serum samples to send him."

He looked over at the girls, both now sitting up. "I'll be damned. C'mon outside for a minute, will you, Sid? We need to talk."

We left through the rear door, a warm Santa Ana wind blowing in from the Mojave Desert, where it all began. The scent of desert sage filled my head and then vanished like a mirage on a hot asphalt road. I looked up at the mountains. Someone had fixed the 'H' and the lights of the Hollywood sign twinkled in the clear night air.

"Sid?"

"Yeah."

"We were lucky today."

I nodded.

"You know," Ray said, "before we can save the world, we need to save ourselves."

"What do you mean?"

"C'mon, Sid, don't play dumb. We just took care of a few hundred patients without the proper facilities or staff. My doctors are quitting on me, I can't hire good ones because of the workload. Hell, you know as well as I do, one of two things will happen, and I'm not about to do anything that compromises quality of care."

"Neither am I, Ray. That's one thing I'll never skimp on. I know how bad things have gotten. It's almost as bad up north. I'm setting up a meeting with

Kaiser and the Board at Henry's place in Lake Tahoe. I want you to come. We need to make sure we have the right facilities and staff before we enroll one more patient."

"Okay," Ray said. "I'll be there. Let's just hope it's not too late."

## CHAPTER 30

### Santa Barbara

## December 4, 1948

Henry waved me over. "Sid, let me help you with that bow tie."

"I got it, I got it."

"For a surgeon, you're all thumbs. No Best Man of mine is going to have a crooked tie. Now hold still, for God's sake."

No use. Better let him do it. His fingers went around my neck and my tie was in perfect harmony with my tuxedo in less than ten seconds.

Henry, standing in front of a mirror in the men's room at the Biltmore Hotel in Santa Barbara, fiddled with his own tie.

"Is this all about what we discussed years ago on the plane to Chicago?"

"Of course," he said. "I'm following my own advice. And believe it or not, Bess, God Bless her, told me to marry Allie if anything ever—she knew I couldn't live alone for long. Now what about you? Have you seen Victoria today? Both she and Allie look ravishing." He laughed, deep and raspy from the bottom of his throat.

"Yes, she does. Look, Henry, we need to talk about the program. We're growing faster than we have staff. And frankly, it's compromising quality. And—"

"Sid, Sid. It's my wedding day. Can't this wait?"

Outside, it was a brilliant, picture perfect day without any moisture in the air to obstruct the Pacific view. The Biltmore, a Mediterranean style masterpiece with plastered pink walls, had long rows of palm trees rising like Burma Shave signs that stretched down an endless road. The wedding was small by

Kaiser standards, with less than forty friends and family in the courtyard under the early autumn sun. Many of Henry's family members and business associates, shocked by a wedding so soon after Bess' death, had refused to come.

"Let's get up there, Sid." Henry took a step, then paused. "I'm as nervous as the first time. Hell, now that I know what I'm getting myself into, maybe more."

He might have been nervous, but I was petrified as I took my position under the white canopy covered in hundreds of roses. I closed my eyes, breathed in the fragrant smell, and imagined my father next to me, wearing that same three-piece suit, telling me it was time to settle down. *My son the doctor, it's time to get married and give me some grandchildren.*

Henry whispered, "You remember the rings?"

I opened my eyes and intentionally hesitated a moment. "Rings?"

"Sid!"

"Relax, I have them."

Victoria looked breathtaking in her long pink dress. Maybe Henry was right, *and my father was right*, maybe it was time to ask Victoria out again. I extended my arm to her as she made her way to the canopy. She interlaced her fingers with mine and brushed her lips against my cheek.

The minutes flew by. A pianist played as we strode down the aisle behind Henry and Allie, everyone standing, applauding, smiling. We glided over thousands of yellow rose petals, lining the path from the ceremony to the restaurant Henry had rented for the night. I cringed when two newspaper reporters ambushed us just outside the reception, one with a new Kodak camera, the kind with the bulbs that allowed them to work indoors as well.

"Dr. Garfield, is it true that Miss Chester is pregnant? That's the reason for the rush to get—"

Victoria interceded. "Why gentlemen, I'm the only Miss Chester and no, I'm not pregnant," she said warmly, then added, "yet."

The camera flashed and momentarily blinded me.

"As her sister, then, do you know why she'd—?"

"Because they love each other." She took my arm as another bulb flashed. "Is there any other reason to get married?"

"Come on, now. The age difference, and only three months after his wife died, I mean—"

Henry and Allie caught up with us. "Gentlemen, please. This is a private party. But I'll answer your questions anyway. I'm in my sixties. I don't have the time to do what a young person does. I'll always love Bess, but I'm in love with my new wife. I'll be a sweeter, simpler, and more useful person because of her. We'll pose for one more photo if you leave us after." He shook both the reporters' hands. One more photo and they tipped their hats and left.

Side by side, the four of us strode into the Biltmore's restaurant. "My, aren't we the perfect couples," he said.

"Henry, we do need to talk," I said.

"Not now. After my honeymoon. We'll meet up in Tahoe. Until then, I'm sure you can keep things going."

# CHAPTER 31

Oakland

December 31, 1948

"Dear Sid:

Last night I was disturbed when you remarked to me that you had nothing to do and no longer controlled anything. I know, I was gone on my honeymoon for two weeks and I promised to talk to you about the program. Now that I'm back, I looked up the records of the last hospital meetings on December 5, 1948, and find from the charts and resolutions that you are—

1. Executive Director, The Kaiser Foundation
2. Executive Director, Kaiser Foundation Hospitals
3. Regional Director, Southern California Region Kaiser Foundation Hospitals
4. Executive Director, Kaiser Foundation Health Plan
5. Regional Director, Southern California Region Kaiser Foundation Health Plan
6. President-Trustee, Kaiser Foundation School of Nursing
7. Executive Vice-President, Kaiser Foundation Northern Hospitals
8. Executive Director, The Utah Permanente Hospital

And in addition Personal Physician to Henry J. Kaiser.

Too bad, Sid, you have nothing to do and don't control anything! It looks to me like I'll have to find something else for you to do as these duties apparently are not enough. I'll have you fix my foot in the morning.

All my love.

Henry J. Kaiser

P.S. Should you be neglecting any of these responsibilities, you might advise me."

The letter was Henry's way of telling me that I was no different than him. That I hated having anyone else in charge just as much as he did. There could only be one boss and I'd never been good at delegating or taking orders. Even Dean Keating would have agreed with me on that. I loved taking care of patients and I loved running the group. The problem was, we were too big now for me to run alone and the disharmony in the group was partly my fault.

I put Henry's letter down, smiling at his sense of humor. After eight p.m. on New Years' Eve, I sat in my office, finishing off my charts for the day. I had an hour before Henry's party and Victoria was meeting me there. I scribbled a note on the chart of Mrs. Randall, a forty-six-year-old woman with gallstones.

"Sid, old boy."

No one talked in that preppy "old boy" way except for one person I knew. "Chandler? What brings you to the enemy camp so late?"

"Touché, old buddy. I knew you'd still be working on New Years' Eve. Mind if I sit?"

"Go ahead. I swear we're not advertising, we haven't hired any unlicensed physicians, no one was turned away from our ER—"

"Sid…I'm here because I need your help."

I closed the chart and looked up at him. He was beginning to show his age. A little too much around the middle and too ruddy in the cheeks from alcohol. But he still had that tan, a full head of dark hair meticulously brushed back, and he was still married to Judy. "Sid, did you hear me?"

I nodded. "My help? With what?"

"A patient I want to discuss with you."

"Okay. But I'm surprised you came to me."

I noticed the manila X-ray envelope in his right hand. He handed two of the films to me. I got up from behind my desk and snapped them on the view box above the file cabinet. It was hard to miss the abnormal shadow on the top of the right lung. "Apical thickening, here." I pointed to the first of the two. "Much larger on the second one. What's the date on these?"

"Six months apart." He hadn't bothered to get up, just sat there staring at the wall while squeezing some of his newly sagging neck skin between his thumb and index finger.

"The first could have been old TB, but the second…well, something's definitely growing here." My office phone rang. "Just a sec."

"Do you want me to leave?"

"No, no. Stay. Hello?"

Henry sounded buoyant as always. "I talked to a friend of mine in Washington. Seems the draft board was under pressure. Some old Medical Society friends of yours called in favors."

"They never give up trying, do they? But getting me drafted... well—"

Chandler straightened in his chair, looking nervous.

Henry laughed. "Nothing in Washington happens by chance. Hell, you're not even forty. I'm almost seventy, why not draft me? I told them they had their choice of fighting Henry Kaiser or the AMA. Happy New Years, Sid. Consider yourself undrafted."

I gripped the phone. Even though we'd been arguing over control of the medical group for months, Henry still did everything he could to help me. "Henry, I can't thank you enough."

"Well, don't thank me yet. But there is one thing," he said in a conspiratorial tone.

"What?"

"Allie's wondering what's going on with you and Victoria. What's it going to take for you get together again? What better time than tonight's party?"

I laughed. "Henry, you know what a yenta is?" I was on my feet, Chandler fidgeting in his chair. "Can I call you back? I have another doctor in my office. We're going over some X-rays."

"Of course, Sid. But, promise me you won't be late."

"Don't worry."

"Sid," Henry said.

"I'll be there by nine." I hung up.

"They drafted you again?" Chandler asked.

"Yeah, you know anything about it?"

"Sid, we're old friends."

"Old friends." I nodded. "Sure." His eyes met mine and for the first time I realized what was really going on. "These are your X-rays?"

He nodded.

I flicked off the view box. It took guts for Chandler to come see me. He had to know my first reaction would be to tell him to take a hike. But he knew me too well; I couldn't abandon him or anyone who needed my help. Not like Foster had done to my mother. "It's the cigarettes, you know."

"Why?" Chandler asked.

"Why? Because there's evidence they cause cancer. I know the cigarette companies want you to think they're as healthy as apple pie." I tried to think how I'd feel if I were in his shoes. "What can I do to help?"

"I want you—*you*—to operate on me." He sat there, unmoving, his face without expression.

"At Permanente hospital?"

"I know how big an ass I've been to you over the years. But, I've...uh, done my homework. Permanente has the best cancer outcomes in town. And Sid, I know you. You'll do anything for your patients; you never give up. Remember that blood transfusion? Well, I need a little of that...that Garfield stubbornness now. You've seen the X-rays. Without you, I don't stand a chance."

I pointed to the right upper lung mass. "You know we might have to take the innominate artery. Which means you could have a stroke or embolism or worse."

"I still remember my anatomy," Chandler said. "I'm already dying, there's nothing worse."

"What does Judy say about this?"

He looked down. "I haven't told her."

"What?"

"We haven't been close in years. She's thinking of becoming a stewardess. She's always loved flying and they're looking for nurses. God knows we have enough money...she just says she wants to travel. Hell, it'll be best for both of us if she's not around at the end."

I said nothing.

"You need to know something else before you agree to operate on me."

"Go on."

"The reason Judy married me."

His words knocked the air out of me. "What are you talking about?"

"C'mon, Sid. She was in love with you. You must have thought there was something...some reason she'd marry me. Well, there was." He stared down at his hands as he talked. "My family ruined her father. We bought an area near Palm Springs called La Quinta that he was trying to develop. He'd spent everything he had getting the county approvals, the engineering reports…then we outbid him. He went bankrupt. The deal…well, the deal was I gave it back to him as a wedding present. I'm sorry."

Knowing the truth after all these years made the reality of what happened no easier to bear. I remembered that night I'd gone to her apartment, her words to me: "*I waited months to even kiss you and then I cried that night because I thought I was going to lose you.*"

She'd agreed to the bargain; he hadn't tied her up and forced her. She'd been the one that was bought and sold. I hoped the deal had made her father happy. I studied Chandler, his face beginning to show the early ravages of cancer, the look of sadness or guilt or maybe only self-pity. I'd never know. In the background I heard music blaring from somewhere across the Bay. "You want me to operate even though the Board is still trying to take away my license?"

He looked down. "I'll do what I can, you know that."

"No, I don't want you to do anything. If I operate on you, it's for one reason only. And that's to help you. There is only one string attached."

"What?"

"You'll have to become a Kaiser member."

"Will they take me?"

"We take everyone."

# CHAPTER 32

## Oakland

## January 2, 1949

"Tell me again how he talked you into operating on him?" Cecil looked at me above his OR mask with an expression that said I was out of my damn mind.

"Concentrate on the surgery." It was twice as hard to operate on someone you didn't like compared to someone you cared for. How do you reassure yourself you did everything if you let feelings get in the way? We'd finished cracking the chest and had the self-retaining rib retractors in place.

"Looks like the ballgame is over," Cecil said. "Pleural mets. Let's close."

Covering the lining of the lungs were at least a dozen pea-sized tumors. The cancer had already spread from inside out. Poor guy. Even Chandler didn't deserve to go this way.

"We can resect the pleura along with the tumor."

"Give it up, Sid. You might be able to take out the visible ones, but we both know there are cancer cells everywhere that will grow back within the month."

I ran my gloved finger over the firm lump as Chandler's lungs rose and fell under my hand. Chandler was right about one thing. I wasn't going to give up on him. "Get Goldstein in here," I said to the nurse. "Tell him we need him now."

"Goldstein, the radiologist?" Cecil clamped one of the intercostal arteries, running along the split second rib. "Sid, you don't need an X-ray to tell us his chest is full of tumor."

I shook my head. "You've been watching too much Milton Berle. You ever read your journals?"

"Funny. Can you quit the jokes and put a tie on this vessel?"

I placed a knot and the oozing stopped. "There was a case report from Mayo. Just like Chandler here. They did a radiation implant and the patient's still alive at a year."

Cecil cut the silk suture above the knot. "What the hell is a radiation implant?"

"Just like it sounds. We sew catheters all around the tumor, then —"

Goldstein, dressed in scrubs a few sizes too small, came wheezing into the OR. He looked at the open chest. "Shit. It's worse than the X-ray."

"You know anything about radiation implants?" I asked.

"Sure, read about them. Wait a minute, you're not thinking..."

"Yeah, I am. You have a better idea?"

"Okay. Let me get this right." Goldstein scratched his nose under his mask. Something a surgeon could never do while gloved. "You, Sidney Garfield, the same Sidney Garfield who used to make us turn in pencil stubs, wants me to order radioactive gold to implant into this doctor who for years has done his best to put us out of business?"

"Yeah, Irwin, that's exactly what I want you to do." I stared at Chandler's cancerous lung. "I want you to order the gold."

"That's enough pencils for a few thousand years," he said.

"Go order it. When will it be here?"

"We're lucky. Berkeley has the stuff from Livermore. I'll have it first thing in the a.m. You sure?"

I nodded. "What size catheters you need?"

Goldstein shrugged. "Never done one. I don't know, at least 20 French. How many you going to put in?"

"They did three back in Mayo." I looked at Goldstein. "Get four."

"Okay, you're the boss." Goldstein stopped at the door. "Remind me to come to you if I'm ever a hopeless case."

With Goldstein out of the OR, I glanced at Cecil. "I know what you're thinking. But you know as well as I do, we skimp on pencils not patients."

"Hey, especially ones married to..."

That surprised me. He'd guessed my thoughts.

"I'm sorry, Sid. What are we going to use for catheters?"

"NG tubes." I looked at the circulating nurse. "Liz, open up four sterile nasogastric tubes, 20 French in diameter."

She nodded and went to the back hall to get them.

"You ready to take this thing out?"

Cecil nodded. "Looks like it's right up against the innominate artery."

"Abutting, but hopefully not invading. We'll need to take the subclavian vein though. It's right in the middle of the tumor."

"Your lead," Cecil said.

I extended my palm. "Scissors, please."

It took four hours to get the primary tumor and pleural mets out. We fed the catheters between the ribs and directly overlying the surface of the involved lung. "Do me a favor, will you Cecil?"

"Sure." I knew he still felt bad about his remark. "Can you stay with Chandler tonight in the ICU? Kaiser invited me to dinner. Victoria will be there. Maybe it's time to start dating her again."

"I didn't know you wanted to," he said.

"Neither did I, until now. Look at Chandler here. Top of the world a few weeks ago. Now…well, like they say, life's too short."

Henry Kaiser's mansion in Lafayette Park, a few miles from downtown Oakland, was big enough to fit three, maybe four of my original Desert Center hospitals. What Bess had decorated in dark, muted colors, Allie livened up with flowers, pastels, and the latest silks from Asia.

I knocked and Ida Washington answered the door. "Evening, Dr. Sid."

She led me to the living room, and I felt dwarfed by the thirty-foot ceiling. Victoria gave me a kiss and a warm hug. A towering Christmas tree, trimmed with gold ornaments and ribbon, reminded me of the Kaisers' New Years' Eve party a few nights before.

"Hello, Sid." Her eyes were questioning, unsure.

"Sid, you look beat." Henry held out a glass of champagne. "How about something to drink?"

"Thanks, but I had enough on New Years' Eve to last me for a while. And

I'm going back to the ICU later so I'd better stick to coffee."

"Okay." Henry put his right arm around me and his left around Victoria. "What's it going to take to get you two together?"

I felt the blood rush to my face. "Henry, I appreciate what you're doing. But this is between Victoria and me."

"Sid's right, dear." Allie said. "We shouldn't butt in."

"Then, listen to my offer." He tightened his arm around my shoulder. "Sid, you two need some time away from here. I'll order you a volcano just like at Trader Vic's...only in Honolulu. I've arranged a little vacation for all of us next week. You game?"

"If Victoria wants to—"

"Dr. Sid," Ida called from the hallway. "Dr. Cutting's on the phone. Says it's urgent."

Knowing instantly that something had gone wrong with Chandler, I hurried to the phone. "Cecil?"

"Chandler's thrown a massive pulmonary embolus. Most likely a saddle one."

Which meant a giant blood clot had blocked off the flow to Chandler's lungs. "Is he on heparin?"

"Yes, of course. It did nothing. He's non-responsive. Sorry, Sid, I don't—"

"Goddammit, don't say it. Take him to the OR now. We're going in after it."

"That never works, you know—"

"Cecil, *now*."

I returned to the living room. "Emergency. Sorry."

Shortly after, I was in my scrubs and hustling through the OR to room three. Cecil had the chest sutures out and the retractors in. He looked up at me. "This is nuts, you know. He won't make it off the table alive."

I snapped on a pair of gloves. "Feel there." I squeezed the pulmonary artery and felt the rock-hard clot between my fingers.

"Give me the scalpel." I couldn't keep the edge off my voice. I sliced into the artery and saw the purple clot that may have already killed Chandler.

"Suction...no, two suctions. Frasor tips, full bore." I started sucking on the clot. "Shit, it's too long." I made another incision eight inches lower. This time, blood shot up and soaked my mask.

"Pressure. Cecil. Hold your finger. Nurse, I need a Fogarty." She looked at me blankly. "Fogarty, balloon catheter."

"Sorry, I've never seen one," she said.

There wasn't time to search for anything. It had been at least ten minutes with minimal oxygen going to Chandler's brain. Chances were, it didn't matter. I grabbed one of the NG catheters we'd placed a few hours ago for the radiation implants and yanked it out of the chest. "Hook this up to suction." I ran it through the upper artery incision, suctioning out the jelly-like clot until blood shot up, soaking the OR light and giving the room a red glow.

"I'm not getting a pulse." I hadn't noticed the anesthesiologist, Stan Adams until he spoke. "Pressure's...dammit, can't get a pressure."

"Cecil, clamp off the aorta," I ordered.

"What?"

"You heard me. Clamp it."

I reached into the chest, pushed aside the left lung and started squeezing directly on Chandler's heart. Cecil looked at me like I'd gone mad.

"Getting anything?"

"Maybe...maybe." Adams had his stethoscope in his ears and was tapping on the blood pressure gauge. "Maybe."

"Okay, release as I push on his heart," I told Cecil. "His brain needs some blood flow."

He let go of the clamp and blood oozed out as I squeezed his heart as hard as I could.

Cecil put a gloved hand on mine. "He's gone Sid. There's nothing more you can do."

Chandler's heart was flaccid in my hands. Not a hint of a beat. Half his blood covered the OR, along with soaking me and everyone else in the room.

I looked at Cecil, the OR crew and at Chandler's lifeless body. I'd disliked Chandler since the first day we'd met in residency. He was selfish, self-centered, with an ego that...why was I feeling this way? I'd lost patients before. He was dying of cancer after all. *But he was my patient.* And no matter what, he had deserved everything I could do for him.

Under the bright OR lights, Chandler looked pale, like a dime store mannequin. Sweat ran down my face and I rushed out of the OR feeling as though I was about to lose everything I'd eaten for the past year. I needed fresh air, but I had to stop…stop just in case Judy was in the waiting room. For the first time since we'd met, I was hoping she wouldn't be there.

I walked into the waiting room, Cecil's words still ringing in my head. *There's nothing more you can do.* Judy, wearing a powder blue Pan Am uniform, leaned against the counter.

For a moment we stood in silence, though I'm sure she knew. "I'm sorry, Judy. I tried. I really tried."

She looked at me with the eyes that had haunted my dreams for almost twenty years. Then she wrapped her arms around me and held me. What I felt for her, I'd never felt for Victoria. Was it fair to either of us? Seconds, minutes, I wasn't sure. Then she moved back slightly, her uniform covered in her husband's blood. She gazed at me not with grief or sorrow or forgiveness, but with understanding. No tears, no sobs. I looked into her eyes, the darkness of her pupils engulfing me.

She pulled away and stared through me. "I knew he was dying and I hoped he would come to you."

I felt a chill, a sad finality.

"Thank you," she said. Then she kissed me on the cheek and was gone.

# CHAPTER 33

Sacramento

## May 20, 1949

Cecil drove up Highway 5, while I re-read for the tenth time Section 2392 of the Business and Professions Code. Cooper v. State Medical Board. Moran v. State Medical Board. My appeal before the California Medical Board was at nine a.m. and I was scared as hell.

I looked down at the papers on my lap. Staring at the pages without my reading glasses, unable to think, my vision started to blur. I'd use every bit of instinct and intuition to keep my license. Every bit and more. I wouldn't let these bastards win. We rode in silence for at least half an hour.

Cecil glanced at me as he turned into the parking lot. "Sid, you'll keep your license. I know it."

I didn't answer.

The courthouse clock chimed nine and my heart raced at ten times that number. The California Medical Association's boardroom, where these hearings were normally held, was under construction and they'd rented the main courtroom on the fourth floor of the Sacramento County Courthouse. I went inside first, followed by Cecil and my attorney. The elevated judge's bench, the gold seal of the State of California, the formal carved wood pillars—all made me feel like a criminal on trial.

"Hey, Doc!" Mike Everett, my old friend and patient, gave me a thumbs up.

"We're here for you, Doc." In front of Mike sat Mark Sullivan, the teenager who'd recovered from polio. I looked around; of the hundred or so seats, at least half were filled with former patients smiling, waving, hoisting their thumbs. The fist that had gripped my throat the moment I'd walked into the court started to loosen and I took in my first real breath. I thought of the surgeries I'd done on these people and the days afterward, rounding on them in the hospital, encouraging them to get out of bed and get well. Now the tables were turned and they were here supporting me.

I shook hands with a few patients, but couldn't come up with the right words to tell them how much their being here meant to me.

"Thanks…thank you…I appreciate you…" I was rambling and I knew it. I might be a good surgeon, but I was definitely not good at finding words at times like this. No matter what else happened, this was one of the proudest moments of my life.

I whispered to Cecil, "You knew about this?"

"I'm as surprised as you are." He suppressed a smile.

"Sure you are."

I reached the front table and sat down. My attorney, William O'Brien, bifocals perched on his nose, three-piece suit hanging off his thin frame, sat next to me and shuffled through papers. "O'Brien may not look like much," Henry had said, "but he's fearless, ruthless, and smart, three qualities that the opposing side will quickly learn to hate."

Paul Foster smashed his cigarette into an ashtray and tapped the microphone in front of him. "Let's get this started. Will everyone please take their seats? There will be no talking during the proceedings." The four other members of the State Medical Board flanked him. Foster cleared his throat and continued in his raspy smoker's voice. "I'm going to first summarize the facts in this case."

Sandwiched between Cecil and O'Brien, I shifted uncomfortably in my seat and looked back at the crowd for reassurance. The first row was lined with reporters, busily scrawling. An article on a doctor stripped of his license sold papers. The rest of the courtroom had its smattering of County Medical Society doctors, twenty or so staff from Permanente, and, of course, my former patients. I thought of a sports team with its hometown fans yelling for a home run or touchdown and hoped that, with so many supporters, I'd have the same home field advantage. But instead of the smell of hot dogs and popcorn, the room reeked of sour cigarette smoke and pungent furniture polish.

"The first count against Dr. Garfield is for employing unlicensed physicians, including Dr. Clifford Keene. In addition, we are charging Dr. Garfield's medical group with unprofessional conduct: advertising and solicitation of patients, placing mass production ahead of the health needs of the patients, preventing patients from having free choice of physicians, and rendering inadequate service in understaffed hospitals."

I'd heard all this before and wondered if anything would change their minds. God knows, I had the evidence on my side. I looked around the courtroom again and my gaze—and heart—stopped on a woman in the last row. *Judy.*

"Dr. Garfield, are we boring you?" Foster said. "Please face the Board while we're talking." His lips tightened. "Sidney Roy Garfield, are you aware it's unlawful to practice medicine in the State of California without a license? That the care provided by unlicensed doctors places the public in a great deal of danger?"

I asked O'Brien, "Can I answer him now?"

"This isn't a court proceeding," he said, loud enough for everyone to hear. "Go ahead."

I took a sip of water and stood. "Gentlemen," I held up our Residency Charter, "Permanente Foundation Hospital has been and still is approved by the Medical Board in the State of California to train interns and residents. All of the physicians named in count one except Dr. Keene were graduate students registered with the Board. Dr. Keene—"

Foster interrupted. "Have you considered the ramifications of your actions? We are all saddened by the death of Dwight Chandler at your hospital. And our heartfelt sorrow goes out to his wife, who is here with us today. Your gross malpractice and negligence has resulted in the loss of one of our most esteemed physicians."

"Dr. Chandler came to me because he knew our quality was second to none. He voluntarily became a member of Kaiser Permanente. I did everything possible to cure his cancer and I'm saddened by his death, but the issue today is Dr. Keene. He's Board Certified by the American College of Surgeons and has more experience than 99% of surgeons in this state—"

"Dr. Garfield," Foster snapped, "that's not the question here. Was he licensed, yes or no?"

"Yes, he was licensed in Michigan. And yes, he was a member of the American College of Surgeons. And yes, he provided the best of care."

"Dr. Garfield, I don't care if he was licensed to work at the Mayo Clinic, the issue is that he was not licensed in California. Correct, Doctor?"

"Yes." I looked at O'Brien and then at Cecil. This couldn't be going any worse. They were bringing up old news and now adding Chandler's death. I glared at Foster. The courtroom felt as hot as August in the Mojave. Sweat poured down my face. A camera flashed. *Guilty*. I looked guilty as hell. "I've shown you the evidence. We are running a certified intern and residency program. I have the call schedules, pay stubs, medical school certificates, everything to prove that your accusations are false."

Foster looked beyond me to the gallery. "Is that all, Dr. Garfield?"

"What do you mean is that all?" I opened my briefcase and took out a six-inch stack of papers. There was much more at stake here than just losing my license. A whole way of practicing medicine could be destroyed. Feeling like I was sliding helplessly toward a fall, I braced myself.

"You must consider these facts." I held up the papers to the whole room. "We've followed all the regulatory rules. We invited the California Medical Association to come to our hospital and look at comparative mortality rates. No one showed, so we completed the study ourselves. I have the results here, certified by Dr. Ray Lyman Wilbur, past president of the American Medical Association and president of Stanford University. The results show that Permanente Hospital is the best in California in overall mortality rate not only for pneumonia, but also for cases of perforated peptic ulcer, for appendicitis with peritonitis, and for childbirth, including by Caesarean section—"

Foster gripped the microphone, his fleshy face glowing red. "Bring your documents forward. Is Dr. Wilbur here today to confirm these results?"

"No, he's in Washington this week. But I'm sure he's available by phone."

Foster's chair squealed against the wood floor as he leaned forward and took my papers. He stood and pointed to one of two uniformed policemen in the first row. "Marshall, we have enough evidence now to close down Kaiser Hospital. I am instructing you to lock down Fabiola Hospital and transfer the patients to hospitals where they will be out of harm's way."

"You can't do that!" I shouted. I looked at my attorney, waiting for him to say anything. He just sat there, poker-faced.

"Just a minute." Mike Everett's voice came from the back of the courtroom.

"You are not recognized." Foster said.

"I don't give a damn!" Mike Everett shouted. "You're going to listen. None of us would be here today if it weren't for Dr. Garfield."

Foster shook his head.

"Wait! Just, wait," Mark Sullivan said. "Dr. Garfield saved my life, never gave up. Never turned his back on us as you are doing to him."

Mrs. Sullivan took out a piece of paper and began to read. "I'm Mark's mother and I have a letter signed by over two hundred of Dr. Garfield's patients demanding that the Medical Board not revoke his license."

I remembered my father's words that day back in the desert. He had looked at me like when I'd graduated high school, college, and medical school. *"I'll help you build your hospital."*

I wasn't going to let it end here. Henry and his lawyers could help, but in the end, I'd do my own fighting. My mother had died because of Foster and doctors like him. I stood up. "What you're committing today is murder."

Foster rolled his eyes.

"Our prepaid system, which you are trying so hard to destroy, has stopped the dying that happens every day when patients are too afraid to come in because they cannot pay private fees. They come to us with the first pain in their abdomen, when they first catch their colds, and we treat their appendicitis before they rupture and their pneumonia before they are terminal."

"Your arguments are not recognized here," Foster said. "And whether or not Dr. Garfield may have helped any or all of you in the past is not in question. Where is Dr. Chandler today? If it were not for Dr. Garfield, he would be here."

"That's a damn lie!" Judy walked up the aisle and stood next to me. "My husband asked Sidney Garfield to operate on him, because he knew Dr. Garfield was the best surgeon around. Because he knew Dr. Garfield would never give up, he'd do everything he could to save his life. Unlike you, Dr. Foster, Sidney

Garfield knows he's not God. His heart is where every doctor's should be. *Healing his patients.*" Sunlight slanted in, casting a triangle of light onto her face. Her eyes met mine, her half-smiling look of concern replaced by tears.

Foster banged his gavel against the table. "I'll have quiet, please. Dr. Garfield, please come forward."

I approached Foster, my mind a million miles away. *Judy.*

"Sidney Roy Garfield," Foster continued, "we find your method of taking care of patients violates the doctor-patient relationship and goes against the time-honored practices that for years have been the backbone of our Medical Societies. You have hired unlicensed physicians, unlawfully advertised, and committed gross malpractice."

I clenched my hands into fists. When I looked around, Judy was gone.

Cecil stood next to me. "She's gone, Sid. Let's see what these morons decide."

I turned my back on Foster. "Thank you all for being here," I said to my patients. "This means more to me than…well, thank you, thank all of you." They were about to rule that the last ten years of my life had been an utter waste of time. Maybe I couldn't stop them today, but I wasn't going to let them get away with it.

Foster continued: "Because of these unlawful actions, we have no choice other than to—"

"Give him his license! Give him his license!" The shouts filled the courtroom. "Give him his license!"

Foster tapped the microphone. "Quiet, now!"

O'Brien stood up and bellowed, "The Medical Board should be aware that we believe there is a conspiracy by you as individuals and the Medical Society as a whole to restrain Kaiser Permanente's practice of medicine. Your act of ordering the Deputy to close our hospital confirms this. By the laws of the State of California, we will be obligated to proceed with the dissolution of the medical associations of this state." He pointed to the front row, where a County Marshall held out four sheets of paper. "I suggest you drop this matter now. If not, we have instructed the Marshall to hand each of you a subpoena, requiring you to appear in front of a court of law to face charges of falsifying documents, libel, and defamation of character. Gentlemen, I can assure you, we will use all of the resources of Kaiser Industries to convict you, dissolve your associations and bring justice to Dr. Garfield."

"You can't pressure us," Foster snapped.

"We do not bluff, gentlemen," O'Brien said. "You will lose." He pointed to the second uniformed officer in the front row. "Marshall, can you please—"

Foster grabbed the microphone, his hands shaking. "This has gone far enough. Based on the evidence, Dr. Garfield's medical license to practice in the State of California is revoked." The four other members of the board looked at one another and nodded in agreement.

Boos resonated in the courtroom. I crumpled into my chair.

"Dr. Garfield," Foster rose and pointed at me, "we're closing *you* down. These proceedings are adjourned."

# CHAPTER 34

Lake Tahoe

## May 22, 1949

A warm afternoon wind blew in off Lake Tahoe, carrying with it the scent of a thousand pine trees. I hurried across a path covered in brown pine needles toward Henry Kaiser's great stone lodge, the centerpiece of his one-mile waterfront estate in the Sierras. Henry called it Fleur de Lac, Flower of the Lake, and like everything he did, it was bigger than life. In the distance, bulldozers roared, bringing in sand where he was trying to turn his tiny beach into Waikiki. Henry controlled everything he was involved with, business or nature. And our medical group was no exception. Kaiser Permanente, after two years of phenomenal growth, could end today and everything I'd worked for all my life would be over. Was it time to start over like I'd done back in the desert? Find a small community without a doctor, far from the clutches of the AMA or Henry, and do it on my own? I had lost my license. How much more was I willing to sacrifice for the program's survival? I clutched my briefcase, my answer inside.

I opened the double-wide front door, made of rough sawed timbers, and entered the lodge. The morning sun reflected off the lake through the multi-paned glass window, creating a haze of dust particles dancing in the rays of light. Massive wood beams arched twenty feet high and the largest antler chandelier I'd ever seen dangled from its center. Seated around the central dining room table was the future or the end of our program. Ray Kay, Morris Collen, and Cecil sat opposite Henry Kaiser, Edgar Kaiser, and Eugene Trefethen. Trefethen, a close friend of Edgar's at Berkeley, was a graduate of Harvard Business School. He'd risen through the ranks to become one of the most powerful men in Kaiser Industries. Henry surrounded himself with the best, and Trefethen, who reminded me of a young Harry Truman, worked twenty-hour days and thought four steps ahead of anyone in a chess game.

Coffee brewed on a small log table against the window. I poured myself a cup. I'd been up all night and needed to get the sour taste out of my mouth. Cecil nodded at me; everyone else looked away, afraid to face me. The worst of all arguments were family ones, and Henry and I had come to one that could lead to divorce. We'd stood through tough times together, but if my plan didn't work, we'd be split by the end of the day.

"Good morning, Sid," Cecil said. "Ray's been at it for hours."

"You're right I have," Ray Kay snapped. "We're not going to be Kaiser docs. We'll buy the hospitals if we have to. We're not going to be employees of Kaiser Industries and let Henry Kaiser tell us how to practice medicine."

"Don't challenge me." Henry pointed at Ray. "You're challenging me and I won't stand for it. Where the hell are you going to come up with twenty million dollars?"

I took a sip of coffee. Dammit, too hot. It burned as it went down and I started to cough.

"Sid, you okay?" Cecil asked.

"Yeah," I said in a thick voice.

Trefethen spoke clearly and slowly, as if lecturing a third grade classroom. "We have 400,000 members in three states. This is a business and we need to run it like a business."

"We're the ones taking care of the patients," Morris said. "We make the decisions, period. We decide who can enroll and how many to enroll. We stop playing catch-up and begin hiring enough physicians to provide the care before we take on new patients. That's the only way it can work."

"Okay, listen up," Henry said. "None of us are going to leave this room until we work out a plan. You all know how much I respect what you've done, how I respect all doctors. Let's not lose sight of why we're doing this—the patients you take care of. And the thousands more that need your care."

"Henry's right," I said. "We need—"

"Jesus, Sid," Ray interrupted. "You don't have to agree with everything he says."

"Stop it, Ray," Cecil said. "That's not fair."

"No." I held up my hand. "Maybe it is." I snapped open the briefcase and removed the pages I'd written instead of sleeping the night before.

"I've just lost my medical license and I'm not about to lose my medical group. You all hear me?"

"Where are you going with this?" Henry asked.

Trefethen nodded. "I think I know."

Edgar wiped his glasses on a cloth napkin. "Go ahead, Sid."

"When I first started, back in the desert, I'd keep all the finances myself in a single notebook. That was for 5,000 patients and it wasn't easy. Now, we need businessmen to manage the millions of dollars we're making."

"C'mon, Sid," Ray said. "I'm not about to let businessmen, no matter how good their intentions, tell me how to practice medicine."

"Let him finish," Henry said.

"Effective immediately, I'm resigning from all my administrative positions in the Health Plan, hospitals, and Medical Group." I held up a single sheet of paper.

"Good, Sidney," Henry said. "Good, it's got to be this way."

"Wait a damn minute," Cecil said. He grabbed the paper from me and hesitated as he read it. "You started this group. I won't accept your resignation."

"Cecil, I appreciate what you're saying, but it's the only way to reach a compromise. They've taken away my license and this is the only way to take the pressure off our group."

"None of us will allow you to resign," Ray agreed. "This is exactly the problem. You're letting the AMA and Henry Kaiser force you to resign."

I sipped more coffee. "I'm turning over control of the hospitals to the Board of Trustees and the Partnership to the partners because I have complete faith in all of you. Morris, Cecil, Ray, I hired you and you all feel as strongly as I do about what we're doing. If I can't trust you to run the group, then who can I trust? My resignation is the first step in working out a compromise that will keep our medical program strong."

"You're not thinking this out," Cecil said. "We need you where you are. With all due respect to Mr. Kaiser, we need someone strong enough to deal as his equal. When all is said and done, I'd rather be known as Sidney Garfield's associate than a Kaiser doc."

Trefethen shrugged, "This isn't getting us anywhere. Why don't we outline the issues, one by one?"

Henry stood abruptly. "You do that. As for your comment, Cecil, you should all be proud to be known as Kaiser docs. I've done everything to promote your program, your status, and enable you to take the best care of your patients. Now if you'll excuse us, Sid and I are going for a ride."

I looked at Henry.

"Humor me, Sid. Come on."

"Now?"

"Yes." He grabbed me by the arm. "Let them work it out without us. My bet is they'll get more done. In the meantime, I have something new to show you."

I looked over at Cecil, who nodded. "Okay, sure."

Henry strode to the front door and held it open for me. We walked down the stone path to the boat dock. Around us, two pink Permanente Cement Company bulldozers moved around piles of sand.

Henry climbed aboard his newest speedboat, a four-seater with an engine the size of a truck.

"I'll drive," he said. "You cast off."

I untied the rope and jumped in the boat, pushing us away from the dock.

"Hold on." A second later he floored the boat, his hat flying off his head, the boat roaring from the shore fast enough to knock the wind out of me.

For five minutes, Henry shoved the accelerator to max and headed to the center of the ten-mile-wide lake. He didn't look at me, just smiled into the wind like a kid taking his first bike ride. Then he stopped as suddenly as he'd started, far enough out that his estate was barely visible in the distance.

He looked at me, his smile now gone. "I'm proud of what you did today."

"Resigning?"

"It took a lot of courage to give up the most important thing in your life. How long have we known each other now? Nine years? Since I jumped off that train in Desert Center and first saw the look of pride on your face over that tiny hospital of yours, I knew we'd make a good team. I knew you were a man of integrity. One who would give up personal gain for ideals. I brought you out here to tell you that. To let them come to the same conclusion."

I met his eyes, moist from the wind, and nodded. "All last night, I tried to think of another way. Any other way. There wasn't one. It came down to me or you. And that made the choice simple. Kaiser Permanente can't survive without Henry Kaiser, but it will do just fine without Sidney Garfield."

Henry shrugged. "I'm sorry, Sid. But, we're too close. The physicians don't trust you anymore, thinking you're working for the 'boss' and losing your independence, since many of my ideas have rubbed off on you, just as yours have rubbed off on me."

"Cecil and Ray will come to the same conclusion. They probably did, a minute after I walked out of the room."

Henry leaned over and did something he'd never done before. He hugged me, like a father would his son. Then, he held me at arms length and nodded. "I'm proud of all we've accomplished together, Sid. And what we'll continue to accomplish. This isn't the end of your involvement, just a change, a new beginning. Change is the hardest thing in the world to come to grips with. I have us booked on a plane tomorrow to Washington. We're meeting with the Secretary of Health, Education, and Welfare. I promise you this, Sid. We'll get your license back and bury the AMA. What do you say we head home?"

He engaged the throttle, the boat hurtling forward. Then he whipped it around, sending us airborne as we hit our own wake and bumped hard over and over.

Back on shore, we walked in silence to the lodge, listening to the soft lapping of the water against the new white sand. Inside, Trefethen stood in front of the group again. I opened the door for Henry and we both stepped inside.

"I call it the Medical Service Agreement," he said, holding a stack of papers up. "A simple compromise that will act as our constitution for years to come."

"Listen to this, Sid," Cecil said. "I think we have something here."

"The Health Plan will be responsible for collecting revenue and providing facilities and equipment. The Medical Group will be the sole provider of care. Dr. Collen will be the Medical Director of The Permanente Medical Group in the north and Dr. Kay the Medical Director of the Southern California Permanente Medical Group. There are some more specifics about compensation, net revenue, and retirement funds, but this is the gist of it. Both sides acknowledge the other, both sides agree to work together."

"What do you say, Sid?" Henry asked.

"It's the only way." I looked back at Henry. "It's up to us to make the highest quality medical care affordable to all. To take this idea from California and introduce it to the rest of the country. We've fought the medical societies in the past and we'll continue to fight them—the internal squabbling ends today. Our mission is clear. The road ahead difficult. With this agreement, the new Kaiser Permanente starts today."

A feeling of finality, of an ending came over me. I stared out at the lake and in my mind saw the mirage of heat rising from the sand dunes of the Mojave.

## CHAPTER 35

Over the Pacific

December 7, 1949

A few thousand feet below, the Pacific Ocean glistened as tiny whitecaps broke toward shore. The props of the Pan Am Constellation droned in the background as we left San Francisco on our eight-hour flight to Washington. I sank back into the leather first class seat and looked over at Henry. He was downing his first martini and shoveling in a plate of fresh shrimp. I'd lectured him often on watching his calories.

"Henry, it's a long flight, you sure you want to eat so much?"

"Is this the doctor talking now? Well, if it is, thanks for the advice." He dipped another shrimp in cocktail sauce and devoured it.

"Okay, Henry, it's your body. You know, speaking of advice, remember the last time we flew together?"

"Can't say I do."

"Well, I remember. It was on that trip to Chicago. Remember Fishbein and that hat of mine?"

He laughed out loud.

"Do you remember?"

"Of course. I hope you're not going to blame me for Victoria."

"No. She's a wonderful woman, it just didn't work out between us. But you did advise me to settle down, have a family. No time to wait. Well, now I have time—"

"You'll have another chance." He gave me a fatherly look. "When Bess died, I thought my life was over. But Allie, well, I've never felt so alive. It will happen to you—you just have to meet the right woman."

"Sure. Well, if you don't mind, I think I'll concentrate on getting my license back. And forget the family thing."

"Up to you. I'll make you a deal. You stop lecturing me on food and I'll stop talking about you having a family. But work's fair game."

"What do you think the Secretary can do to help us?"

Henry gulped down his martini. "The AMA can't survive without its Washington lobby. We called Foster's bluff. O'Brien got the injunction that kept our hospitals open. Now, if we turn enough of our friends in Washington against the AMA, get the public involved, they'll have no choice."

"I hope you're right, Henry."

"I know I am. We all have to make compromises." He grabbed his stomach and winced in pain.

"Henry, you okay?"

"Yes, just a stomach cramp. Maybe you're right about eating too much."

He pushed the plate of shrimp to the corner of his tray and one of the stewardesses removed it.

"Can I get you something to drink, Dr. Garfield?" Her uniform made me think of the night that Chandler had died. Judy, wearing her powder blue Pan Am dress.

"Just a ginger ale, Miss." She smiled and made her way down the aisle.

"Henry, you sure you're okay? They have sleeping berths in the back if you want to lie down."

"No...no, I'm fine. Tahoe. We all compromised at Tahoe. The Medical Group gets exclusivity with the Health Plan and the Board of Trustees keeps control of the ownership of the hospitals. Checks and balances. How American can we get?"

The stewardess returned with my ginger ale. I thanked her and took a sip. "Yeah, I guess no one can accuse us of being un-American."

Henry shook his head. "I don't know about you, but since the McCarthy trials, I'm sick and tired of hearing about being un-American."

"Well, at least the Senator got what he deserved."

"From what I've heard in Washington," Henry said, "he's on his way out. Enough politics. You're in charge of facilities planning now until you get your license back. You like my idea about expanding to Hawaii?"

"You think we'll get enough members?"

Henry nodded. "With the ILWU and Restaurant Workers' Union, plus individual enrollments, I'd say 35 to 50,000 within a year."

"I can't get too excited about expanding until we patch things up in California."

Henry squirmed in his seat. Sweat poured down his forehead.

"Henry, what is it?"

"It's that damn cramp again. I've had it for days now. Goes through me like a knife. Don't worry, it will go away in a minute."

"I *am* worried." I signaled to the stewardess. "Can you show us to the sleeping area? Mr. Kaiser needs to lie down."

"Let me get the nurse for you," she said. "She's at her station in the rear of the plane."

"Nurse?"

"Every flight has a stewardess who's also a nurse." She headed down the aisle.

"I'm okay," Henry said. "Just let me sit here a minute."

I felt his pulse. It was racing at over one hundred. "No, Henry. You're going to listen to me."

"Can I help…oh, Sid?"

I looked up. "Judy?"

"Now, this is a coincidence." Henry winked. "Nice to see you, Judy."

"You too, Mr. Kaiser. Let's do as Sid says and let me help you to the back. It's not far, we have the first class berths right—"

"I'm better now," Henry said. "It's letting up."

"C'mon, Henry." I grabbed his right arm, Judy his left. We walked about twenty feet to the rear of the first class cabin.

"Hey, Kaiser, too much to drink?" one passenger yelled out. A few others laughed. Henry, on the verge of collapse, leaned his enormous weight on me as we stopped at a row of sleeping berths, each as large as a full-size bed and each separated by satin curtains. Judy and I helped Henry down.

"Let me feel," I said. He unbuttoned his shirt. His huge abdomen made it hard to feel a mass; it was like flying blind. "Judy, can you take his blood pressure? And we'll need an IV setup."

She nodded and rushed to the back of the plane.

"Okay, show me where it hurts."

"Right in the middle. Goes straight through to my back. C'mon, Sid, it's just indigestion. You're right, I'll start eating less."

"Maybe. Tell me if anything hurts." I pushed on the different quadrants of the abdomen, checking for tenderness of the gallbladder, spleen, stomach, and kidneys.

"Nothing."

I pushed in with two fingers and let go quickly checking for rebound tenderness, which happened when there was bleeding or a ruptured appendix.

"See, I'm fine."

"Where in your back does it hurt?"

"Like I said. Straight back."

"And down your legs?"

"Well, yes."

"One or both?"

He looked at me, puzzled.

"Henry, does the pain go down one or both legs?"

"Both, why?"

Judy returned with the IV and BP cuff.

"200 over 100," she soon announced.

"A little high." It was abnormally high, his systolic at 200 instead of a normal 120. A hypertensive crisis. I felt his pulse. Up to 105. "You still remember how to start IV's?"

"Of course." She had it in and running in less than two minutes.

What was I missing? I had that awful feeling I was overlooking something.

"How many more hours to Washington?"

"Around seven," Judy said. Her eyes met mine and she knew what I was thinking.

"Dammit," Henry said. "There's that back pain again."

"All right, Henry, I want you to take a deep breath and try and relax your stomach. Bring up your legs too."

I pushed down, trying to feel through the layers of fat. "Hold your breath...relax...relax."

I let go, not completely sure I'd felt it, but not willing to gamble if I was wrong.

"Judy. Tell the pilot we have a medical emergency. We need to turn this plane around now."

## CHAPTER 36

Oakland Permanente Hospital

## December 14, 1949

Henry was sitting up in bed, talking on the phone while a second phone rang unanswered. Next to his ICU bed, one of the residents had left the latest abdominal X-ray on the view box. The enlarged shadow of Henry's abdominal aortic aneurysm had been replaced with a normal-looking aorta.

"For Crissakes, Henry. One week after surgery, you should be relaxing, not gabbing away."

He waved at me and said into the phone, "Got to go, my doctor's here."

"How are you feeling?"

"Like I was run over by one of my cement trucks."

"Good, you're feeling better." I picked up the vital sign clipboard and paged to the graph of his blood pressure. Back to normal. "And you're going to have to stay off the phone and take it easy for at least another week."

"I can always count on you, Sid." He patted my hand. "You know, you're as much a son to me as Edgar and Henry Jr."

I nodded. He'd become more of a friend and father to me over the years.

Ignoring my orders as usual, he picked up the phone and dialed. "Send them up."

"Henry, you're supposed to be resting," I protested.

"I am. I am."

There was a knock at the door. "Come in," Henry said, the old force of command in his voice.

The door opened and the Secretary of HEW, John Curry, strode in, followed by Dr. Paul Foster.

"Henry." Curry pumped Henry's hand. "Glad to see you doing well." Curry, a slight man of about sixty, had graying hair combed straight back, and a polished politician's voice.

Henry extended his hand to Foster. "Doctor." Foster shook it. "And this is the good Dr. Garfield that I told you about."

"A pleasure," Curry said, shaking my hand.

"Dr. Foster and I had a chance to talk on our way here," Curry said. Foster looked red-faced. "We have some good news for you, Dr. Garfield. Your medical license is being reinstated." Foster hadn't said a word since he'd entered the room. "And he's agreed to allow your physicians to apply and join the CMA and AMA."

"You can have your license," Foster protested, "but I made no agreement about letting Kaiser doctors join the AMA. It's still a free country and I'm not about to be strong-armed by any of you."

"I'm sorry you feel that way, Dr. Foster," Henry said. He picked up the phone. "Send up O'Brien."

"I don't care what your lawyer says," Foster said.

"Oh, I think you will. There are laws about over-billing insurance companies, aren't there Mr. Secretary?"

"Yes, sir, there are."

"This is rubbish," Foster said, the veins on his forehead pulsing. "You can't threaten me."

"Threaten?" Henry shook his head. "No, Doctor. We're not threatening you. We're arresting you."

The door swung open and O'Brien, followed by three uniformed deputies, marched into the room. "Dr. Foster." One of the deputies held out a document. "You're under arrest for ten counts of insurance fraud." He grabbed Foster by the arm.

"This is all lies," Foster spat back. "I charge what I deserve to be paid. Period. If people can't afford it, they can go wherever else they please."

"Like my mother?" I said.

"Get this man out of my hospital," Henry ordered.

*I hold up the three pennies Mom gave me.*

*The doctor pats my head.*

*"I'll get you the money," Father says.*

*"Sorry. There is the Charity Hospital." The doctor walks out.*

I didn't watch them go. I listened as their footsteps crossed the hallway to the elevator. The elevator door closed with a finality that reverberated through me like my mother's last gasp.

"Sid, I'm going to give you one more piece of advice. I want you to go across the street to my office. There's someone waiting for you."

"Who?"

"Now do what I tell you before you drive my blood pressure up. Sid, you listening?"

"Okay, sure Henry. Anything to keep you healthy. This had better be good."

"Oh, it is. You'll see."

Outside the hospital, the wind carried the scent of sea salt and freshly mowed lawns. A crisp blue sky had a single cloud sailing on the breeze. The elevator whisked me to the sixteenth floor and I entered the waiting area of Henry's personal office.

"Dr. Garfield," his secretary said, "go right in."

I nodded. What was Henry up to? Trying to get me back together with Victoria would be my guess.

I opened the door.

Judy sat on the couch.

"Hi Sid," she said. I smelled her perfume and a long ago image of Judy, one that had been there since the moment we met, danced into my thoughts.

"We need to talk," she said.

I sat next to her and took her hand. At that moment she looked like that young nurse I'd first met in the desert; we both were young.

"Ten years is a long time," she said. "People grow up and leave the kids that they were behind."

"Do they?"

"No, not really." She smiled. "But sometimes, how we act and how things seem aren't really how we feel." She put her head on my shoulder and I held her. For now, it was enough that she was here.

# EPILOGUE

New York City

## October 27, 1977

"I'd like to welcome Dr. Sidney Garfield and Mr. Edgar Kaiser." Joseph A. Califano, Jr., Secretary of HEW, the Department of Health, Education, and Welfare, spoke clearly into the microphone with the polish of an experienced speaker. A crowd of two hundred doctors, many from Kaiser Permanente, some from the AMA, the doctors' families, plus politicians and reporters, filled the meeting room in New York's Waldorf-Astoria Hotel. I'll never forget the date: October 27, 1977.

Califano, in his fifties with thinning dark hair, of medium build, wore a traditional gray business suit with the top button of his white shirt undone. The air conditioner was so cold, it sent chills down my back. Or was it the ceremony that did that?

"Today is a happy day and a very important milestone in my department's efforts to give every American an opportunity—an opportunity to obtain good quality, comprehensive and cost-effective health care."

It had taken more than forty years, but Califano's words meant everything to me. Califano smiled as he spoke into the mike, sounding as proud as if he were Henry Kaiser himself. Henry had died back in 1967 in Honolulu. He'd survived the aneurysm for years. The man who had been so important to me, so much bigger than life, took his last breath on the morning of August 24th. Allie and I were with him at the end. I remember how she'd looked up at me as the heart monitor gave its final beep. She broke into tears. We both did.

With Kaiser gone, his vision and will faded and the Kaiser industrial empire disintegrated. Of all his efforts—the cars, washing machines, housing developments, dams, roads, aluminum, cement, steel—the one thing still going strong, and the endeavor he would be remembered for the most, would be health care.

"From its beginnings on a California desert serving aqueduct workers," Califano continued, "from Henry Kaiser's request of Dr. Garfield to provide medical and hospitalization services on a prepaid basis to the Kaiser Shipyard workers, has arisen the classic model for health care. Kaiser Permanente today provides the highest quality prepaid medical services in California, Colorado, Oregon, Ohio, Washington, and Hawaii, to more than three and a quarter million people. They have voluntarily chosen its services because of its quality, accessibility and cost. In Northern California, for example, nearly 30% of the eligible civilian population has chosen, has elected to sign up with Kaiser."

Califano gestured toward Edgar and me in the front row. "I'd like to acknowledge the presence this morning of two of the principal founders of the Kaiser Permanente plan: Dr. Sidney Garfield and Edgar Kaiser. In my judgment what will put Edgar Kaiser and his family in the history books is what he's done for medical care in this country, what the Kaiser Permanente Health Plans have done for patients in this country. I would like to now introduce the former first lady of the United States, Lady Byrd Johnson."

Her rose perfume overpowered the room. "Thank you, Joe. It's my pleasure to be here today, to present the 1977 Lyndon Baines Johnson Foundation Humanitarian Award to Dr. Sidney Garfield. Millions of Americans go to sleep every night without adequate health care, unable to afford the basics. The health care plan that Sidney Garfield and Henry Kaiser launched forty years ago gives Americans a chance to afford the health care they deserve. Kaiser Permanente is now a reality that enriches life for millions of Americans. It is, in 1977, an idea whose time has come, an idea worthy of serving millions more. We can no longer deny care based on cost. Thanks to Dr. Garfield, we are going to do everything we can to encourage that idea because every American citizen deserves this opportunity. Let us honor Dr. Garfield not just for the idea he gave us but also for the pioneering spirit and the courage that made that idea a reality."

"Get up," Cecil Cutting whispered in my ear. "Don't make the First Lady wait."

Jonas Salk, the first recipient of the award, patted me on the back as I stood. We'd kept in touch since I'd sent him those polio blood samples back in the early fifties.

I walked to the podium and Lady Byrd wrapped her arms around me, a petite Texas woman possessing the strength reminiscent of a Kaiser bear hug. One by one—led by Cecil, of course—everyone in the room stood and applauded. My eyes blurred with tears, something I found I'd started to do more and more as I entered my seventies. I waved to the back of the room for my wife to come join me. She made her way forward, her graying blonde hair neatly tucked under her blue hat. The spotlights filled my eyes. I blinked to clear them and then there was only one figure visible. My wife, Judy.

\*   \*   \*

# AUTHOR'S NOTE

Born out of the challenge of providing Americans medical care during the Great Depression and World War II, Sidney Garfield's model, Kaiser Permanente, is now the nation's largest *non-profit* health plan, serving 8.2 million members in 10 states, and employing over 136,000 people and 11,000 physicians. Garfield was responsible for changing the face of American medicine, helping to make it more affordable and improving the quality of care by encouraging early detection and treatment of illness. The system that he and Henry Kaiser started, a non-profit plan of health care, now known as a Health Maintenance Organization (HMO), devotes all revenues to patient care rather than shareholder profit, helping to make health care accessible and affordable to more Americans.

Our predominant fee-for-service model of health care encourages doctors to do more of everything: more visits, more tests, more hospitalizations, more surgery. The sicker you are, the more business they get. Not a penny goes for preventive care. On the other hand, HMO's are prepaid and are motivated to keep you healthy. They do everything they can to encourage you to come in for mammograms, diabetes testing, colonoscopy, vaccinations, weight loss programs, no smoking classes, and the list goes on. The less sickness, the less cost.

But there's more to it. Not all HMO's are created equally. There are two models of HMO care: *for-profit* and *non-profit*.

In the *for-profit* heath plan, when fewer services are delivered, the profit margin increases so there is more money to distribute to the shareholders and staff. In other words, an outside bean counter, not a doctor, manages costs instead of managing the quality of care.

A *non-profit* HMO health plan, like Kaiser Permanente, reinvests all revenues back into quality patient care rather than out to shareholder profit or huge CEO salaries. Its incentive is to keep you healthy, by actually preventing illness like heart disease and cancer, because healthier people require less costly care. In other words, all efforts to contain costs are not done for the profit of the doctors or administrators—they are done solely to provide quality health care at a price you can afford. It's no surprise that a recent *Consumer Reports* study of 20,000 people showed that patient satisfaction rates were much higher in *non-profit* HMO's.

Most physicians want nothing else other than to keep you healthy. But no matter how dedicated we are to the Hippocratic Oath, no matter how much we want to be Good Samaritans, in the end, to keep our practices going, doctors have to bill. Fee-for-service doctors employ office staff to "code" their fees in a manner that maximizes their reimbursement. If a doctor owns expensive equipment, e.g. MRI's, endoscopy suites, minor OR's, they need to use them to recoup their investment. Every week, I receive three or more letters in the mail to take a "coding course" to help "increase my income." As I throw them away, I breathe a sigh of relief that in my practice, I don't have to play this fee-for-service game. All of my decisions on care are based on what's best for the patient. We're on the same team. That's why I've looked forward to going to work every day for the last 25 years.

As my seventeen-year-old son would say: "Dad, it's a no-brainer." We should pay doctors for keeping us healthy. To put it simply and to quote Cecil Cutting, "Fee-for-service medicine is a 'sick plan' while managed care is a 'health plan.'"

As the numbers of the uninsured (45 million Americans, one in five Californians) spiral out of control, I believe that Sidney Garfield's model of competing *non-profit* HMO's may be the best solution to our nation's health crisis. Trust me, I'm a doctor.

# ACKNOWLEDGMENTS

In writing this novel, I have tried to respect history wherever doing so served my purposes as a novelist, but wherever it did not I have, cheerfully, and without regret, ignored it.

I would like to thank the many individuals who helped in the writing of this book. The Asilomar Writers' Consortium for their suggestions and critiques, including "Professor" Jerry Hannah, Dr. Barry Slater, Daniel Houston, Susan Vreeland, Grant Farley, and special thanks to Dave and Mary Putnam for their friendship and countless suggestions.

To Mike Sirota, the "world's best editor" for helping to transform this novel from its first rough draft, and to the members of "Mike's original group," including Ed Jones, Angela Hurst, and Mark Fogg. A special acknowledgment to Steve Gilford, "Kaiser Historian extraordinaire" for his "On This Date in KP History" series that provided some of the important background information used in this novel and to the Head and Neck Surgery Administrative Team and physicians for their friendship and support: Carolyn Felder, Peggy Wilshusen, Kathy Peterman, Janice Polk, Gail Jauck, Alex Favish, Michele Biggerstaff, Stephen Saltzman, MD, Roberto Cueva, MD, Peter Martin, MD, John Burnett, MD, Bruce Edens, MD, Alex Battaglia, MD, Greg Stearns, MD, Dave Londo, MD, Victor Schorn, MD, Shane Zim, MD, and Todd Broberg, MD.

Deep gratitude to my parents, Fred and Rosella Bernstein, and my brother, Mark Bernstein, MD, for instilling in me the values and dedication that led to my career in medicine.

And finally and most importantly to my "beacons" and inspirations, my wife Judy A. Bernstein and son, Clifford Bernstein, who encouraged me to put my interest and admiration of Sidney Garfield onto paper.